I0638386

CHOWBINGO
The Creator's Canine

PHILIP I. AMOS

Philip I. Amos, LLC
Editors and Publishers
Hermosa Beach, CA

Philip I. Amos

Philip I. Amos, LLC
1634 Prospect Ave
Hermosa Beach, CA 90254
www.PhilipAmos.com

Publisher's Note: This is a work of fiction. Names, characters, places, and incidents are a product of the author's imagination. Locales and public names are sometimes used for atmospheric purposes. Any resemblance to actual people, living or dead, or to businesses, companies, events, institutions, or locales is completely coincidental.

Book Layout © 2014 BookDesignTemplates.com

Chowbingo/ Philip I. Amos -- 1st edition
ISBN 978-0692568873

Dedicated to Diane Amos
My wife, my love, and my best friend

*This only I want to learn from you: Did you receive
the Spirit by the works of the law, or by the hearing
of faith?*
—GALATIANS 3:2 (NKJV)

Philip I. Amos

Prologue

Although this started as a children's book, it no longer remains as such. I now choose to call it a "creation fairy tale".

I have found that the books and movies of lasting interest to readers and viewers, with a capacity for imagination, are the likes of The Hobbit by J.R.R. Tolkien, C.S. Lewis' series, The Chronicles of Narnia, and J.K. Rowling's Harry Potter books. These aforementioned books are fictional, although some offer allegorical content. Nonetheless, each character and their settings are clearly established and leave little to the creative imagination. Universes are set forth and clearly defined with their characters placed neatly therein.

The story of Chowbingo provides an atmosphere in which characters, from another environment (Heaven & Hell as it has often been relayed to us), immerse themselves in Earth's environment in a manner that is not disruptive of the belief systems of adults yet remains available to captivate the wonderment of youth.

Chowbingo and his companions operate beneath the radar of the book's adult characters as they enter into an open relationship with Val, a pre-teen youth who is just approaching the end of his life's first decade. I believe that Chowbingo's adventure will provide a "fairy tale" environment that enables readers to insert their own imagination into this story as it is being told.

It is my wish through inspiration, and a bit of my own obedience, that you too may come to believe, through your faith, that a spiritual universe of goodness does truly co-exist with this physical environment in which we live.

(Author)

Contents

Philip I. Amos

Cast of Characters

Father	Creator of All Universes
Schezak	Father's High Priest
Chowbingo	Father's Canine Companion
Jabez	Chowbingo's Scribe
Esau	Chowbingo's Friend, Lucy – Talking Cow #1
Khasmar	Neveah's Messenger, Maria – Talking Cow #2
Xeres	Evil Adversary, Owari, or the Magnificent Seraph
Angelina Patadarski	Mother to Val and Widow to Salvio
Salvatore Patadarski	Deceased Father to Valentino
Valentino Patadarski	Angelina's Son aka Val
Dominique Bellingeri	The Village Candy Maker
Yuri Kolvalenko	The Village Butcher
Sam Emerson	The Village Grocer
Sam Ellison	The Village Dairy Farmer

Philip I. Amos

Chapter 1

Home

H i, I'm Chowbingo. You would probably now look upon me, in my earthen form, as a plump, under-sized, yet furry chow puppy with a purple tongue and small black inquisitive eyes. My reddish-tipped fur is mostly sandy blonde and extends outward from my body, simulating the plushest of powder puffs. My unique ball of fluff is interrupted by my short black snout, my eyes, and my two over-furred, triangular ears. Add to this my four legs, terminating in creamy white paws, and there remains not much to separate me from a singular fur ball.

However, I pray that you be admonished, before in foolishness you consider me as such. I am, in actuality, a solitary warrior sent on a specific mission by Father. My mission began without instructions and its purpose was then yet unknown to me. I now have become that which I was to be, and therefore I am able to share my odyssey with you in the hope that you too will join me in the knowledge of its purpose.

Be prepared to go where you have never been, to learn the yet untaught, and to believe in the unspoken.

My home is where I hope you may be favored to go and from where I have come. Mine is a place where the differences from Earth are both great and unexplainable to you. Even as I then began my entrance into your place, I found myself unable to possess either descriptive ability or understanding.

Now that my trip is complete, I find myself possessing your language, your thoughts, and your emotions. Nonetheless, even though I am strong in the gifts of spiritual discernment (the language of my homeland), nonetheless I still find myself woefully lacking in the communication skills that you call speech and literacy.

Therefore, being slight of words and unaccustomed as I have always been to communicating through any except my home language, I have asked my companion Jabez to set to script that which, although I am most qualified to discern, nonetheless I find myself unfortunately most limited to express.

———————

I, Jabez, through the fervent request of my good friend Chowbingo, herein commit to script the story of his journey, as it has been spiritually recounted to me.

It was, for Chowbingo, a warm and most beautiful day. Father's light had just begun to pierce the translucent silver shield that separates light from dark. Chowbingo had relaxed his spirit and extended his vision, to the extent that it would be most practicable for him to soak the warmth of Father's love into the very being of his inner essence. The nourishment of Father's love continues to provide the sustenance by which we, and Neveah's others, are able to live, move, and have our being.

Chowbingo can never remember a beginning nor has he ever heard of an ending. All Chowbingo ever knew was that he is, and that his spirit existed within his being, here in Neveah. Food is never a requirement for nutrition but only a luxury to be sampled and enjoyed at will. Vegetables are delicious, meats are unknown, and fruits continued to change their flavors in agreement with our tastes.

Sickness and disease, before his journey, were both unknown to him. Simple tiredness, from a long healthy run across the verdant heath, was then nonexistent. Chowbingo, unlike Khasmar or myself, always felt as if he had recently stepped from a cooling shower and been rubbed, to a ruddy red, with the likes of a gloriously thick, terrycloth towel. Charged and energized, as was his nature, he was forever ready for the next joyful engagement that might be sent to cross his path.

Chowbingo always knew that he would finish his meditations, followed by one final languid stretch, before seeking me out with the singular intent of disrupting my coveted, solitary continuum, of pondering, thinking, and planning.

I only wish that he might understand that I was habitually given to such processes. Could he not realize, it was because of these very endeavors of mine, that he might be led to request that I author this record of his adventure? Then, as we always had done together, Chowbingo would enthusiastically join me to seek out our beloved friend, Khasmar. Although deeply cherished by both of us, Khasmar nevertheless was known to be distant, aloof, and mostly of a separate mindset.

Chowbingo, at the time, did not know what manner of temperament he had, nor was it then of any importance to us. He has forever been Father's beloved and a loving companion to both Khasmar and myself. He was simply Chowbingo and that was, to him, the all of it.

It was a day in Neveah, which I was then pleased to call today. It was to become the day when all that Chowbingo understood would change for he was to have a formal audience in the presence of Father.

Suddenly, without warning or thought, Chowbingo along with Khasmar and Schezak, found themselves before Father, blinded by the very light of His being. Chowbingo, at the time, heard His voice as if from a dream. It was a voice delivered with the clarity of chimes, yet ominously silent in sound.

These meetings, they were always according to Father's will and without notice for preparation or appointment. This was His way, never early never late.

The voice, speaking with a conviction of leadership, said, "Turn your eyes from My light lest you be blinded. Look now only to My reflection."

The second voice then announced, "Listen to me, I am Wisdom. I was there with Truth, and Knowledge, and Understanding when all of the universes were first formed. I was there at a time before limits were set for where the seas could go, where rivers could run, and the directions to which the clouds, stars, moon, and sun would rotate."

There was silence for a time, and then for a time again, before the next voice spoke. Then the Spirit of Knowledge spoke to Chowbingo. "Chowbingo, you will soon go to a place that you do not know nor will you understand. Fear not, for you will meet there a friend, also without ending."

Again He spoke, the "Father of Truth and All Things". Now, however, it was a strong commanding voice, yet still filled with love. It seemed to come from beyond Chowbingo's personal being. Unmistakably, again he recognized it to be from Father. Now, however, it was a voice speaking from authority, rather than one of solace and comfort, such as Chowbingo had always before known.

"Chowbingo, now hear this," spoke the "Father of Truth and All Things." "I have purposed you for such a time as this. I am the great, I AM; I am the Spirit of Light; I am the Fountain of Love; and I am the Creator of All, even of that such as may become known to you to be without beginning or without end.

"Wisdom is now being ignored, but through you, my little one, it will again be established.

"Chowbingo, you have always been My loyal companion. Now I am sending you to a place to be a companion to others that they might again learn, through your loyalty, to have fellowship with Me."

"Huh?"

"Man was created to be in My image, and he has become a disappointment to Me! You are different; you are not man, but you are beloved. Chowbingo, you will not tarry. Your mission is important to all who are to become beloved. I sent my son and still they failed to turn from their wicked ways. Now it will be you whom I elect to send."

"But . . .!"

"Fear not, my faithful Chowbingo! I am sending ahead a counselor to provide you with assurance and guidance."

Before he could utter a response, Chowbingo had already found himself immersed in space and falling through time. He might have guessed himself to be suspended in place were it not for the colors that appeared to be spinning upwards toward him. He was, in actuality, cascading downward and passing before a flowing curtain of glowing, multi-hued rock. It felt, as he later relayed it to me, that while his speed increased the passing rocks changed, first from solid to molten, and finally to a creamy liquid. More fluid and more beautiful they continued to become; a falling, cascading, kaleidoscope of colors. Intermittently he would find himself interrupted by defining layers. Strata, which Chowbingo later learned, could be identified as jasper, sapphire, chalcedony, emerald, sardonyx, sardius, chrysolite, beryl, topaz, chrysoprase, jacinth, and amethyst. Seven were Neveah's foundation, while the others still remain unknown to the both of us. Chowbingo had just fallen through the foundations of Neveah and into that abyss of weightlessness called space. Blackness followed. He then experienced a darkness that can only be identified as, "an absolute absence of light." After time, and then time again, a dark blood-red light began appearing. Dimly at first, and then becoming more, ever more, apparent. It was unlike any light that Chowbingo had ever before witnessed. It did not radiate outward nor did it emit warmth. It was a light that could only be called a selfish light, a light that was totally contained within its own origin. It was most frightening.

Chowbingo's fur stood on end and his tail went straight up. A sudden cold passed between the toes of his stubby paws. Chowbingo was passing through his metamorphous. He found himself, without warning, in an earthen body – restrictive, perhaps, might best describe it.

There, just as suddenly as he had entered, Chowbingo moved from a place of permanent darkness into an illumination of celestial bodies, displaying shapes and types too numerous to recall. It was, there, while being transported through that celestial arena that Chowbingo encountered angels of types and of beings such as he had never before imagined nor encountered. These angelic beings, an "Angel's Club" might be a proper definition, were of common cause in that they all moved about with similar intent, task, and purpose; all of which was then indiscernible to Chowbingo. There, as his gaze became increasingly settled, more balanced, and more fixed to his continually evolving surroundings, Chowbingo began to notice that these angelic beings moved not only with order and purpose, but also in arrangements of caste and class. Their shapes and raiment varied greatly between them. There were angels, clad in robes, with massive feathered wings attached to their backs, which reached from well above their heads to within inches of the soles of their feet. When immobile, they appeared as alabaster statues. When in flight, those eighteen-foot-tall behemoths transmitted beams of pulsating gold, purple, and crimson hues. They appeared to be emitting purposeful dialogue but still remained absent from any discernable order or sequence. Just the sound of their movement was hurtful to his ears. It might sound to an earthling like separate claps of thunder with every beat of their wings.

There were angels who appeared to have body parts that were separated, one from the other. Yet, these separated body parts moved in harmony, as if connected to a single mind.

Celestial rocks covered themselves with ever-shifting colors, in continually fluctuating hues, and with uninterrupted brightness, as they sped across the foreground of Chowbingo's vision. They would dart into his view and just as suddenly they would disappear. They sped across his celestial canvas, some as solitary projectiles, oftentimes, as massive galaxies. Intermittently, they moved in random appearance, not unlike geese winging their way along their flight paths, destined to fulfill their predetermined appointments.

There were the strangest of beings, ones who appeared to be part angel and part crafted material, as if formed from alabaster. They moved, sometimes as a united individual, but oftentimes as a colony of flesh and stone. These angelic units clearly moved under the direction of their singular intellects and operated as singular bodies, in all that they performed.

As he continued to fall through space and time, Chowbingo, in accordance with his best remembrance, also witnessed, in addition to angelic beings and intelligent formations, inanimate formations. There appeared crystal galaxies formed from the remains of living galaxies which long before had passed. This was Chowbingo's first view of a crystal galaxy and he became very frightened. His round, furry body had increased in speed as he tumbled downward, head over tail, through a lifeless abyss. This was Chowbingo's first encounter with death. He did not understand it and it terrified him.

Chowbingo has always understood the concept, "intelligent being". He is one. Father is one. Khasmar, Schezak, and I are also well known to Chowbingo as such. Angelic forms and galaxies are also "intelligent beings", which although strange to him, were nonetheless accepted by him, and comfortable to him as living creations.

However, a galaxy that was once intelligent, and had since lost its intelligence, was certainly foreign to his understanding. Here, before him, appeared a crystal galaxy, frozen in time. It could never grow, or form new bodies, or change on its own, or move, or react. It, as a crystal, was absent of all intelligence. It could only deteriorate. Where had its intelligence gone? This is death! Death can't come from Father. Father is the giver of life and light. He can't abandon it now, nor Chowbingo reasoned, would he.

"Where does this harbinger of death come from," Chowbingo later asked me. "Does it perhaps come from the selfish light that I had formerly passed, the blood-red one with the light that caused my fur to stand on end? Is that where death came from? Is that where intelligence goes after death? Is that where we find angel's burning? Is that where the paths to evil lead?"

I informed him that I would later refer his questions to Schezak, Father's high priest, if he wished, or following the completion of our transcription, he might choose to inquire of Father directly.

Apologizing for the interruption, Chowbingo recounted that he was with Father, as His companion, during the week when all that was to be formed was formed. Wisdom, Knowledge, and Understanding were all there. Father had foretold of angels and saints to come but death had never been included, or even introduced, during those gatherings.

Chowbingo then continued his story. His passage through the crystal galaxy ending, he began to feel his fur push harshly against his belly, as his unimpeded velocity moved him into an unfamiliar realm, gravitation. He began to watch his entire surroundings being transformed to bluish white. Advancing toward him, at tremendous speed, appeared what he would learn was a planet. Looming before him, it appeared first as an indistinguishable object, new to his vision and still distant. Later, it presented itself as a small sphere but then rapidly grew to where it encompassed his entire forward field of vision. Simultaneously, Chowbingo began to feel an increasingly strong pull drawing upon his body. Finally, felt himself being pulled, against his will, toward a place he did not yet know. Its name, he would learn, was Earth.

Philip I. Amos

Chapter 2

A New Beginning

That was Chowbingo's first absence from Father, and it had raised a level of anxiety and discomfort previously unknown to him. Such feelings, in Neveah, were never experienced nor were they known. Although seemingly terrifying at moments, Chowbingo's travel from home had, nonetheless, been a mostly comfortable adventure. Inwardly he knew that Father's hand was upon all that he had experienced. His introduction to death, which he had first encountered while passing through the crystal galaxy, remained for him both foreboding and frightening.

Chowbingo knew that he was in a strange place, very strange indeed. While he was involuntarily being pulled toward Earth he had cried out for Father, but there had been no response. There were moments, moments like those when he found himself filled with uncontrollable fear. This power that was pulling him to a place he did not know, this was not Father,

This was not His way. Chowbingo knew Father by His nature. The power had come from a malevolent force, one that he had never before experienced or felt. Chowbingo, for the first time, was personally experiencing evil. Greater and greater had become its pull. Faster and faster had become its speed. Chowbingo's body had been pressed against itself to where it was no longer able to properly function. He had been firmly caught up within a force from which he was, absolutely, unable to escape. Later he told me, he remembered nothing else. Chowbingo had never before been unconscious. He did not know it then nor can he understand it now.

Chowbingo tried to spiritually stretch and awaken his inner being, as was his custom. Everything, as he had known it from before, had vanished. The two blue moons that cast their reflected light outward toward infinity, the purple haze cast upon the golden fields; it was all gone.

"Where is the mist that cools the surface?" he then asked.

Space without limits appeared to have ended for Chowbingo as he found himself now gazing from horizon to horizon.

"Why can't I see forever?" he asked. It was as if "all" had suddenly become "some".

"Where is my father? His heat, His light, His warmth," wondered Chowbingo. *"It just doesn't make sense—so unreal, so artificial."*

The sounds of glory, praise, and adoration that used to fill the voids—he found this now to be missing. This was, for him, scary. This was an absence that was truly terrifying.

"As I had then attempted to move in freedom, I found myself withheld and contained," explained Chowbingo. *"I was trapped, limited, restricted. I called out, as I was accustomed, but there came forth no answer! I couldn't hear Father or find Him. I missed His warmth and His love. I was isolated, set apart, confined, and abandoned. My faith, it had been ripped from me. I was afraid! What was this that so constrained me?"* he had asked. *"Where was I?"*

Frustrated, afraid, confused, lonely, and exhausted, Chowbingo had fallen into a deep slumber. That following day he was rested and, for the first time, hungry. He stretched, not unlike he had done many times before in Neveah. Now, however, he needed food. His new physical body ached from the voyage and the chill of the morning air permeated his bones. These were feelings that Chowbingo had never before known. Just like from a caterpillar to a butterfly, or from a tadpole to a frog, Chowbingo, during his journey, had experienced a metamorphosis. He had gone from being a free Neveah spirit, to that of being trapped within the canine suit of a chow dog. No longer was he able to experience telepathic communication, to exist without pain, to live without tiredness, or to continue to survive without nourishment. Chowbingo had never before been unconscious. He did not know it then nor can he understand it now.

Here, because of the barrier Father had established between Neveah and Earth, following the incident in His garden, Chowbingo was unable to speak to Him in his spiritual language. He was beginning to feel isolated and very much alone.

Now, fully awake and alert in animal form, fear and trepidation began coursing through his bones. Reacting in a manner that might then be considered instinctive, Chowbingo spun full circle and gingerly shook his fur. Finally, with his tail turned down, he cautiously made his way into his new environment. Animal instinct now seeming to have replaced spiritual discernment he, nonetheless, knew that this was still Father's plan for him. Without hesitation, Chowbingo accepted his charge and settled into his best form of obedience, knowing that any rebellion, or failure to trust in Father's directions, would certainly not avail, for him, any benefit.

Perhaps the first that Chowbingo recalled, after awakening on planet Earth, were the colors he found to be primary to the area. He distinctly recalls seeing the bluest of blues, luscious multihued greens of the most vibrant shadings, and many-layered browns of every shade and description. On display, seemingly for his personal enjoyment, he also found streaked and speckled nuggets of silver and gold interspersed with mottled pearlescent granules. There were low-growing ferns to enclose him with warmth and towering palms to shield him from an overbearing sun. There were pathways seemingly untouched for centuries and fruit trees of every imagination, each bearing its own fruit providing, for him, offerings of uniquely delectable tastes. These were encased in skins, bearing individual colorings, of the most vibrant shadings. Each fruit he found to be enclosed beneath its own individual leafy canopy, a most spectacular presentation, each to its own. The stem of each fruit was either formed of burnished gold, or polished silver, as might best be found to complement its color. Chowbingo learned, upon the picking of the fruit, that the stems would quickly disintegrate into the dust of the soil, dead and valueless.

There was one particular tree, however, that appeared quite different from the others. It was a solitary tree that Chowbingo chose to name the "Death Tree". Rather than luscious fruit hanging from its limbs there were, instead, petrified fruits of the most hideous distortions. These were the fruits of the shrunken heads for civilizations that were still yet to come. There were also sister fruits that were bloated and resembled gargoyles, each one of despicable countenance. Apostles of death and minions of another world, they were adroitly encased in the leathern skins of long-dead fruits.

Sprinkled across the Death Tree's grotesqueness were large scales that shone resplendent in the rising morning sun. Every color and hue imaginable to Chowbingo, from Neveah, was displayed in its brilliance and majesty.

Chowbingo found himself standing before this tree, captured by awe and bewilderment. He was both shocked and stunned. Then, just as fast as Chowbingo's new puppy legs could transport him, he found himself running again, overcome by fright. He felt abandoned by Faith and Hope. He knew that he was running from Father's love, but yet he didn't know why. He had never before felt the air rush across his whiskers and blow into his ears as it did at that moment. Chowbingo ran so fast it felt as if his hind feet were climbing right up the pads of his fore paws.

Finally, just as quickly as he ran, he suddenly stumbled and fell. He recalls that he tumbled head over tail multiple times before finally coming to rest, firmly on his back. All four paws ended straight up in the air, definitely not the position where a mission-minded servant of the Father might expect to find himself. Bewilderment then began to settle in, overtaking fear.

Startled and confused, Chowbingo unwittingly began to discover that he was instinctively responding to newly acquired "fight or flight" animal responses. He jumped up and ran again. This time he saw things that he had not seen before, and he imagined events that previously were not there. The more he reacted, the further he found himself becoming distanced from Father's love. Nonetheless, moving and dodging in random patterns, he attempted to flee the unseen evil that he felt was surely bearing down upon him.

Having just recovered from his prior tumble, he found himself once again falling, actually tripping. This time, though, he immediately returned to his feet and shook himself free from the dust which he had again accumulated. As he looked about for the cause of his tripping, he spotted the probable cause, bones of a long since dead animal. Chowbingo was now not only more afraid than from before, but he found that he was also further perplexed. Within Neveah, from where he had come, death was nonexistent. That would be the purview of Xeres – or could it be from another? Moments later, as his canine curiosity began to overcome his fear, he sniffed at the dry bones in the manner that inquisitive puppies, of which he had recently become one, are want to do. While fixing his eyes on the sun-bleached skeleton, he noted there were scoring marks that circumvented the four leg bones at the hock, or ankle areas.

Chowbingo, having taken note of this anomaly, found that it left him more perplexed and assuredly more nervous than from before.

_____

He noted as he walked, wondered, and sniffed his way through the area, that this new locale appeared to actually be a self-contained garden of special uniqueness. Here was a place that presented special offerings unlike any other that might be considered familiar to him. Although seemingly similar to the gardens that he, Khasmar, and I are accustomed to moving through during our idyllic days here in Neveah, there was certainly something uniquely different in Earth's special garden, where Chowbingo had found himself.

Although the foliage was different, and the colors were unlike those to which he was accustomed, there still remained, in like and same manner, a familiar sense of extraordinary, incomparable beauty—Father's imprint! However, there also remained the Tree of Death, and those dead animal bones, which were clearly out of place. This was surely a mysterious and most troubling place.

In a fleeting moment, and without warning, a gazelle had burst from the thicket and jumped through a bush, as if it were flying, before settling back in a sudden rush of noise, whereupon it disappeared as suddenly as it had arrived. The tension of silence having been broken, animals began to appear. These are animals familiar both to Chowbingo and myself. They are the self-same animals whose natures we enjoy here, at our home, in Neveah. However, on Earth the animals do not play in their garden together, nor do they share their fellowship while standing side by side, like the spirits who frolic, side by side, along the shorelines of our crystal ponds, here in Neveah. There, on Earth, the lamb, rather than lying in the noon day sun with the lion, runs upon seeing it. I fondly recall how Chowbingo would often pause to commune with all of Neveah's citizens, as Father's constant companion it was required of him.

Chowbingo informed me how, following his arrival in Earth's garden, he began to notice that as the animals approached a pond, there would often be snarling and even biting, especially between the disparate species. Some, it seemed, would always approach boldly with the assurance that they were dominant, while others held back, steeped in submission. Others would simply run, in fright, from their neighbors.

Chowbingo, somewhat aware but not yet comfortable in his new milieu, was about to settle in for a brief respite. Then, seemingly by design, but yet without warning, he found himself about to be trampled by a charging bull. The animal, although of the same nature as ones we know from Neveah, had absolutely no interest in sharing the field's fragrant aroma and its blooming flowers with Chowbingo. His sole interest lay in removing Chowbingo from his temporary position of rest, in the lush golden meadow, and dispatching him upward and outward, in the manner of an airborne projectile.

All thoughts, which Chowbingo may have then had to the contrary, would have been permanently erased had it not been for the fact that, at the last moment, he fortunately avoided the trampling hoofs and lowered horns that were preparing to catapult him into the upward branches of an awaiting tree. Chowbingo, catching the threatening shadow of his unwelcome visitor, executed an oblique dash to the right. This sudden defensive maneuver only succeeded in ensuring that he would be propelled up and over the garden's protective floral barricade, rather than alighting in some far tree's upper branches. The bull, apparently satisfied that he had delivered Chowbingo unceremoniously into the bordering stream, returned to his grazing.

Water soaked and pulled down from the weight of his abundant fur covering. Chowbingo began choking, coughing, and sputtering as he was being carried unceremoniously downstream. Unable to swim and unaccustomed as he was to his new body, Chowbingo found himself rolling about and out of control, akin to a barrel being transported along through a twisting river. The water was angry and the shoreline was neither inviting nor beautiful. It was most quite unlike the blue-white, crystal-clear, meandering stream that he had discovered in the garden from where he had just been expelled.

All remembrances of where the garden's location might have been or any chance that he might eventually return to it were firmly shaken from his mind, never to again be recalled. It was only the presence of the garden itself that remained implanted within his spirit. Almost as abruptly as he had discovered himself in the river, Chowbingo found himself being expelled from its torrential forces, where he was set in a most unkindly manner, wet, bruised, and exhausted, upon its bank. Unable to completely catch his breath, and still firmly disoriented, Chowbingo heard a voice calling.

Looking upwards, he believed that the voice was coming from just beyond the river's embankment. It sounded as if its source was from beneath the solitary, canopied tree, there just to the right of the clover-covered knoll.

"Chowbingo," the voice called.

"Who's calling? Who knows my name out here?" Chowbingo barked.

Startled by sounds that were guttural rather than linguistic, Chowbingo paused to consider the source and origin, but not before first turning his attention to a more primitive and compelling need; that of shaking the muddy river water from his fur, which he did, with a sense of enthusiastic verve.

His metamorphosis was complete.

Again, the same voice spoke from the knoll. "Come over here, warm yourself, and dry out. I have a fire started for you."

Chowbingo, now drenched in uncertainty, promptly bristled his fur, lay back his ears, and prepared to run in the opposite direction, just as fast as his new puppy legs might carry him. During his brief time in this new place he had been in the presence of evil, witnessed the remnants of death, and almost been thrust through by a bull. Chowbingo did not feel, for the moment, that he needed to make any further acquaintances.

"Over here! I'm under the mustard tree. Come up here and rest yourself for a spell." Chowbingo did find something intriguingly familiar about this voice, but he was still feeling too fuzzy of mind, from his recent experiences, to identify the caller.

"Unfortunately," thought Chowbingo, *"he probably wants to do to me what was done to that animal in the garden. After all, aren't I just another four-legged animal now, a strange animal in a strange place? I don't have any place where I can think to run."*

Finding himself weak in faith, he felt that Father had surely abandoned him.

"Such is my fate; it truly must be over for me, I guess, if death is to be my fate. Perhaps it's just better for me to die here right now rather than later."

23

Head hung low, tail turned down, and with his back slouched, Chowbingo slowly walked to meet his executioner. Here he found himself: Chowbingo, a spirit from before galaxies beginning and formerly without ending, now in this place. A place to which he had been unwittingly transported. He couldn't understand why he had been abandoned, so unwanted, so unloved, alone, and forsaken.

"Why have I become one of 'them'? Why am I here, captured in a body not unlike the soil that surrounds it? Here I find myself trapped, constrained by beginning and soon by ending. I find that I am no longer the free spirit I once was, gifted to abide in the company of Father, forever.

"How is it that I, who once was to live with Father for eternity, chosen from before time began to be his constant companion, now committed to death in this miserable puppy suit—one that is even beginning to smell bad?"

Chowbingo chose not to look up as he stumbled forward hesitantly yet with resolve, prepared then to end the matter. He would not allow his executioner the satisfaction of seeing his frightened gaze.

"Where are you, Father?" Chowbingo cried out from the inner recesses of his spirit. *"Where's your love? I know you! You can't abandon me! You're Father! I'm your companion."*

He continued to cry out as he resolutely placed hope against despair. He once again feebly declared the fullness of his faith against the fear that was continuing to envelop him. Nevertheless, even against his best efforts, within a matter of only brief moments, Chowbingo again found himself absent from all hope and stripped of his faith. Valiantly, in hopeless, helpless faith, he bitterly screamed again for Father.

"*Aaaargh . . . Faaaarrrk!*" Try as he might, his most desperate cry was, nonetheless, still a bark.

In its natural course the heat of the sun dissipated, and Chowbingo, from his downward gaze, noticed a large shadow being cast across the ground. He had made his way from the wetness of the river's bank all the way to just under the shadow of the massive mustard tree. Yet, still, he refused to look up. Again the voice, a familiar one he was now quite certain, came from directly in front of him, certainly from less than an arm's length away.

"Chowbingo, I've been waiting for you. Please sit and rest awhile. Perhaps then we can talk."

Again, the voice! It was close and familiar, yet Chowbingo still hadn't recognized it. Cautiously, raising his gaze skyward, he finally came face to face with his host. Chowbingo found himself immediately shocked to discover that such a uniquely familiar voice would be originating from such a completely unrecognizable being. Vexed and perplexed, Chowbingo, nonetheless, mustered his resolve and immediately demanded an accounting from the individual who stood there before him.

"*WHO ARE YOU?*" asked Chowbingo, while simultaneously recoiling from the sudden aggressiveness of his own voice, a voice that he later recalled was spiritual, in language—of the type used in Neveah.

The stranger responded, in like kind, with a soft measured voice. "You know me, Chowbingo. I'm Schezak, Father's high priest. Now lie down and sleep. We can talk later after your earthly suit has rested and been rejuvenated."

"Sleep, rest, restored—I don't understand. What are you talking about?"

"Those are earthen things. Don't worry, you'll catch on. Took me a while, too, with this wizard suit and all."

Chowbingo then, for the first time since his arrival on planet Earth, found himself feeling warm, safe, and at peace. He knew he was with his friend Schezak, his mentor from Neveah. Father had not forsaken him. Schezak was surely the wise counsel whom Father had promised.

Chowbingo then slowly sauntered over to the trunk of the mustard tree, where he circled about his own body before falling on all fours, quickly to the ground. Tucking his muzzle, securely near his tail, he was soon asleep. He moved in and out of a deep slumber whereupon he recounted those parts of his journey that previously he had failed to consider.

There had been the city suspended in open space, which had been lit by the five moons reflecting the lights of Neveah. There was the silver ladder with rungs wrapped in golden threads. Chowbingo had been most impressed; he recalled, that the end of each rung had been capped with single, white alabaster pearls, each at least forty carats in size. Who, he later had asked me, were the ones he had seen descending that ladder when he passed alongside it, on his way to Earth, and who, he asked me, were the two he had seen battling in space, if I knew?

He recounted that feathers flew from one and from the other dislodged scales showered the skies. Each of the two had appeared as shooting stars in the night. One combatant had celebrated, using the vilest of words, while he parried each thrust of his adversary using his jewel-encrusted sword, the hilt of which was uniquely fabricated from black onyx and rubies of the darkest hue. If further inquiry were to be made of him, Chowbingo might describe it as the color of spent blood. Surrounding this embodiment of evil, Chowbingo witnessed hideous little monsters, who arose as a chorus, following each vile word that was emitted.

His opponent singularly fought without chorus or support. His strength, Chowbingo noted, had come from his faith and from his inner resolve.

"What about the black hole, that space folding in upon itself, where nothing rolled inward to further nothingness?"

Chowbingo asked this of me, with great interest, as he considered his voyage. Such a place of darkness he had never before witnessed, nor was it one that he could presently even consider. Within were the burnings, from which came unimaginable heat. And emanating from the conflagration came putrid smells of such foul odors as he had never before encountered. He reminded me that it was truly such a terrible stench that it could only be referred to as "indescribable". The surrounding blackness was beyond understanding, and then came the sounds. They were as if they might have been the screams of a million times a million. They had been deafening for Chowbingo to hear, and still they remain painful for him to recall. Within this, the indescribable, each was contained. Separately each was isolated unto itself. It can be said that they were all together, yet totally apart.

Their presence, Chowbingo was only partially able to witness because of the reflective nature of Xeres, the great scaled dragon's, mantle. Xeres, that creature most magnificent and beautiful to behold, shone like a thousand lights. Each of his scales stood out with the luminescence of a thousand rainbows.

"Could you surely have been there, back in the great void, or were you only dreaming?" I had to ask this of Chowbingo.

"I don't know," he pensively replied, after due consideration. He then continued to narrate his story to me just as he had experienced it.

————

The sun, slipping below the horizon, glared directly into Chowbingo's eyes, causing him to reluctantly stir from his position of rest. There, partially awake and rested, he looked toward Schezak sitting against the tree and thanked him for allowing him his fifteen minutes of rest.

"Chowbingo," Schezak began. "My sweet little friend, you have been asleep for the past seventy-two hours!"

Rested but still only partially alert, Chowbingo jumped straight up, shook his fur, and with his hind foot dispatched one final itch from behind his right ear. Finished, Chowbingo bringing himself to as much of a commanding presence as one small puppy might muster, looked at Schezak and challenged, *"Really now, why are we here? What's going on here? I insist upon an answer!"*

Schezak smiled, ignored the urgency of the question, and replied with a slight chuckle. "Chowbingo, you certainly don't look like the person who I knew back in Neveah. Perhaps you should walk over to the pond, near the still part of the river, and consider what you see in its reflection."

Chowbingo obediently left the coolness of the canopied mustard tree and sauntered back down toward the river's edge. Somberly he glanced toward the reflection, assured that he would immediately be able to end this foolishness once and for all.

The clear, perfectly mirrored reflection stared back at him. It moved its head, then lowered its gaze, and finally licked its chops, all in perfect harmony with Chowbingo's every movement. Chowbingo jumped back with uncontrollable alarm and froze in place. The exception was his fur, which continued to bristle as if he had been exposed to a firm jolt of static electricity.

"What's going on," he wondered. Schezak was not appearing before him as Schezak, and he certainly did not appear to be Chowbingo. *"What is this place called Earth and why am I here?"*

Schezak again called for Chowbingo to leave the wetness of the bank and join him. This time Chowbingo,
determined to shake off the remaining remnants of sleep,
dragged himself, slowly and doggedly, back up to the spot
where Schezak was patiently waiting. " *I don't understand*," uttered Chowbingo, to which Schezak responded,
"I know you don't understand, that's why I'm here. I'm Father's high priest, remember? Now settle down, rest,
listen, and please allow me to share my knowledge with
you, so that I can prepare you to undertake Father's mission."

Chapter 3

The Mission

C howbingo, you are seeing yourself in your earthly form and me in mine. Now please relax so I can speak to you.

"Your mission, Chowbingo, is to restore that which was lost in Father's garden, a relationship between Him and His beloved, with their faith restored, as it was in the beginning. You will start with the chosen one to whom you will later be introduced."

"What?"

"Don't worry, it will all become abundantly clear in Father's time: you recall, never early, never late, as is His way."

"Perhaps you'd like to start from the beginning," Chowbingo murmured, mostly to himself, not wishing to annoy

Schezak, who tended to have a short fuse when challenged—and who was, as Chowbingo saw it, possibly his only way back to Neveah.

"Chowbingo, about two thousand some odd years ago, Father and I were talking. He took the occasion to share with me that it was lonely being the Light of the Universe, such as you and the others have always known Him.

"He explained that He also yearns for friendship and companionship. I find that I am insufficient to fulfill that need because His knowledge, wisdom, and understanding always have exceeded my ability to comprehend His eternal knowledge. Try as I might, we would always end with Him being perfect and myself being imperfect.

"He wanted a place where He could go, a place of relaxation as it were, to socialize with others. I took His concerns most seriously and, after cautious thought, recommended to Him that He might consider creating a people whom He could communicate with, people in a location away from the distraction of Neveah, a people with their own free thoughts. Unlike you or me, they could express disagreement or agreement with Him such as they might find appropriate.

"Father took my counsel, which was not at all unwarranted, since He had established me before time began to be His high priest without time beginning or time ending. However, as He always did with our discussions, He turned my imperfections to perfection. Therefore, when He created these humans, He established protections that exceeded even my wisdom.

"These people, humans they were later called, would have free will. But this time their free will would be subject to limitations more restrictive than what He had first allowed the Master Counterfeiter, that master of evil. Humans would become accountable for their own free will. They would reside on Earth where they would have a beginning and finally for their fleshly bodies a temporal end. They would have freedom of choice, but with that freedom there would come responsibility. Humans could freely exercise their choices, and by those choices they would establish where their spirits might later live."

"Schezak, I only knew Neveah with Father. What are these other places where spirits might later live?"

"When you left Father's presence you were transported through space and galaxies here to planet Earth. Here you found yourself in His garden. Remember, while passing through the void of space, you encountered two places: Lambda, the 'city of regrets' or 'land of the unfinished,' and Strakula, the 'city of despair' or 'land of the endings.' Lambda is illuminated by the reflective moons from Neveah, and Strakula is dark except for the residual lighting that shines solely from the eyes of the dragon's presence.

"While you were being transported through the crystal galaxy you witnessed death, frozen in time. After landing on Earth, in His garden, you viewed the Tree of Death with all of its decay. That was, at one time, the Tree of Life. Again, you felt it when you tripped over the bones of the animal. On each occasion, Chowbingo, you felt the absence of spirit."

"Yes, Schezak, I find that I sorely missed their spirits. These silly garments, which you and I now find so restrictive, must we keep them?"

"Welcome to planet Earth and the first day of your mission," replied Schezak as he neatly sidestepped the question. "Here we must live in these physical bodies so that we can help His humans, you as a chow dog and me as a wizard."

"Schezak, do these humans live forever and ever like us?"

"Yes, Chowbingo, but unlike us, humans have a beginning for both their bodies and also for their spirits. It starts when they are first created by Father. It's called 'birth'. Then, after a time, their bodies die, just like the crystal galaxy, the fruits of the Tree of Death, and the body of the animal that you tripped over.

"However, unlike the galaxies, these humans have spirits and their spirits will never die. Human spirits leave their bodies at death and are then transmuted to new locations."

"Why?" asked Chowbingo.

"It all occurred because of the great scaled dragon!

"It was Father's wish to create all human spirits in His likeness and in His image with each having his own FREE WILL. Then, He would be able to communicate with them in His private garden. He would be able to bless them with all grace and goodness. There would never be a discouraging word, or hurt, or harm because He would not create them to know evil. He provided plants, animals, galaxies, and living creatures of every sort to amaze and delight humans during His absence. He only asked for their un-divided fellowship when in His presence, so that He might bless them with His never-ending love. Father's desire was for them to live in a state of perfect love and to walk in happiness, forever!

"He had created His garden and all was well and all was good. There was peace, there was love, and there was harmony. All of the garden's subjects were vegetari-ans. The plants were so plentiful that each could share its foliage to feed His creatures and none would have to sac-rifice its root. The monkey would climb the neck of the giraffe to gather in the morning sunrise. Hyenas would entertain bear cubs while their mothers rested. The wolves taught social manners and leadership to the er-rant offspring of migrating herds. Alligators provided transportation across lakes and rivers to egrets, nutria, and ewe. Eagles flew bunnies to their hutches. The lamb lay down with the lion, and His beloved humans would manage, categorize, and befriend them all.

"Every species was resplendent within its own coat, each was attractive to its own mate, and all were humble before Father. All that is except for the dragon, a creature of resplendent colorations, who was fond of amazing, dazzling, and delighting all those who encountered him. The magnificent Xeres, the great scaled dragon, a crea-tion from times past, delighted in wandering to and fro through Father's garden where he was only wont to coun-terfeit, challenge, or abuse all of that which Father had created.

"He traded love for hate, and he diverted honor and glory, not to Father but to himself. He continually preened his scales and polished his colors so that all glory might be deflected from Father to him. He cried out mightily and unceasingly for all to follow him, to adore him, and to covet him because of his body's magnificence and its beauty. However, his cries sounded without response and his magnificence was ignored by all because creation didn't, then, know evil!

"That great dragon thought, pondered, watched, and observed, and finally he understood. He had to teach just one human to know evil. Then all of creation would certainly know evil.

"The great dragon planned and schemed and then he schemed some more. He would teach the humans envy, lust, greed, gluttony, jealousy, and hate. He would teach them lying, stealing, hurting, and killing. He would teach humans to want things they didn't need and to need things they didn't want. He would mostly teach them to want their bodies to shine gloriously like his.

"The dragon knew what to do and he knew, very well, how to do it. He would overwhelm humans with earthly delights that could not last, and joy followed always by disappointment. He would entice them with beautiful objects, trinkets, clothing, and comforts. He would titillate them with sounds they had not heard, gossip, strange music, sounds of pain, agony, and confusion. The peaceful sounds of Father would be replaced with the dragon's sounds of bewilderment. He would entice humans through their eyes, their ears, their touch, their taste, and their smell because he was unable to reach them through their spirits. Father had freely given, to mankind, the gift of free will. Xeres, a creature who was truly Mephistophelean in all of his cunning, would use Father's gift of free will to turn humans to his evil ways."

"Why did Xeres want humans to do evil?" asked Chowbingo.

"So that he could separate them from their relationship with Father. Then they would adore only him."

"How is evil able to separate a human from Father?"

"Father cannot be in the presence of evil," replied Schezak. "It is against His nature, just like it is against your nature to walk under water. Whomever Xeres draws to evil, Father cannot bless with fellowship, or give to them spiritual gifts. This deeply hurts Father, but it brings overwhelming joy to the dragon."

"Schezak," asked Chowbingo. "Why can't Xeres, the great scaled dragon, and Father both enjoy the fellowship of humans together?"

"At a time, and then a time again before the garden, Father created the dragon. I was there with him. Wisdom, Knowledge and Understanding were also there with us. It was a glorious time when Father spoke and said, 'Today I will create a creature of such awesome beauty that whosoever might gaze upon him will know and recognize him as the majesty of My creation.'"

"That must have been a wonderful event, Schezak."

"Yes, Chowbingo, it was truly wonderful, but unfortunately it did not end the same way. Xeres was created with the knowledge of good and evil. Father had created the dragon to magnify Himself but not to replace Him. The more Xeres' beauty and magnificence became apparent to him, the more he viewed himself as first equal to, and finally greater than, Father.

"Not unexpectedly, Father became enraged over his behavior, and He expelled Xeres from Neveah along with all of those who had chosen to join him."

"Where did they all go?"

"To Strakula, 'the land of despair.' There they are to remain separated forever, existing within the error of their ways."

"Will they ever see Father again?" asked Chowbingo.

"Never again will they be able to enjoy the warm, giving light that is the Father. His light, which illuminates Neveah by day and warms it by night, will never be known to them, except in remembrance. Their spirits will only be illuminated by the reflection, which comes from Xeres, as a remembrance of things past. His is that selfish reflection, which caused your fur to bristle, as you passed far from it, on your voyage here to Earth."

"So-o-o, then that's the end of it? Xeres, the great scaled dragon and all of his friends are in Strakula, while all of Father's humans are on Earth. Did I get it right?"

"Unfortunately, that isn't the way it all turns out. Xeres, the great scaled dragon, from the time of his beginning has always been able to move to and fro as he pleases. Remember, Chowbingo? He was made to display Father's magnificence throughout all of the universes. Later, when Father created His special garden to fellowship with humans, to show His love, and to give them spiritual gifts, that wily ole Xeres found a way to be there too. There he hid and awaited his opportunity to teach evil to just one human.

"Father was so excited about His garden and His gift of 'free will' that He elected to outfit all living beings born to Earth with their own personal bodies, just like you presently possess as a chow puppy and I as a wizard. Now each of us, with our spirits within our bodies, can live and operate here in Earth's realm. Father even selected for Himself a suit for His times of fellowship in the garden. Sadly, because of the great disappointment, He never wore it again after that day."

"What is 'THAT DAY' about which you are speaking, Schezak?"

"Well, Chowbingo, it happened like this. Father had created His special beings. He called them humans and blessed them with their own free will. They were made in His likeness and His image and He blessed them in every way. He graced them with a very special garden. It was a most special place, beautiful to behold and magnificent to see. Then, with all preparations complete, Father slipped into His earthly suit and descended into His garden for fellowship with them.

"He called throughout His garden, but the only response was from the sound of running and scurrying, not to Him but from Him. Father sat patiently and waited for a time. Finally, sheepishly, two humans emerged from the undergrowth. They were scratched and torn from the shrubs; each was wearing a garment made of sheep skin, and they were both found to still be dripping from an animal's blood.

"Father knew because their bodies were covered in blood that each had experienced evil; and therefore they were hiding their shame. He had made them perfect and now they stood before Him imperfect. They knew evil! They had killed the lamb for their covering, the one whose bones you saw, and now they knew death."

"What did Father do?" asked a shocked Chowbingo.

"Before Father chose to respond, Xeres stepped out onto the garden's pathway. He was right beside the fruit tree that you now call THE TREE OF DEATH. Lifting himself to his proudest stature, he looked at Father smugly, and addressed Him with a voice that sounded as if it had been distilled through venom. 'Father, I am greater than You,' he began. 'I am more perfect than You. I am more beautiful than You. Now I have shown You that I am also cleverer than You.' He then finished his announcement displaying all of the smugness that his vile countenance could muster.

"Father, then, said not a word.

"Xeres, the harbinger of all that is evil, continued uninterrupted. 'You created Your humans in innocence and provided each with his own free will. You knew that if they never witnessed evil, they'd be faithful only to You. I've changed that! I taught them evil, right here beside this fruit tree, and they, the fools, bought into it. They exercised that very same FREE WILL that You gave them. Now, Father, those beautiful children, they're mine!

"'They will spend their days in evil ways and they will do evil things. Evil will always be on their minds. When they try not to think of it, they will recall it. They will not be able to dismiss it. Evil thoughts will pass to father and mother, brother and sister, aunt and uncle, grandmother and grandfather. They will pass through to descendants as fast as galaxies give birth to stars. Evil will be with them always, until the end of time.'

"Almost finished with his rant, Xeres glared at Father, before declaring in parting words, 'I curse this fruit tree and claim it unto death as a covenant, between You and me, in memory of what I have done this day.'

"Father slowly stood and gazed at His newly created children with the sadness and sorrow that only a loving parent might feel or understand. As he stepped away to depart, Xeres, that great scaled dragon, bellowed in a final, parting, salvo, 'Earth is now mine and all that is found within it.'

"Earth, and all that it contained was then filled with evil. It had become sin and all that it contained immediately became sinful.

Suddenly powers appeared from Neveah as had never before been seen. The garden was emptied of the serpent and all humans were expelled. Left behind, as a remembrance, was the dead tree and its fruit. Xeres' scales remain scattered about. The bones of the lamb still remain, the one from which the skin had been cut for coverings."

"What happened to Father?" wailed Chowbingo, now truly upset.

"He returned to Neveah, cloistered the garden, and never spoke of the matter again. That was until you."

"Me? What can I do, Schezak?"

"You can show humans how to turn from sin to love. You will return them to the love of Father."

"I can't do that! Look at me. Now I'm just a dog. I can't even talk to them, I can only bark—and I don't even do that very well. What am I supposed to do, roll over, fetch, beg, and look cute?"

"Chowbingo, you have been Father's faithful companion since before universes began. You have observed his every action because that is what loyal companions do. You have been there for him in sadness, to share his joy, and when appropriate, you sit quietly by until the loss, hurt, or pain leaves.

"Although Father has been forsaken by humans, He has not forgotten them. His love, which He holds for them, is everlasting and never ending. Unfortunately, now He can't commune with them because the perfect Father cannot present Himself in the company of imperfect, sinful humans.

"Now that you are here, you will be changing that soon, beginning with your meeting with Father's elect. So, off with you. It's time for you to get started."

"Who, me?" Chowbingo replied in a voice mixed with emotion and desperation. "I'm just a dog," he again repeated one of his now-familiar protests. Then he was asleep and just as suddenly Schezak was gone.

Chapter 4

The Meeting

Chowbingo awoke to find the ground moist and un-comfortable. His underbelly was soaked. Unlike many other dogs, Chowbingo had discovered that when a chow's stomach becomes wet, it can become saturated and quite unbearable. He promptly arose onto his stout but stubby legs and began to furiously shake, dispelling the water from his fur with almost cyclonic force. He then did what most sane dogs are inclined to do; he went about the task of getting dry.

Finally, up then and partially awake, it was time to investigate his surroundings.

"How did I get here?" he murmured quietly to himself as he gazed about.

Set forth before him there lay a wooded passage, filled deep with leaves. Seemingly, its only purpose appeared to be to restrict his northerly progress, and thus it did; leaves piled upon leaves! Why he elected to go north, Chowbingo later acknowledged, was without rhyme or reason. Nonetheless, it seemed appropriate for the time.

Trudging forward, with his undersides repeatedly being dampened by the saturated leaf bed strewn before him, Chowbingo finally chose to accept all of it as part of his fate while he just quietly "continued to continue". He knew that Father was behind this, and there was just no arguing with Him, at least if he expected a proper outcome!

Slowly, into his peripheral vision, began to appear familiar forms, silhouettes of shapes that might be found throughout Neveah. Glancing directly toward the source of all that his eyes were able to envision, he saw wet, blackened limbs from ancient trees now lining his pathway. Although the limbs still held remnants from the last of the season's fall foliage there was something else, something that was foreboding, and very much present.

Chowbingo, with a slight tremor from beneath his fur, turned his focus toward the direction of his travel. During that slight movement he caught it, those faces! Hundreds of them, embedded in the trees. They were all immobile of course, part of the trees' structures, one might say. Yet, there were the eyes. The eyes which never moved. They were all focused on him! Meaningless? Yes. It was meaningless. Just pieces of bark from old trees depicting random images. After all, Chowbingo later learned, as he relayed it to me, humans, as children, were sometimes known to spend lazy, idyllic days, lying on their backs.

There they would watch varied images display themselves from within the clouds passing overhead.

It was with sudden recall that Chowbingo remembered those faces. They were the faces he had encountered during his trip to Strakula, the "land of despair." Those strakulian faces were all represented here: gargoyles, nymphs, the dark angels, his minions. The most frightening of all were the faces of the humans. Those portrayed were the ones lost forever and moaning in unrequited despair.

The further Chowbingo walked, then sprinted, and finally ran, the narrower the path appeared and the taller became the trees that loomed above him. When the sky, as was its nature, began to darken, those faces, now familiar to him, not only followed his every step with their gaze but also began to leer in countenance, as if to say, "This is Xeres' victory and Father will never be permitted to claim it as His again."

Here was evil. It wasn't about the remembrance of lost humans, crystal galaxies, or applauding minions. This was about evil in its purest form. This was Xeres' personal introduction to Chowbingo. Xeres was declaring to Chowbingo that he was Earth's master. He was its lord, and evil was to remain his conquering weapon.

Chowbingo perhaps hadn't yet understood the completeness and complexity of his mission but Xeres had, and the gauntlet had been thrown. Xeres wasn't about to give in or lose this time. After all, hadn't Father already shamed him and expelled him from Neveah?

Chowbingo, afraid, frightened, and realizing that he had nowhere to turn, continued on the path that lay before him. He lowered his head and restricted his gaze to that of glancing only at the leaves passing beneath him. He knew that Father was with him and that he wouldn't neglect him, BUT!

"Where am I?"

Slowly the low-lying fog began to work its way through the trees, a few wisps at a time. Softly wrapping each tree, as if in soft gray blankets, the forest seemed to fall quietly asleep, except for Chowbingo who found himself to be separate, alone, and fearful. Gathering his resolve, he slowly took a few cautious, exploratory steps forward into the thickening gray envelope, until he made out, coming from the north, a blurred yellow light, glowing as if it were from some distant candle.

The light, he felt assured, was from Father. Now with security, and a new sense of urgency, Chowbingo moved forward with a proper sense of purpose and a newly found determination. No longer did he fear the images of evil nor did he even consider the wetness of his underbelly. Focusing on the light before him, he moved forward until it turned from a beacon to the outline of a small village. Stumbling unexpectedly onto a cobblestone pathway, he shook the remaining leaves from his fur and paused to take in his unravelling surroundings.

Sensing a slight movement from behind his left ear, he turned unexpectedly with a start. There he found a young boy, standing quietly, who was staring at him quizzically.

Straightforward and without pretension, the youngster immediately walked up to Chowbingo and announced, "Hi, my name is Val, what's yours?"

Dumbfounded, and as a dog unable to verbally respond, Chowbingo just stood with his ears perked forward and his tail wagging. Val responded by reaching down and scratching Chowbingo behind his right ear.

"Well now, that certainly felt good," exclaimed Chowbingo. *"I've never had that done before. Maybe this Earth thing does have some side advantages,"* he thought.

Gently, Val took Chowbingo by the nape of his neck and led him forward through the front door from where he had just come. Once inside, Val cried out with giddy enthusiasm, "Mama, Mama, I've just found me a puppy. Can I keep him for myself? Please, please!"

Stepping forward, from within the darkened recesses of the humble cottage, appeared a middle-aged woman looking well beyond her probable years. Hunched over, with straggly brown hair now turning gray, she moved forward as if the weight of the universe were upon her shoulders.

"Val, you know I can't properly feed us. How might I also now feed this animal?" She spoke her words in a saddened, resigned voice.

"Mama, it's late and it's cold outside. Can't he just stay until morning?"

"All right, but tomorrow he goes," she replied in a voice filled with determined resolve.

Feeling the tension and not wishing to become a topic of dissension, Chowbingo quietly settled down before the diminishing embers of the cabin's bleak fireplace. As the night's air grew colder, Chowbingo curled into an ever-tightening ball while the fire's embers turned from a heat-giving orange-red to a warmth-robbing steel gray. The discomfort of the cold continued to strip Chowbingo of any possibility for sleep until, finally sitting up before the cold fireplace, he chose to seriously consider his plight.

Here he was sitting on a cold hearth, in a poverty-stricken cabin, where all of life's enjoyments were being sucked from this widowed mother and her young son. This could not be Father's best nor was it even His hand. This was darkness and evil. This was the hand of Xeres. Evil was his weapon.

"My new friends live in despair and Xeres laughs. I must find a way to change this," mumbled Chowbingo, seated there without an idea, in the cold dark of the night.

Finally, completely awake and visibly distraught, he began to tread a circuitous path about the cabin's interior. It was there that he first began to notice a gleaming of the moon's light through the cabin's cellophane covered opening. Instinctively, as if by inspiration, he walked directly to the doorway, slightly set ajar, and stepped out onto the moon lit walkway.

It was here where Chowbingo found me waiting, beside a humble hand-hewn rustic bench, along with our mutual friend Khasmar. He had, at the last minute, chosen to accompany me from our home in Neveah.

"Hey, what the . . .? It can't be! Who is it? Is it really you? Jabez, Khasmar, what are you guys doing here—how did you get here?"

I watched with amusement as Chowbingo continued to blurt forth his retinue of disbelieving expletives until Khasmar ended it in his very understated and simple manner. "Yes, it's us."

Then, obviously besides himself to see the two of us, Chowbingo followed with his customary, direct, head-on approach once again. *"But, how'd you two get here?"*

Again, in his normally aloof and seemingly disinterested manner, Khasmar replied, "We came down Neveah's ladder, certainly a bit more civilized than the manner in which you tumbled here, wouldn't you think? How else did you expect us to come – get sucked down by gravity like you?"

"But why'd you come?" queried the still-startled Chowbingo.

"Because Schezak told us that you were in a bit of a jam, and, after all, we are friends!"

"Well, it is quite cold sleeping on that hearth, without Father's heat, I must admit. I haven't been nourished, and the wet leaves sticking to my belly haven't been pleasant, and this doggy earthen suit is most restrictive and . . ."

I found opportunity to interrupt.

"Chowbingo, we did not travel all this way just for your comfort. Please understand that a trip down that ladder is more than just a little trying, especially at our ages. We have come here to assist you in the fulfillment of your assignment.

"Now Khasmar, give the amulet to Chowbingo, and let's be off," I instructed a bit rudely. Moments later, following my selfish little outburst, I apologized with contrite solemnity and then personally affixed the chrysolite amulet about Chowbingo's neck with a bit of vine that I found strewn along the pathway. Khasmar, not wishing to be excluded, took care to remind both of us that this was a remnant from Neveah's foundations and therefore was not to be treated with the same carelessness as I had used to affix it about Chowbingo's neck.

I was genuinely miffed at Chowbingo for his selfish response. This trip was not for his own individual pleasure but rather to redirect the hurting, the suffering, and the disenfranchised into Father's embrace. Chowbingo's mission was to first becoming acclimated to Earth's mannerisms through Father's elect. He then would be free to select and change one individual. Through the changing of just one person others would be able to observe and to learn. Ultimately, through association, they could discover the excitement of believing by faith. Each then could, through the knowledge of faith, finally be brought before the Father's light, where he could share in His joy and in His happiness.

The amulet had been taken from Neveah's seventh foundation which was always known to us as the "Foundation of Completion". Our amulet, this one small piece of rock, was to serve as Chowbingo's reminder to take his assignment seriously, and to move with resolve. Contained within it there would be no power or magical qualities. Its sole purpose was to serve as a reminder of Father's power and His willingness to answer, when called upon with sincerity and in accordance with His way.

Dawn had not yet arrived before Chowbingo wandered slowly back into the cabin. He really had nowhere else to go for the moment. So, after entering, he quietly settled down onto the wood plank floor, alongside the stone hearth, then too cold to touch.

Soon after, with dawn giving way to full light, Val arose from his straw mattress, which was covered in cotton flour sacks. The designs and logos of multiple flour processors, still imprinted on them, provided their own special motif. Eclectic as it was, nonetheless, it did serve to provide a bit of whimsical brightness to an otherwise dark, dank, and dingy environment; the only other object of brightness was the large copper-clad kettle that hung from the fireplace's singular wrought iron fixture.

Standing almost erect, Val slowly began the process of fully awakening as young boys are inclined to do. Then, upon spotting Chowbingo at the far side of the room, he sprang from where he stood, recovered as he almost slipped from crossing over the stone hearth, and finally lunged toward Chowbingo, grabbing him by the tail before he could entertain any thoughts of escape. Chowbingo jumped up and let out a painful yelp, more from surprise than from any actual pain. He pulled loose and immediately fled for the door reacting to his inner-dog "flight or fight instinct". Val quickly bolted for the solitary door behind him. His mother, responding to Chowbingo's yelp, arose confused, and also followed, trailing the both of them.

"Val, I said you can't keep the dog," she yelled out toward a direction but to no one in particular. Val, in the interim, had already moved far beyond their garden and was around the corner, in pursuit of Chowbingo whom he finally caught with a flying tackle. His mother, still believing herself to be in the chase, unknowingly had turned in the opposite direction. There, not having found anyone to pursue, she returned to her cottage. She left Val and Chowbingo to their own activities, confident that she would confront the two of them later.

Wrestled to the ground, Chowbingo squirmed and tossed in an attempt to rid himself of the sixty-five-pound Val who had pinned him to the still wet ground. Tired of being pressed into the soft, wet soil, Chowbingo, with a singular burst of reserve energy, attempted to slide out from under Val's grip.

Finally, after lengthy runs and harrowing dashes between pursuer and pursued, through the forest's web of entangled labyrinths, Val once again had his puppy, all of which added to Chowbingo's frustration and dislike. Trying, as he was capable, to renew his grip to that of a more favorable hold, Val mistakenly found himself grasping the amulet, rather than the fur he had expected. Slightly startled, and therefore taken back by the unfamiliar feel of the stone, he involuntarily loosened his grip from around Chowbingo's neck.

Stone then still in hand, all wrestling ceased for both Val and Chowbingo. The chrysolite that Val fingered beneath Chowbingo's neck was, in color magnificent to behold, to the touch smooth, and of a warmth that might be called unexpected. It might have been not at all unlike a translucent emerald reflecting the rays of the noonday sun. However, for Chowbingo, this had become an overcast afternoon in an aged village, deep down within the Vesdre Valley of Eastern Belgium.

Finally, free of their wrestling activities, the two began to walk side by side in silence. Moving through the winding ways of the textile town, Val glanced, as he so often had before, toward the workers' serpentine line working its way toward the factory gates. He often recalled that his father, before the accident, had been one of them. Those had been Val's happiest days. He so loved it when Mama would smile. He remembered, so fondly, the day that Papa had returned from the factory with his copper kettle. It was still Mama's proudest possession. It had been awarded to Papa for outstanding service as a line supervisor. The engraving even stated it.

That was just two days before they lost Papa to the "accident".

They never did find his body. The other workers who had been with him said that the structural timbers supporting the building began to squeak and groan. Said it sounded to them like the human screams of people in mortal pain. Then suddenly the pressure and tension caused the timbers to snap like toothpicks.

Papa, who was in his cubicle within the inner office, was caught up in the splinter of timbers. All the beams and their supporting posts, broken and fragmented, plummeted down upon him as if by agreement. Papa, caught up in the entanglement, disappeared into the rubble. Mama never smiled again.

Continuing along the path, as they were, Val began to notice renewed glances in his direction. He hadn't recalled being noticed like this since the days when he first walked down those same paths hand in hand with his dad. Those were the days when he had been referred to as Salvio's son.

Val lifted his head as the rising sun seemed to greet him with a new brightness. It reflected off Chowbingo's coat to where it shone as if it were emitting its own amber glow. Men waved in his direction as his eyes met theirs. The women looked his way with engaging smiles. This was a beautiful day.

It was the chrysolite amulet. There it was hanging from Chowbingo's neck for all to see. Surely all who came near it were being touched by its powers.

"Look, Puppy, the stone—the stone! See."

Chowbingo, of course, was unable to see the stone. Hanging from his neck, it was not visible to him and, as a dog, he couldn't point that out to Val.

Val, now exuberant, began carousing through the village while dragging a bewildered Chowbingo along on a makeshift leash. There was hardly a place that they had not visited or revisited, throughout the village, as the hours fell behind them.

Turning one of the corners, with giddy enthusiasm, he saw the candy store, which he had not visited since his father's death. He hesitated, but then, remembering the amulet and the powers he had newly witnessed, he entered the store alongside the bewildered Chowbingo.

Mr. Bellingeri warmly greeted him, as if he were his own son.

"Val, how are you, my boy? It has been so long since we've talked," he blurted out in his heavily accented, old world Walloon accent, a dialect inherited from the "langues d'oil".

Val started to withdraw, but them remembered the power of the amulet about Chowbingo's neck, and exclaimed, "I haven't been able to visit you since Papa was killed."

"I know about your father's death, and I am very sorry, but why haven't you come to visit with me before now?" responded Mr. Bellingeri.

Val's first reaction was to immediately run out of the store, never to return. Then, from the corner of the doorway, he spotted Chowbingo and the amulet. The stone, with all of its power, was right there beside him.

"My young Val," began the shopkeeper, as he reached into a large candy barrel, "there has always been candy at my store for you. Your smile was always sufficient payment enough for me—here, enjoy."

Val hesitated, glanced at the amulet, smiled, and reached his hand forward to receive the candy. Ready to put the candy in his mouth, he hesitated, looked toward Chowbingo, and then stared directly into Mr. Bellingeri's eyes, whereupon he remained silent.

After some uncomfortable moments, Mr. Bellingeri asked, "What is it, Val?"

Val replied, "Can I have a piece for my new friend? I don't think he's eaten since I found him yesterday."

"Candy isn't good for animals, Val. Walk down the street a couple of doors with me and we'll see if we can take care of your friend."

Mr. Bellingeri, without hesitation, stepped out of his store and turned left onto the sidewalk without ever glancing back. Chowbingo and Val looked at one another, and then quickly fell into step, tagging along behind. No sooner had they caught up than Mr. Bellingeri was at his destination and stepping through the entranceway to Kolvalenko's Fine Meats.

"Yuri, I would like you to meet my good friend, Val Patadarski, and his furry companion. We were wondering if you might have a spare bone that you might give to his dog. I understand that he hasn't eaten since yesterday."

Yuri, the butcher, looked toward Chowbingo. Val noticed that Yuri was looking directly at the amulet before he spoke, saying, "Yes, of course, I have a bone for your friend. Take this one, it even has a choice piece of meat still on it."

"Well now, that's settled," replied Mr. Kolvalenko, as he gently inserted the bone into Chowbingo's mouth. "How's your mother, Val?"

Val began to recount the same hardships that he had recited to Mr. Bellingeri just a few minutes before. After listening compassionately, Mr. Kolvalenko reached into his display counter, pulled out a nice roast, and began wrapping it.

"Val, please take this to your mother with my love," he said. "Tell her, whenever she needs more, to drop by. I always have special prices for your mom. She was a very beautiful woman when we attended school together. I am sure nothing has changed."

Butcher Yuri took one last glance toward Chowbingo before saying to no one in particular, "That's a pretty stone around your dog's neck. Better be careful lest someone takes it."

Then stooping down and looking directly into Chowbingo's eyes he said, "Young puppy, this bone is all yours but that roast belongs to Angelina."

Then he winked and stepped away.

Chowbingo, both perplexed and confused, gently accepted the bone in his mouth. Then, realizing that he was dismissed, started on his way.

Mr. Bellingeri took a moment to look out the window, whereupon he noted the darkness beginning to descend onto the valley floor, as was the custom for the season. He quickly admonished Val to follow Chowbingo's lead and get started for home lest his mother should suffer added worries.

The two of them, Val and Chowbingo, began the journey back through the village toward Val's home. Darkness was beginning to displace what remained of the retreating light. The glow from the amulet, which soon disappeared, seemed to be replaced by the sights and sounds of the night. Ghosts, goblins, witches, and witchcraft; they may all seem part of a child's reality, yet a parent may differ.

Nonetheless, shall it be called permissible to deny children their "visions of the night" while also insisting that they acknowledge the religious spirits of their elders? I think not, nor did Val, as he made his way toward the cabin with Chowbingo in tow.

Val, firmly convinced that whenever it turned evening evil spirits were sure to appear, spontaneously sprang forward, entering into a broken field run that would bring smiles to the face of even the most seasoned football coach. The faster he ran the quicker he felt them following. The more he darted, the more numerous the apparitions seemed to appear. They were not visible, of course, but the hair rising up the back of his neck verified for Val, nonetheless, the reality of their presence.

Reluctantly, Chowbingo was again finding himself being tugged by Val's makeshift leash, but this time it became wrapped around three of his four legs. Rolling and sliding through the grass, Chowbingo did all he could to untangle the leash and right himself. All while still being pulled across the ground by a panic-stricken Val. Finally, for the brief moment that it took for a frightened Val to stop and determine his next course of direction, Chowbingo was able to free his legs and stand erect. Freedom, however, was only to be short lived. Unexpectedly, he came to a harsh, sudden stop that provided him with his first earthly taste of certain sharp, and unexpected, pain. His was a pain that was hurtful, lasting, and piercing. It was unlike the discomfort that his body had experienced after being pummeled out of the garden before splashing down into the cool river. Here, he had just jammed the butcher's bone, which he had been carrying between his jaws, into the fork of a bush.

Val, witnessing his recently acquired little friend sprawled on the ground and yelping in pain, suddenly came to his senses. The thought of spirits immediately disappeared from Val's imagination as he knelt down before his injured Chowbingo. Val gently removed the bone from Chowbingo's mouth where it had been jammed betwixt his rear-most teeth. Finally, free of the bone, Chowbingo continued to yelp both from the fright as well as from the pain. These were not feelings that he had experienced while in the company of Father. Pain—this was an experience from Earth, and Chowbingo didn't like it.

Now that they were finally just a few short yards from the cottage's door, Val set down the bundle from Mr. Kolvalenko and then carefully placed Chowbingo's bone on top. Next, stooping down, he gently picked up Chowbingo and headed for the front door.

Unexpectedly, just seconds shy of his arrival, the door swung open as if it were operating on its own accord.

There, before Val could react, his mother filled the room's emptiness with her presence as she began to scream at him before, momentarily, regaining her composure. "Where have you been? I thought this darkness scared you. You have never stayed out like this. You've made me almost sick from my fear for you. Why did you . . . oh, that dog again. I told you to get rid of him. Val, we can't feed him and now here you come in late. Boy, what am I going to do with you?"

"Mama, please, my puppy is injured," pleaded Val.

"My puppy, now it's my puppy," wailed his mother. "I suppose now you think perhaps I must not only feed your puppy, but I should also fetch your puppy a doctor or maybe even a specialist. If only you had listened to me last night and put him out as I had asked you . . . Never mind, now he is injured and we must care for him as best we can. Carry him over here and lay him on my bed."

Val did as he was instructed, and Chowbingo's yelps slowly were reduced to sickly murmurs. Val then briefly recited, to his mother, Chowbingo's encounter with the forked branch.

Chowbingo did, however, find it important to later inform me that Val, to protect his personal bravado, had managed to overlook the matter of "his flight from the night spirits" as he had recounted the events to his mother.

Angelina Patadarski picked up the oil lantern and moved it closer to where Chowbingo lay so that she might more properly attend to his wounds. Noticing the blood around the corners of his mouth, she instructed Val to stroke the embers as she gathered together some kindling wood, to reignite whatever dormant logs remained in the fireplace. Hopefully, they would soon have enough water heating in her copper kettle to properly cleanse his wounds

Waiting for the water to boil, she returned to her verbal scolding of Val for his disobedience, while absent-mindedly running her hands through Chowbingo's fur as she looked for additional injuries. Inadvertently, striking the chrysolite amulet, she unconsciously grasped and lifted it from the recesses of Chowbingo's fur where she brought it into the reflection of the lantern's light. Immediately, noticing its green glint, she exclaimed to no one in particular, "What's this? Why, it's beautiful!"

Val answered, "Yes, Mama, it is very beautiful." Angelina continued, more to herself than to Val, "I don't know what it is but it looks like it is very valuable. This animal must belong to a very wealthy owner."

Then she continued, expressing a renewing interest in Chowbingo, "Perhaps, if we are careful in caring for him, we might find the owner and he might reward us, richly.

"Val, the water is boiling now. Wet the rags and bring them to me. Not too hot now, I don't want to burn his mouth."

Val looked at his mother and cautiously responded, "Mama, I don't think he belongs to anyone; I think he has magical powers and I think that green stone is what he uses. You should have seen what happened when we were walking toward Mr. Bellingeri's candy store. . ."

"Val, you're starting to talk foolishness. Now please bring those rags over to me so I can tend to this dog and perhaps get us a reward."

"Oh, oh," exclaimed Val as he suddenly bolted for the door and dashed into the darkness. "I almost forgot!"

"Well I'll . . . there goes that crazy fool son of mine again," muttered Angelina, before she had an opportunity to grab him, as was her wish. "What has come into his crazy head now? First I lose my husband, now I'm here caring for someone else's dog that my son says is magical, while he takes off, running around in the dark."

Just then Val returned with Chowbingo's bone and his mama's package.

"I told you he was magical, Mama," he loudly exclaimed, as he handed Chowbingo's half-eaten, freshly broken meat bone, to his mother.

Angelina Patadarski slowly pulled away from Chowbingo, stood straight up, and compassionately looked toward Val, as only a loving mother could. "Val, are you okay?" she asked.

Val responded, now more excited than before, "Mama, look at this," he exclaimed. He thrust the wrapped package into her hands. "Open it, open it," he begged.

Returning to her sitting position on the bed, Angelina careful began to unwrap the parcel. No sooner had the corner been opened before Chowbingo's canine instincts took over. He sprang to attention, apparently healed, and immediately positioned himself next to her, and of course, her package.

"Well, you certainly seem to have returned to your former self," she said, smiling at Chowbingo.

Then, as she completed opening the package, containing the one kilogram of prime beef, she believed she knew the reason for Chowbingo's sudden recovery.

How could she possibly know, from his actions, that Chowbingo truly had no interest in eating meat? He was for the moment, inwardly struggling between his newly acquired animal instincts and his more familiar spirit. This internal conflict was a new encounter for Chowbingo, and it was startling to him.

"Val, where did you steal this?" The tears began to flow down her cheeks as she spoke. "First I lose your father and now you do this to me, and all since this dog has come into our lives," she gasped between her sobs and her tears.

Val tried his best to console her, but no amount of effort seemed to work. He finally just gathered Chowbingo into his arms and went over to a seat, beside the fireplace, where they quietly waited for her to stop sobbing.

Later, when he felt it was appropriate to speak, Val quietly said, "Mother this is a gift from Mr. Kolvalenko to you. He said he remembered you from when the two of you attended school together. He told me that you were very beautiful."

Angelina looked down at her hands, and then she looked at the roast resting in her lap. Slowly she raised her eyes and looked toward Val, and finally then over to Chowbingo. She captured each of them in her gaze and then, softly, began to weep all over again.

Val looked at Chowbingo curled in his lap, and just sighed with resignation as he carefully crossed his legs to afford Chowbingo a more comfortable spot while they waited quietly in the cabin's solitary fireside chair. Chowbingo, comfortable and undisturbed for the moment, quietly thought about Father at home and wondered if he really cared, or even understood Mrs. Patadarski's plight. Looking toward the warming fireplace, they both started to doze off together, Chowbingo and Val.

Philip I. Amos

Chapter 5

Other Worlds

The embers began to ebb and fall, almost as if they were in harmonious concert with Chowbingo's breathing. Slowly, as he began to slip away into a slumber, Chowbingo saw them again: the faces. These were the same faces that he had seen melded into the forest trees, but this time they were in the flames dancing, smiling, grinning and leering. Chowbingo, in the twilight of "half-sleep", tucked his head, inward toward his chest, to avoid their gaze. It didn't work. The faces, flashing upward from the hot embers, seemed to bypass his vision and assault his innermost mind with an intensity not unlike that of a frozen treat consumed too quickly. Try as he might, he could not dismiss the vision.

These were more than just animated faces. These were inviting, beckoning spirits, who began by cajoling and enticing Chowbingo to release control of his mind so that his spirit might be free to join them. This was a vision, which had been cast for Chowbingo, and its invitation was clear. The hollow tunnel that appeared through the flames' center was certainly inviting to behold. It shone a warm orange, deep from within its bowels, there where it had first been formed. Nestled, within the epicenter, were bright red and cold yellow flames, which, without pause or interruption, repeatedly darted upward. Ascending the flames arose climbing ever higher, as they rode the chimney's draft. Enticed upwards, by the winds passing overhead, it was as if all was being choreographed by an outside intelligence.

Chowbingo drifted away into a deeper, quieter sleep, as he unceremoniously allowed his legs to fall, one by one, from the sides of Val's lap. He relaxed, appearing as a stuffed animal, carelessly abandoned at the edge of some spoiled child's dresser.

Peace however was not to remain his. The apparition continued to unfold as its allure permeated Chowbingo's thoughts. He felt that he was being transported to within, and he wondered what the end would bring. As if in response to his question, and without time for preparation or warning, it just simply began. The inner core, a fluid wall, cascaded down upon itself showering forth liquid gems: rubies; emeralds; topaz; and pearls colored in black, silver and white; diamonds, brilliant white, yellow and brown; sapphires, onyx and amethysts. It was a cascading waterfall, showering fluid jewels whose reflections were being captured as if by a sunrise. It was magnificent and truly beautiful to behold, tantalizing, and mesmerizing.

Chowbingo had entered within. Was it with his mind or with his body? I, even as I now set this to script, don't know. Chowbingo only recalls that it was stunning! Turn to the left or turn to the right? He selected the right and it was in this manner that his journey continued.

Deep, deep down from within the smallest recesses of his heart, Father's quiet, small voice of love and concern cried out to him. "Don't go there!"

Further and further Chowbingo continued, drawn more and more inward by the beauty and by the enticing call, a siren's song. *"Perhaps I should stop? Perhaps I should turn about? Perhaps I shouldn't be here?"*

And so he pondered his questions as the music continued toward its crescendo. Lightly and almost quietly at first, perhaps as if in a whisper, one might say, it started. Later, as if sung by choirs of angels, the beckoning melodies covered his every thought. Chowbingo was being drawn further and further into an abyss that he now began to fear. Nevertheless, he submitted to its allure and allowed for it to continue.

Steadfastly he progressed deeper within, as with each summoning step the walls became higher, the lights reflected brighter, and the music, the music became ever more beautiful and mystical in its calling. It all coalesced into a crescendo of lights and sounds, first reaching and then finally overwhelming.

It was then over. The beauty, it had ended.

Chowbingo, after he finally snapped to attention, found that he had been unable to discern reality from fiction. The fur on his back felt as if it had been standing straight up. He clearly recalls that when he attempted to awaken, his heart began beating at a feverish pitch. He felt sure, with a certain sense of diminishing certainty, that he had awakened to find himself running, ever so fast; just as quickly, he recalls, as his little puppy legs would permit.

Then, fear had taken hold. Fright froze him in time as it overcame his ability to run. He tumbled and fell flat on his back, where he found himself looking straight into the direction from whence he had just come. There was no longer light, nor music, nor flowing jewels. The gorgeous pathways had turned into dark steaming pavement; warm, in fact a bit hot, to the touch. The bejeweled walls were turning to cliffs of black granite. The music, yes the beautiful, beckoning music had become the screams of the eternally dying; those who would continue to exercise their wails of hopelessness, never to be satiated, so long as eternity should continue, time unending.

Chowbingo, sensing he was presently somewhere other than in his dream, awoke to find that he had just been returned to reality, or so he imagined.

He sprang to his feet, or was it as he thought? He knew that he was being constrained by his surroundings. His little furry legs felt as if they were being pulled onto warm pavement, preventing him from going anywhere. Captured in the warm bituminous mix, through his own foolishness, Chowbingo found himself stuck to the pathway as he continued to watch, with mixed emotions, the vision unfolding before him.

Val, who had been slumbering erect in his chair, shifted position and began to slump toward the floor. The weight from Chowbingo's four draped legs afforded the final pull necessary to unseat Chowbingo and drop him, without ceremony, to the hearth beneath. Likewise, Val simultaneously slipped smoothly from his chair leaving both of them firmly setting before the fireplace. Val on the hearth and Chowbingo sitting in his lap with his furry paws pushing through the center of Val's crossed legs.

Not measurably disturbed by his unexpected repositioning, Chowbingo felt the pathway begin to release him to continue his journey. Again he traveled, no longer into pitch blackness, but rather into a new garnet-red environment, quite like the color of spent blood returning through arteries for re-cleansing. Faintly at first, and then more clearly, the cavern's walls undertook their transformation into the faces of angels; dark angels would be a most appropriate name. They were the same faces that Chowbingo had seen before, once upon a time in Neveah; but they had been from a time that was before time.

The faces, as they became more animated, directed their voices toward Chowbingo, orchestrated as if they were a choir. These, however, weren't the voices of sensitivity and beauty that might be expected from a well-rehearsed assembly. No, these were voices filled with a vile harshness of pure evil. These were voices meant to intimidate. These voices were assuredly not meant to encourage.

From the recess of this cacophony, a singular voice began to arise, becoming more and more distinctive. That sound carried to the forefront, a cry like the sound of rolling thunder, delivered its message with unmistakable certainty.

"You are Chowbingo. I know you. You are not of this kingdom. This is privileged ground upon which you are not welcome. Cannot evil too, also have a place to rest?"

"I don't understand."

"You have been sent by Father. He is not welcome here and neither are you."

Chowbingo uncurled from Val's lap, and his body temporarily became rigid as his legs reached outward seeking support. His paws reached closely toward the fire.

The voices turned quiet. The choir dimmed. All movement stopped as Chowbingo began to arise. Feeling, then, that he was stepping out of his body did not concern him as he was finding it to be quite the nuisance. After all, hadn't he found it to feel dirty from the places where, since his arrival, he had found himself traveling? More times than not it was sore, like the night when he had caught his mouth on a branch because of Val's foolishness. He recalled, painfully, how it had continued to smart.

Imperceptibly Chowbingo again felt himself moving, as if he were leaving his body further and further behind, or so it seemed. The hot black pavement, where his body seemed to have been imprisoned, continued to retreat from under him sliding further behind. Chowbingo felt like he was being moved through an open chasm. The void, appearing before him, was vast without measure. Afraid, he tried to cry out, to yell; but he was not to be heard, not even by himself. He felt himself being transported; he was moving and it was not of his own will.

Looming before him, slowly appeared the silhouette of a large dark mountain. Black and angry well describes it. The closer it began to appear, the more Chowbingo's speed was felt to increase. Focusing on the approaching mountain, he faintly began to view, from within it, an open tunnel perched just above its base; a massive, beckoning, black tunnel, into which Chowbingo feared he would soon find himself being catapulted.

The mountain rumbled and firebrands belched from deep within its cavernous belly. Unexpectedly, as if from an earthquake, a tremendous roar began. It was a sound beyond natural. It could only have come from the deepest forces of depravity. There, immediately before him, that black mountain was transforming itself into the nemesis of all that represented goodness and light. There he was, Xeres, that great and magnificently evil serpent that Father had cast from His garden.

Faster and faster Chowbingo was moving. He was being sucked, as if it were by a vacuum, toward that serpent's mouth. Then, just before Chowbingo's entry, there was a great belching. Xeres' eyes brightened like polished rubies in the noonday sun. The serpent's great mouth was cast open by a reflux action that was not of his own choosing.

Chowbingo's amulet began to glow its bright emerald green and it swiftly radiated its beam outward from the recesses of his furry underbelly. This time, though, Chowbingo found that his amulet's rays were being bent back toward him. Chowbingo's green laser rays were involuntarily submitting to the force of a second light coming from deep within Xeres' inner bowels.

This was a light brighter than white. Its intensity was such that Chowbingo instinctively looked away from its direction of travel. The light momentarily hesitated, as if engaged in thoughtful consideration, and then it left Xeres' mouth with such a violent roar that Chowbingo felt as if his very spiritual being would be destroyed at its passing. Quickly the light passed Chowbingo, and narrowly missed him, before it continued outward and upward providing the pathway for that which was to follow: a pure white unicorn with a coat that was woolly white. Upon its horn were stacked crowns, too numerous to count, and upon its flank was emblazoned a script, which, because of the speed, Chowbingo was unable to decipher . . . and then the mighty Xeres collapsed.

Chowbingo recovering, began to feel a most nauseating tugging as he was being pulled from atop the serpent's scales.

"Wake up, wake up you two," Mrs. Patadarski exclaimed. "You're both lying on the hearth, and you're too close to the fire. Those stones are too hot and too rough. You are both going to be the worse for it if you don't get up quickly. That fire's certain to burn the two of you."

Chowbingo jumped up with a yelp, perhaps more from Angelina's pull on his leg than from any heat on his paws. Val awakened, with a start, from the commotion that was beginning to happen around him.

"Hey, what's going on here?" he yelled, jumping up. "There's something burning here and it smells like fur."

"Of course it does," responded Mrs. Patadarski. "You were sleeping while this poor animal here was about to burn up—and you weren't too far behind him."

Chowbingo, by then fully awake and totally confused, jumped aside to avoid the hearth, before cautiously returning to position himself as close to the fire's warmth as he thought to be prudent. Mrs. Patadarski, seeking to restore a sense of calm, to events that she did not fully understand, began her futile attempt to restore order between the two. They, by then, however, were settled into fulfilling their own separate agendas.

"Mama, Mama," interrupted Val. "Can we talk about my dream from last night? I know it was real, Mama, I just know it was."

"Okay Val, but first what's that on your dog's feet? It looks like he just got some tar stuck to the bottom of his paws."

"They all feel like they're dry, Mama, so they shouldn't hurt anything here. Funny though, there's nothing with tar on it like that around here."

"All right Val," Angelina exclaimed, with a faintly disguised inflection of impatience in her voice. "We'll speak a little about last night if you'll please just calm down. If now you sincerely feel it's all that important, I'll hear you out first, before we do our chores."

Chowbingo obviously had quite a "nightmare" of his own to share. Nonetheless, trapped, as he was, within his chow puppy earth suit, there wasn't any way for him to share the evening's events, which had also just befallen him.

"Perhaps it had just all been a dream, or . . .?"

Stuck in his role as "puppy of the world," such that he was, Chowbingo finally elected to just follow his canine instincts and lie down beside Val.

All that was about to occur was going to become "people talk" and that wouldn't be anything that was going to interest him. After all, as a puppy, he was mostly attuned to body language. Verbalization of the human language was foreign to Chowbingo and mostly of no interest to him. After all, it was not as though he were speaking with Khasmar, Schezak our high priest, or myself. Chowbingo has always been accustomed to communicating through our spiritual language. In our manner of communicating we transfer thoughts and ideas through "total concept portrayal," which is akin to delivering thoughts in picture form rather than through sequential word form. The word form always takes so long to convey that it often leaves much open for misunderstanding. Personally, I have always wondered why Father designed humans to communicate using the inferior "word" language.

Val began reciting the story of his events as Chowbingo, doing his best to exhibit his most condescending posture, rested his lower jaw on the floor between his front legs. Looking directly at Mrs. Patadarski, Chowbingo could not help but wonder what her body language might convey.

"Mama, last night I fell asleep in the chair, but I know I didn't stay there. I was swept away with Puppy. I found myself trailing right behind him when he almost hit a waterfall of flowing colors. I've never seem colors so beautiful, Mama."

"Well now that's real nice," replied Angelina, her voice trailing as she prepared to move the subject back to the prior evening's events.

"No Mama, you don't understand. I wasn't dreaming. This was real. I heard a lot of really scary music. It was all very loud. I know that Puppy heard it too. I saw a dragon with big red eyes. Then a bright white light came and jumped out of his mouth. Then it took off just like a bright flash except that I was able to watch it disappear from sight. Mama . . . it looked just like a shooting star that you, Papa, and I saw that one night, except that this one was a million times brighter."

Then he exclaimed, yelling, "Ask Puppy, he was there. He was in front of me. Ask him!"

"Val dear, you know that I can't ask the dog. He's just an animal. He can't possibly know about such things."

"Mama, Mama it's true. I know it's true. I was there!"

"Val, if you say it's true then I know that you believe it's true and that's good enough for me," she replied in a most polite yet condescending manner.

"Val, now that I've heard of your adventure, please tell me some more about Yuri Kolvalenko."

Before answering, Val glanced over and looked into the eyes of Chowbingo. His eyes confirmed it for Val. They had both been on that adventure together.

"Yes Mama, what would you like to know about Butcher Kolvalenko?"

"Did he really ask about me?"

"Yes Mama, he did."

"Why, what exactly did he say?"

"He said that he remembers you from your school."

"Well, is that all he had to say?"

"Like I told you last night Mama, he said that you were very beautiful."

Chowbingo, of course, didn't yet understand human language, but his sensitive spirit was picking up a very clear picture of what was then being discussed between mother and son. His understanding of the language was assured to become clearer as their relationship continued in its growth.

Mrs. Patadarski had an interest in Yuri and she wanted to know, without revealing it to Val, if he still cared for her after all these many years.

Her face flushed.

Chowbingo immediately knew her wish, but how could he, a mere puppy, be of help? Even Val then believed that, perhaps by seeing Butcher Kolvalenko, his mother's spirit might be uplifted.

"Mama, we have to go thank Butcher Kolvalenko for the meat. Let's all three of us go right now."

Angelina hesitated and then spoke, "I'm sorry Val, but I can't go with you. You'll have to go alone and thank him for me."

"Mama, why can't you go? I really believe that he'd rather see you than me. The two of you are grown-ups. I'm sure he would have more fun if it were just the two of you.

"We know how you adults are when we hang around for too long. Don't we, Puppy?"

Chowbingo, who was by then taking it all in, exhibited no discernible sign of interest.

"*What to do? What to do?*" wondered Chowbingo, as he watched the events unfolding before him. The very manner by which Angelina began to adjust her hair in front of the dingy mirror, the one which had been installed by Mr. Patadarski, as a loving gift to his wife, said it all.

Angelina, who for years had avoided looking into that mirror, now suddenly found herself confronting her own reality. She was too humiliated to see her old friend. Her hair was too gray and her figure was obviously not what it had been since she was a student. Her precious mirror, once a gifted remembrance of pleasant times past, had become an unbridled harbinger for fears yet to unfold.

Angelina Patadarski, as she stood before it, watched herself changing from one of a loving mother, to that of an aging old woman, presently realizing that all of life's gifts and graces were swiftly eluding her.

Chowbingo, as he looked toward the same mirror, saw rather than the reflection of Angelina, those smirking faces formerly found encased within the barks of the forest's trees. They looked straight at him, laughing voraciously, with a hilarity possessing such evil that even the sound from their voices refused to participate.

"Mama, Mama, quit looking at yourself in the mirror," chided Val. "We have to go and thank Butcher Kolvalenko. Isn't that what you and Papa always taught me to do?"

"Time for a quick exit," he thought, as he sauntered over to the front door and scratched it with his front paw.

"Hmm, I think I'm kind of getting used to this 'puppy suit'."

The wretched sound made from his nails startled all three. "Quick, let that darn dog out. We don't need a mess in our house. Val, PLEASE—let him out."

"Well," thought Chowbingo, *"that worked quite nicely."*

Then, as he considered his past few minutes, Chowbingo absent-mindedly glanced toward the brush off to his left. There he caught a foreign reflection. Momentarily having set aside his immediate concerns, as puppies are apt to do, he allowed his curiosity to direct him closer toward the glittering object.

"Well I'll be! Schezak, what are you doing here?"

"I go up. I go down. Then again I go up and, then once again, down. How often must I repeat myself, Chowbingo? This is a very long ladder upon which I have been asked to travel. And . . . please try to understand that for me to have to coordinate my mind, which is older than time's beginning, within this quite intolerable earth suit, is truly very frustrating."

"Schezak, it's really good to see you! I truly do miss you, Jabez, and especially Father. How are they? What are they doing? I guess I really mean, what were they doing when you left?"

"Enough of your chit-chat for now, Chowbingo. I'm here on a mission, with a purpose, and that purpose just happens to be you."

"Well, I can tell now, by the tone of your voice, that this is not exactly a social call, Schezak."

"You're right, Chowbingo. I'm here to tell you that you're not exactly on Father's 'A' list at the moment. And after coming all the way down this ladder, you're not too popular with me either."

"But, what did I do wrong? Actually, I haven't done a thing!"

"That's the problem, Chowbingo. You haven't done anything. You're supposed to make the people here feel like we do in Neveah."

"Golly, Schezak, how am I supposed to do that? Neveah and Earth don't even look alike."

"Chowbingo, it's not about what someone or something looks like. You know Father has never been interested in that. That's why, when we're in Neveah, we're not confounded with these silly earth suits. You and I have always been valued for who we are, and never for what we look like, or what we have."

"Okay, I get it, but what's all that got to do with me?"

"That's the point, Chowbingo, it's got nothing to do with you, but it has everything to do with our lovely Mrs. Patadarski. The poor woman is absolutely miserable right now. It's your job to fix that, so please get on with your assignment."

"But how? What shall I do? How come it's up to me? That's just not fair.

"Schezak, come back here. Oh no, you're not going to do your disappearing act on me again, are you?

"It's not right! You're ditching your earth suit while I'm stuck here in mine.

"Schezak, I know you can still hear me, even without your earth suit; it's just not fair!"

Disillusioned and frustrated, Chowbingo wandered back toward the cabin where the door had remained open awaiting his return.

"Why do I have to stay here, in a darkened room, filled with misery and unhappiness, while Schezak is able to return to Neveah and the light of Father? It just isn't right. Okay, orders are orders, I guess. But I still don't know what to do," thought Chowbingo, as he slowly and methodically continued to circle within the cabin, pondering his fate.

"It's time to go, Mama," urged Val. "Let's take the puppy and go see the butcher so that we can thank him."

Angelina looked at her son, with sadness in her eyes and hesitated before finally speaking. "Val, I'm sorry but we just won't be able to see Mr. Kolvalenko. I must find another way to thank him."

The room fell suddenly quiet and its silence was deafening.

"Now," said Mrs. Patadarski sheepishly, "let's see if we can prepare some of Mr. Kolvalenko's fine meat for this evening's supper, and a bit for your puppy here also."

Val, as children will do, immediately captured the opportunity to advocate for Chowbingo's permanent residency.

"Wow, thanks, Mama. Does that mean Puppy can live with us now?"

"Val, let's not jump to any conclusions. I'm allowing him to have dinner with us since it was the two of you that brought the meat home. That was not meant to imply that he would be a member of the household. Now, how about you and the puppy taking a walk through the woods to see if you can find some wild mushrooms and vegetables that I can prepare to go with Mr. Kolvalenko's fine meat?"

"Okay, Mama.

"Come on, Puppy. Let's get going before she changes her mind." And with that the two of them bolted out through the front doorway.

Running then, as fast as they could, their paths began to crisscross each other as they dodged the tree trunks, skirted bushes, and broached the trickling stream. Soon exhausted, they both found themselves panting as they collapsed upon the moist earth with Val laughing hilariously.

Momentarily, as he lay on the ground with his nose pressed to the earth, Chowbingo detected an odor that caught his attention. It was not one of the peculiar smells that naturally emanated from the soil, but rather the small voice coming from the recesses of his spirit, which prompted him to investigate further. Standing now, he purposefully circled the particular spot of interest, before cautiously beginning to paw at it.

"What are you doing?" asked Val. "This is no time to be digging dirt. We're supposed to find vegetables for my 'he will let you stay with me as my puppy."

"Oh swell," thought Chowbingo, picking up a bit of his Earth's language. *"This kid wants to keep me here, stuck in this earth suit, to be his personal play toy. Well, that's certainly not my plan. Let him go and find some of those 'favorite vegetables' if he thinks he can! I don't even like that kind. I'm going to stay right here, dig my hole, and try to discover what this smell's all about."*

"Now, see what you've gone and done Puppy," thought Val, as he stood back to see the outcome of Chowbingo's little excavating soiree. "You've just unearthed a bunch of root bulbs, and you're probably also stopping some pretty flowers from coming up."

"Just had to do what I had to do," thought Chowbingo, not fully understanding, but taking in Val's apparent dissatisfaction, nonetheless.

"Get out of the way, Puppy. Please just sit over there while I gather up your root bulbs. Perhaps Mama will let me plant them so we can have some pretty flowers in the spring; certainly much better than leaving them here to spoil. You just didn't need to dig them up."

Chowbingo responded to Val's body language and did as he was requested, even though he knew, from the smell coming from the "bulbs", that there would never be flowers blooming from them. He remembered them from Father's garden. *"These were bulbs for another purpose."* Miffed over Chowbingo's digging, and with his bucket partially filled from the remnants of his puppy's efforts, Val headed deeper into the woods. Chowbingo, unconcerned, trailed aimlessly behind.

"Look Puppy, there by the stream. See all those greens? Mama is going to be so pleased. We're going to have a wonderful meal, and then she'll let me keep you for sure. Oh, and look over there by that oak tree. C'mon Puppy, let's go over there and take a look. I want to see what's been all dug up, over there. Looks like a few of the forest animals must have discovered something that they liked."

Chowbingo cocked his head and listened attentively but inside he didn't have a clue. Again, moved to consider his possible role as a pet to Val, he immediately started to run. But instead of continuing, he found himself abruptly halting. There was that aroma again. It was coming up from the ground directly in front of him. Again it captured him as strongly as if he were being held fast by an invisible hand.

Val looked back over his shoulder only to see that Chowbingo was again stopped in his tracks. It was becoming most apparent to Val that Chowbingo had no intention of willingly following him to find a vegetable patch.

Retracing his steps, Val approached Chowbingo and swiftly circled behind him. There without warning, he firmly grasped him by the ear, and once again they started off to look for the vegetable patch. Chowbingo yelped and winced as he was involuntarily dragged across the rut-filled field, stumbling over his legs, and bouncing off of nearby shrubs. Sadly, for him, all of his futile attempts to escape Val's firm hold began to diminish the closer they came to Val's purposed destination.

Arriving finally, at what appeared to be a wild, un-tended, vegetable patch, Chowbingo paused to look at Val with a gaze that only a puppy could muster. This was a gaze that masterfully expressed his personal dissatis-faction for having been recruited to such a seemingly distasteful task. Nothing was verbalized, but the look was clear.

"C'mon Puppy," urged Val. "Let's walk through here and select the best greens for our supper." Chowbingo responded by setting on his haunches and refusing to budge, a tried and true defensive maneuver passed, from adult to puppy, through countless canine generations.

"Well then, Puppy, you can just sit there and be as stubborn as you like but, in the meantime, I'm going to pick the choicest greens that I can find. I know that Mama will enjoy the meat, and now I'm going to add these greens to make it a perfect supper for her."

"Okay," thought Chowbingo, "that selfless attitude is one that will surely bring great pleasure to Father. Per-haps I better join in and help."

Just as he prepared to jump in and return to his joyous, happy, puppy dog state of mind, he once again found himself being distracted by that same, peculiar smell.

Again, it was coming up from the ground. And again, unable to resist the seductive odor, he started pawing at the soil. This time, however, he needed only to scratch the surface before he uncovered what appeared to be a root bulb; only this one, rather than resembling a deformed ping pong ball, better resembled a man's clenched fist.

Val, seeing what had been found, forgot about his irritation with Chowbingo and sat beside him, beneath the tree, to better examine their findings. Other than its size, the only other unusual characteristic was its smell, both unique and pungent.

It was late mid-day when Val and Chowbingo finally returned to the cabin. They entered to find that Angelina had already started the fire and the flames had since silently settled down to become the type of embers that might be considered appropriate for roasting.

"Val, you're just in time. Now will the two of you please go right back outside and find me a firm branch that I can whittle down for a spit to roast our meat. And be sure it's a green one; we don't want to see our lovely meal falling into the fire. You know what the fire will do to wood that's not moist and green."

Val and Chowbingo, after a short time outside of playing "catch the stick" returned with a useable branch, albeit somewhat chewed at one end. Angelina, after properly thanking them, then went about the task of sharpening a point, at the narrower end, to pierce the meat.

"I sure do wish that we had some garlic and sage that I could slip under the skin of this roast," Angelina murmured. "It would add so much flavor to it."

"Mama, can I run to the market and get some?"

"We don't even have a proper steel spit with which to roast the meat. We certainly can't afford the luxury of spices. We'll just make do with what we have here and be thankful."

"Mama, I want to show you something," offered Val, as he reached down and brought forward the bundle that he had gathered from the forest.

"Oh my, what lovely greens," exclaimed Angelina, with unabashed delight. "These will make such a wonderful addition to our meal. What an abundant supply! There's so many here that I will need to use your father's pot to cook them. It would surely be nice if we had some accent flavor to add to your greens; a spice or herb with its own unique flavor would be nice. Something that would stand out and give a little 'oomph' to our meal."

"It's not Papa's pot, Mama. He gave it as his special gift to you, remember? It's your pot."

"Yes dear, I'm sorry that I misspoke."

Chowbingo's ears perked as he listened to the latest exchange between Val and his mother. *"Such kind sounding words. What a lovely family they are. Why did Father allow Mr. Patadarski's death to happen? He surely could have stopped it. I wish I was with him now so that I could ask him. Darn this outfit. It's so restrictive."*

"Mama, look what I brought besides the greens. They're here in between," he exclaimed, as he separated the pile of greens from the root balls beneath, allowing them to release their distinctive odor.

"Val, where did these come from? I've surely never seen anything like them before, and I certainly don't recognize that odor."

"I know Mama . . . and the odor, I can tell that it's kind of strange, different like; but I thought that maybe you could use some of them, perhaps to add a little flavor to the meat."

"Val, you know, that's a wonderful idea. I'm going to take your suggestion and try it. I'll wash them and then cut some into slivers to slip under the skin just like I used to do with garlic."

"Okay Mama, but please don't wash more than you need. I want to plant the rest of them around the house. I want to see if maybe we can get some flowers in the spring."

"I expect you'll get some really strange flowers, if any at all, with a smell like that. Nonetheless, they're your find; excuse me, they're you and your puppy's find. So I'll just leave the replanting to the two of you. Perhaps later he can help you with the digging and then you can do the replanting. Now though, how about helping your poor old mother wash these greens?"

"Sure Mama, and I'll wash a couple of the root bulbs for you also.

"C'mon puppy, let's go outside and wash a couple of these for Mama, and while we're there we can plant the rest of them for spring. That is, if you'll start digging the holes, like Mama suggested, so I can follow behind with the bulbs."

"How'd I get this job? First, he tries to make me a pet and now I'm here digging holes. Good thing I'm starting to understand their crazy language. I don't get it. I'm too important to be doing this. After all, from where I come, my assignments require me to perform important tasks, not to just stand around and dig holes for kids, like Val, who think they're gardeners."

"Hey Val, how're you doing?"

"Well, I'll be," exclaimed Val, as Mr. Bellingeri walked up the pathway.

"Where ya going Mr. Bellingeri?" asked Val, who by then was unable to restrain the enthusiasm in his voice.

"Actually, Val, I'm here purposefully, to see if your mom might be in."

Before Val could answer, the door flung open and out stepped Angelina, unable to see through the late afternoon's sun.

"Who is there with the two of you?" she asked, still trying to adjust her eyes to the bright sun's rays.

"It's me, Mrs. Patadarski. Dominique Bellingeri from the candy store."

"Oh ma' gosh," exclaimed a very flustered and embarrassed Mrs. Patadarski. "I certainly didn't expect company. I just heard some noise and figured that I ought to check on Val and the puppy. They were supposed to wash some roots for me and then come back in. It's been a bit longer than I figured it should have taken. I just figured that perhaps they might need some checking up on.

"Well anyway this really is a pleasant surprise; although I must say I wasn't expecting company. I'm sure I look an awful sight."

"But, Mrs. Pata . . ."

"Hush, now if you don't find my looks too distasteful, you're certainly welcome inside. I'm certain, that as a single man and a single woman, there won't be too much gossip with our ages as they are, especially with Val and the puppy here as our chaperones."

She looked coyly at Mr. Bellingeri for a brief second and then blurted out, "Remember at our school dances, they had more chaperones than students. That was such a long time ago. Those were wonderful times!"

"Yes, they certainly were, Mrs. Patadarski."

"Oh, and please call me Angelina, or even Angie, as you all used to call me back in our school days."

"Thanks Angie, and you can call me Dominique, just like you did back in those days."

"Thank you, Dominique. Would you care to come in for a bit of tea? I'm sorry but I don't have much more that I can offer."

"Angie, it was not unintentional or by accident that I'm here. I've come to see you with a purpose; and yes, I will accept your kind invitation for tea. Val, here's a couple of pieces of my finest chocolate for you; and for your dog, I also brought two dog biscuits which I hope he'll enjoy."

"Well, how kind of you, Dominique. Now, why don't you join Val and myself inside for a nice, warming cup of tea?"

"Thank you, and will the puppy be joining us? After all, it was he, and his mysterious stone, that actually led to our reunion."

"Yes, we'll certainly have to allow the puppy in for a moment, since he's the one who brought us all together again."

"About time I had some recognition around here," thought Chowbingo, as he followed the others into the house.

"Well now, Dominique, I haven't had the pleasure of seeing you in quite a spell. It's somewhat amazing that it would take a bright stone to get us back together again. You've always been welcome here. Now, to what do I owe this particular honor?"

"Please, let me begin by apologizing for not visiting you sooner. However, following the death of your husband, I really didn't know what I could have possibly said. I guess, because I was less of a man than I should have been, I couldn't find within me the confidence to express the words necessary to convey the grief that I felt for you and Val."

"Thank you, Dominique, thanks for your kind words. I have often wondered what it was that I had done to offend you. We used to be so close, especially back during our school days. Often I have asked myself, what was it that I could possibly have done, that would cause you to so distance yourself from me. However, hopefully, all that is past and behind us now."

She paused and then spoke, "I must say, I'm most grateful to have you as a guest in my home, again. Val, would you be kind enough to prepare some tea for Mr. Dominique and myself so that we might catch up on some of our past?"

"Sure, Mom!"

"Angie, I have a proposition for you. I have been most fortunate in my career as a 'chocolatier,' and my business is rapidly expanding. It is true that I began with nothing more than a burner, a small pot, and a stone slab since we last spoke. However, I set aside many worldly desires that might pursue a man and concentrated on developing my business. From the beginning, I always used the finest ingredients, always measured my products with honest weights, and never failed to give at least ten percent of all my increase to benevolent associations. Sometimes, I even directly gifted the needy. I believe that it is due to my sacrifices, honesty, and hard work that I am now able to stand before you as a prosperous man and offer you, my childhood friend, this most honorable business proposition."

"Wow, this Earth trip is getting more amusing by the day. Mr. Bellingeri actually believes, that he alone, controlled his success. I'm sure that Father is getting quite a chuckle over that one right now. I'll have to remember to share this one with Him as soon as He releases me from this confounded suit of mine. After all, I'm sure He realizes that being a puppy does impose restricting limitations on me."

"Angie, I wish to incorporate your beautiful copper pot into my confectionary business, for which I am prepared to pay you handsomely."

"Oh, my goodness," replied Mrs. Patadarski, "I couldn't do that. I can't ever part with my copper pot. It was the last gift that Salvio gave me before the accident."

She paused as the tears began to well in her eyes.

"What is with these 'earthlings'? Why don't they understand that it is through their faith and not by their works that they receive their gifts of health and prosperity? Work, such as that done by Mr. Bellingeri, is required because faith without any work will not prosper. It simply doesn't work. It's just plain dead. Don't they understand that it is Father who gives them their good gifts? Everything else is counterfeit, and it will ultimately be lost. I surely wish I could give Mr. Bellingeri a piece of my mind. I'd have him straightened out faster than Schezak could make it down Neveah's ladder. I'd tell him, 'Mr. Bellingeri, you faithfully followed Father's universal laws and He blessed you for it. It's all about Him, it never was about you'!"

"No, no Mrs. Patadarski, I mean Angie. Please forgive me that I've upset you. Here, please take my pocket handkerchief. Oh, I'm so sorry. I'm all flustered now. Angie, I'm sorry, I mean Angelina . . . no I mean Mrs. Patadarski . . . Oh I don't know what I mean. I'm just not used to women crying. I don't want to buy your pot or to physically remove it from you. I'd never do that. Don't you know that I, as well as this entire town, still recall when Salvio was awarded that pot for his fine work; and then very soon afterwards he . . . well you know what I mean.

"I'm just going to start over.

"Angelina, it was and it still is, my fondest wish to enter into a partnership with you so that you can assist me in increasing my chocolate candy production. I just feel that your copper pot will make an excellent vessel in which to melt and blend the ingredients for truffle-quality chocolate. I wouldn't ever ask to buy or to possess your pot."

Still fighting back her tears, while displaying a face filled with years of pent-up emotions about to spill forth, she replied, "Mr. Bellingeri your proposition is most honorable and very much appreciated but . . ."

"No, no Mama," screamed Val, as he almost dropped the pot of tea and the two cups that he was carefully balancing on his arm, while making his way toward their table. Hurrying forward, in a walking, sliding motion, Val seemed to have been outrunning gravity before he finally deposited the hot tea and dinnerware, unceremoniously, on the table.

"Well now, that was quite a human feat," reflected Chowbingo, as he quickly scampered out of Val's path. *"We have tea on the table and it's still in the pot. My friend actually challenged Father's 'Laws of Gravity' and survived. I'll going to have to spend more time in my puppy-suit to get that good."*

"Mama, Mama, just say yes, say yes—PLEASE!"

Angelina, now clearly flustered, and fighting for a moment to regain her composure, blurted out, "I know, let's all have a spot of tea, and perhaps Mr. Bellingeri can tell us a little more about his plan.

"Val, why don't you get yourself a cup and join us for tea . . . and, and be sure that the dog has a bowl of fresh water."

"Mama, you know I don't drink tea. You know, you've never, ever, permitted it."

"Well, you're ten now, almost eleven. Perhaps it's time that you should start. Just get something you like, okay. We're here now, to listen to Dominique and not to debate over your choice of beverages," she added, curtly.

"Water? Why can't I have tea in a cup instead of water in this silly dog bowl?"

Chowbingo was now finding himself jumping into the doggy side of his being. Quickly, though, he sensed Father's embarrassment and displeasure.

Ashamed and with a contrite heart, Chowbingo quietly repented, curled into a ball by the fireplace, and laid his lower jaw on the chrysolite stone shining brightly beneath him.

"Dominique, I want to apologize for all of this confusion. Perhaps we're settled down sufficiently now that you might share your plan with us."

"Certainly Angelina. Actually, it's quite simple. As I previously mentioned, I've worked diligently, most of my life, to make my candy store a success. I am now convinced that, through my hard work and because of my continuing faith, I can now call myself abundantly gifted. My customer base, thanks to some recently acquired commercial accounts, following my trip to Brussels, has increased seven fold.

"Val, I'm sure your mother has spoken to you of 'blessings and curses,' hasn't she? Well, I currently find myself in just such a quandary. If I can find the resources to expand my production, then I believe that I will continue to be blessed. If I cannot, then I won't be able to match my production requirements, and I will fail in my commitments to my new customers. Angelina, I've never failed to keep a promise, and if it should happen now, then that would become my curse."

He paused. "It's all my problem now and I guess I'm the only one who can fix it."

He rested again, took a deep breath, and then sharply asked, "Angelina, I can really use your help. Will you work for me?"

"*Well, well,*" thought Chowbingo to himself as he observed from the side. "*These 'earthlings' sure seem to have a problem with their 'pride' thing, 'I'm the only one who can fix it', ha! Too bad he can't understand canine. I could sure help him to take a better direction than this one that he is starting out on.*

"*Dominique Bellingeri, don't you realize that this is not about you and your promise? You're in partnership with Father and then for only so long as He elects. So, if I could speak to you directly, I would cautiously recommend a bit of humility from you. You might even consider transferring a bit of your self-appointed glory for your past and present 'accomplishments' to Him.*"

"Dominique, perhaps we can speak of your business a bit later. I'm sure you can tell now, from this wonderful aroma, that Mr. Kolvalenko's roast is almost ready. I'll have Val pull it from the spit and set it aside to cool for a few minutes. Then, if you'll permit me a moment to finish the preparation of the field greens, we'll be ready for supper.

"You will of course be staying to share supper with us?"

"Only if I can participate in the preparation or the cleanup."

"Dominique, you're really quite silly about all this, but since you seem to be so insistent about the matter, I will allow you to set the table, if you like. And afterwards you can even help Val with the clearing of the table, if you wish.

"There, now does that make you feel more like part of the family?"

"No, but it certainly makes me feel a bit more comfortable."

"Okay, the plates and silver are right over here on the sideboard," interjected Val, only too happy to see Mr. Bellingeri volunteering to assist him in his nightly chores.

"Excuse me, I'm certainly sorry to interrupt, but I'm beginning to feel an earthly call of my own. I know that I can't talk to any of you, but perhaps as I scratch at this front door one of you may again pay a little attention to me."

"Val, your dog is scratching at the front door. Hurry, take him outside before he thinks about making some sort of mess in here."

"Wow! This scratching thing really seems to be providing some quick results. I'll have to remember it for my future needs.

"C'mon Val, now get yourself over here and let me out. You heard your mom," he inwardly expressed to himself, with his own self-centered satisfaction.

"Hey, this evening air is pretty awesome! I'm smelling odors that I've never smelled before. My nose suddenly feels as if I'm ingesting a potpourri of all of Earth's fragrances. This dog thing is kind of fun right now. I'm going to go for a run."

Out the door and just two steps behind him sprang Val, who immediately began to lose ground. "Puppy, Puppy, come back here. You can't just run away like that. Puppy, stop, I can't catch you. You know that you're faster than me. Oh drat, he's gone! I just can't see very far in this shaded light. Mama, Mama he's gone," blurted Val, trying to follow between tears.

And so it all began; Val chased Chowbingo, Angelina chased Val, with Dominique "huffing and puffing" in a vain attempt to keep up. Off into the woods the "merry band" went, with Chowbingo easily outdistancing them all, until it was only Val and Chowbingo who still remained in the race.

Well, there was one thing that Dominique could do well, other than to make candy, and that was to whistle and whistle he did. His whistle, in fact, was so shrill that, not only did it alert Val and Angelina, but it also stopped Chowbingo right in his tracks.

Angelina, now realizing that she was in unfamiliar territory, harkened to the sound of the whistle and returned to Dominique. Val, on the other hand, catching a sudden glimpse of the glow from the illuminated chrysolite hanging about Chowbingo's neck, took off in the direction of his errant, animal friend.

"Well, Dominique, it appears that my crazy son certainly has that dog firmly fixed on his mind at this time. Perhaps this may avail us some quiet time for you to further explain the details of your offer."

"Shall we just return to your home? I'm sure the two of them will be quite fine together."

"Well, Puppy, it was quite nice of you to stop and wait for me. What do I owe to your sudden change of attitude," murmured Val, beneath his breath.

Chowbingo, at the time approximately twenty paces ahead, chose not to acknowledge Val's call or even to acknowledge his presence.

Unexpectedly the light, boyish hairs on Val's arms popped straight up as he stopped to witness a most unbelievable sight unfolding before him. Chowbingo had suddenly dropped his forelegs to the ground and assumed a position of total submission. His fur glowed from the reflection of the light before him. It shone as if it were from the moon on a clear, blue-white night. Yet, within twenty yards toward any direction, the landscape of the forest remained just as shaded as before. Then, most frightening of all, a light appeared before Chowbingo, which was a white light brighter than any brightness that might have been imagined. Yet, strangely and inexplicably, Val was able to look straight into it without it blinding his eyes, to remain in its presence while feeling nothing more than a warm, comforting heat.

"Oh, oh! I guess I've really done it now," thought Chowbingo. *"He hasn't been here since that last time in the desert and, if I remember correctly, people here are still discussing that one."*

The trees began to all bend toward the light. Their tops began to touch the ground, as their branches splayed outward like angel wings spreading across the ground's surface. Even the rocks turned molten, as their shapes changed, edging themselves ever closer to the light.

Val remained transfixed and frightened, yet strangely comforted, all within a single feeling.

Then, just as suddenly as it had occurred, it was over. The trees, the rocks, and the night sky all returned to their former nature. The only difference was Chowbingo. He immediately ran toward Val, but then only to pass by him. He headed straight for their house, where he entered without hesitation, and plopped himself, exhausted, at the fireplace's hearth.

Philip I. Amos

Chapter 6

Something's Different

Mama, Mama this isn't any ordinary dog," exclaimed Val, as he followed breathlessly behind Puppy into his home. "You should've seen the forest," he exclaimed, as he began recounting all that he had just witnessed.

"Now Val, please try to take better control of your imagination," encouraged Angelina, speaking with a mother's gentleness. "You know that you often are inclined to . . ."

"Excuse me, Angie. I know that it is remiss of me to interrupt your conversation but maybe Val has something here. Take a look at that jewel around the puppy's neck."

"Look Mama, look. It's so bright that it's actually lighting or entire home."

"You're right, Val. I'm sorry Mr. Bellingeri. I was so set on correcting Val that I failed to notice the obvious. It's this puppy's jewel, and not the fireplace, that's lighting our home now. The fireplace can't light the room now. You can look for yourself. It's just embers and soft coals in there now."

"What's happened to the fire, Mama? It was roaring when we left just a half hour ago."

"Val, you've been gone for over three hours. If I hadn't been so engrossed in Dominique's business proposal, I would have been in the forest searching for you long ago. Don't you realize that it's now much later than that?"

"Mama, that can't be. I know I wasn't gone for more than an hour."

"Val, look at the embers. Does the fire lie?"

"Angelina, Val, there is definitely something spiritual happening here, and this puppy; this puppy is no ordinary dog!"

"Now I'm afraid! What should we do, Dominique?"

"Mrs. Patadarski, although I don't believe in ghosts and apparitions, I do believe in the spirit world; you know, like angels, demons, and a higher power. We live in a well-defined, organized, and structured universe with the spirit world and our own natural world mostly separated from one another. However, on occasions, the two have been known to merge for a time and for a purpose. I believe that we may now be experiencing such a time as this."

". . . and?"

". . . and now Angelina, Val, I suggest that we all sit down to this beautiful meal that you both have been so intent on preparing. We need to give thanks to our Creator for this food set before us and also to hold Butcher Patadarski in remembrance for his generosity as we begin to dine on this fine cut of beef."

"Hey, how about a little thanks to Puppy here. After all, he was the one who unearthed the tasty roots that we are using to flavor this roast."

". . . and to you also, Val, for the fine greens that you selected from the forest."

"Puppy, you sit here beside me. I've got a special piece of meat just for you."

"Where I come from, we don't eat our friends!"

"Oh Mama, does that mean we get to keep him?"

"Well, I suppose so. After all, he's responsible for this nice piece of meat and the fixings that go along with it. He's also responsible for our renewed acquaintance with Mr. Bellingeri and he's even lighting our home with his jewel. I guess you might say, now he's family."

"No, I'm not responsible; the butcher is, and the same with the candy maker."

"Let's not forget your new career in the candy business," piped in Mr. Bellingeri.

"Or the big smile he's brought to my son," added Angelina.

"So, what are you going to name him?" asked Dominique."

"Why Puppy of course," replied Val.

"Puppy it is," exclaimed Angelina, winking at Dominique. "Now that the name's settled, Dominique, would you say the blessing. Val, you can then place some greens on each of our plates while Dominique carves the meat."

"Angelina, I thought I knew but I didn't want to come up short so I held my opinion. Now I must speak. Those roots Val and Puppy brought home, the ones you are using for garnishing the meat; they may be truffles."

"What's a truffle?"

"Val, a truffle is a fungus similar to a mushroom that grows just beneath the ground's surface. It's a much sought-after delicacy that's desired throughout parts of the world. However, it only grows in certain regions, and it comes in different colors with some being more coveted than others."

"Wow, they're growing right here in our forest. Maybe we can harvest some with our fellow villagers and sell them to make money. Mr. Bellingeri, if Puppy and I go out and get a lot of them, can I be rich so I can help my mom?"

"That's a very generous thought, Val, but for now let's be thankful for what we have and just eat our meal. You have to consider, Val, that if truffles were growing in our forest, then someone would have certainly recognized them and unearthed them before now. Our little town has been here for a very long time—probably where our French, German, and Dutch ancestors passed through previously.

"Yes, but they were so busy in their battles for acquisition that they hardly would have noticed the blessings of our forest, even as they slept on its soft velvet firmament.

"Wouldn't you agree with that, Dominique?"

"I'll just take you at your word, Angie. After all, it was you who was the 'history buff' at school. I believe it was my job, back then, to just concentrate on getting my grades up to yours," she replied with a well-placed grin.

"Touché."

"What do you mean, 'eat your meal'?" thought Chowbingo to himself, quickly picking up on the earth language which was beginning to engulf him. *"Mr. Bellingeri, of course it will make him rich. It will make all of you rich. I should know. After all it was me, not you, who just got his butt chewed out in the forest. All because I wanted to have a little bit of independence and go for my 'happy dog' run. Now I have to not only help Val, but I'm also suddenly responsible for the whole village's happiness, which I guess includes you.*

"It's a very good thing, for all of you, that I can't speak, or I would certainly be the first to give you all a piece of my mind, AGAIN! In fact, I'd bite each one of you, right there where you sit, but for the fact that I'd be back out there in the forest facing Father again."

After a delicious meal, finished all too quickly, Chowbingo, amply nourished from a bountiful helping of greens and truffles, found himself once again sprawled on the warm hearth, thanks to Dominic having previously added wood to the dying embers. It was just a matter of minutes before he was hardly able to keep his eyes focused on his newly found humans. Then, not but a few minutes later, Val was stumbling off to his own bed in a sleepy stupor, overstuffed and satiated from the type of meal that life's circumstances seldom permitted him to enjoy. Dominique and Angelina were left to face one another, now alone, in the quiet of the night.

"Look at that. The dog ate the greens and left the meat. Something is surely very strange about that animal.

"Angelina, although I might be thought of as a mere candy maker, my specialty is that of a chocolatier, or more specifically a maker of truffles. Uniquely, the making of truffles only requires three ingredients; but the proper blending of those ingredients takes many years, and even then it is only mastered by a few."

"Why is something so simple so seemingly complicated? I don't think I understand."

"Angelina, it's like sharpening knives with a whetstone. Although everyone thinks they are capable, it actually takes almost a lifetime to move from a position of apprentice to that of a master.

"The foundation ingredient, for the chocolate truffle, was first discovered about the year 1828 when the cocoa press was first invented. It was the invention of this machine that allowed the cocoa butter to successfully be separated from the cocoa beans. 'Chocolate solids' are what is left after the cocoa butter has been removed.

"After many years of cooking time and experimentation with these solids, I have been able to add, to my mix, a heavy cream and often times my own proprietary sweetener to develop my very own, uniquely smooth, silky combinations: 'ganache' as it is referred to in the trade.

"This ganache not only becomes the inner filling for chocolate truffles, a worldly delicacy, but it can also be altered to create coatings, pastry fillings, and toppings. My unique formula is just now beginning to garner its own following. Your cherished copper pot, lovingly given to you by your late husband, can be most useful for the proper cooking of my special ganache. Since it is copper it maintains even heat distribution. The heat, in any part of the pot, is the same as within all other areas of the pot. Even heat distribution will continually assure us even consistency for each of these products.

"Consistency was not as essential when all I had to do was to display my confectionaries on display trays at my candy store. With my new commercial customers, consistency becomes essential.

"Finally, with my recipes perfected, if I can now combine them with your expert attention to detail and have the use of your copper pot for consistency, I know that we can provide an excellent product for my clients. They will then become our customers, each time, every time."

"Now Dominique, what makes you feel that I have any sense for detail, whatsoever? Remember I am, as you men often say it, 'just' a woman."

"Angelina, I'll always remember our times together as we passed through our schooling, grade by grade. You got all the A's because of your diligence and your attention to detail. More than one boy in our school had to explain C's, D's, and F's to his parents because of you and the confounded class curve that was used. The only reason you never knew of their hostility toward you was because you were the most beautiful girl in the school, and all the guys wanted to date you."

Realizing what he had just said, the red-faced Dominique stumbled for words before he finally blurted it out. "Well, I guess I'll see you tomorrow, Angelina. Shall I return here to your home, or would you prefer to come to my shop where we, we'll begin with our business plan?" he stuttered.

"Dominique, I really don't know the first thing about making candy, but if you have faith in my ability to learn, then I, in turn, owe you the responsibility to try. I'll see you tomorrow at your shop. Shall we say about 8:00?"

"That'll be perfect, Angelina. Thank you for a wonderful and most enlightening evening, for which I will now bid you a very pleasant goodnight," he half-mumbled, while stumbling over his feet, as he unceremoniously exited through the front door.

Chapter 7

A Very Old Acquaintance

Dominique began walking back to his home in the dark of the night. He uncomfortably started his journey by first bouncing off a tree, then a bush, and finally a low-lying dark object, which, to his befuddled bewilderment, he found himself unable to identify. Briefly halting his journey, he stopped for a moment to reconsider his surroundings and to reestablish his bearings, before setting off, with a shrug, on a more familiar pathway.

Angelina, with a shudder of childish excitement coursing through her veins, quickly collected the remnants of their meal to the drain board as was her custom. She began to whistle a soft tune to herself, a melody that she had not whistled since her teenage years. Dishes washed and breakfast place settings neatly arranged, Angelina, with a light dancing step, sashayed toward her bathroom in preparation for a welcome evening's sleep.

The inside of the cabin, recently filled with joy and laughter, suddenly became foreboding, isolated, and as dark as its outside landscape. The embers, quietly dying down again, had all but completely disappeared. That warm hearth, which had been so inviting to Chowbingo, quickly turned to a surface as cold and unwelcome as a mortician's slab.

Jumping up with a start, from a cold stone hearth, which had begun sucking heat from his still warm body, Chowbingo found himself seemingly disoriented as he shook from a freezing tremor.

Odors of the evening meal were still strong and pungent within the room. The normal smells were being overpowered by the unfamiliar odor of cooked meat and spices. For Chowbingo, this was most disconcerting. His canine body had, of course, enjoyed the delicious meal, but his spiritual self was still unable to acclimate itself to the senses that were impacting him, having just witnessed the others joyously consuming the flesh from one of Father's creatures. In Neveah, where Chowbingo's trip had begun, the lion lay down with the lamb. They did not consume one another.

"Yes, this place, Earth as some call it, is certainly strange."

Chowbingo didn't understand. He was in a very scary place. He yearned for Father's intelligence, and of course my insight, to carry him through. He missed his friend Esau even though he never seemed to agree with him on anything. Additionally, Esau was always looking down on Chowbingo. It was as if he existed nowhere other than within Esau's state of unrelenting disapproval.

Chowbingo, at that time, was finding himself confused and feeling very alone.

Finally, the night was spent and the newness of the day awakened. For Chowbingo, the evening had passed, and the warmth of the new day sun had erased his prior night's cares. Mr. Bellingeri, who had, despite the prior night's challenges, made it safely home, was to be found in his shop warming his chocolate pot in preparation for the day's production. Mrs. Patadarski, true to her word, was just then arriving at the final cobblestone pathway leading to Dominique Bellingeri's candy store.

Angelina could not help but to question her purpose and her sanity. Strangely, she felt her slightly overweight, middle-aged body, just seemed to have followed her feet in a mindless progression over which she had no apparent control. Then, before she could conjure the sense of it all, she found herself at the candy shop's entrance, the door to the left and the window display of chocolate enticements situated to the right. Inadvertently, nudging the already-open door as she entered, the tiny copper bell meticulously announced her arrival, by its tinkling. This, for Angelina seemed too overly aggressive for the announcement of her presence, and far too lengthy to suit her quiet demeanor.

"Hello there Mrs. Patadarski, and a good morning to you," joyfully announced Dominique, as he stepped away from behind the kitchen's door to greet his first arrival. "I'm so pleased to see that you have accepted my employment offer. I'm sure we'll both become the better because of it."

Angelina, a bit taken back by the suddenness of it all, could only comment in a timid voice, "I believe it was perhaps your bell that has volunteered. After all, wasn't it the first to speak?"

Next to enter was Chowbingo, quickly followed by Val.

"Well now, I guess this completes the team," laughed Dominique, as he observed the sudden filling of his small candy store's reception area.

"Does this mean that I'm hiring you also, Puppy?" he asked, while looking directly at Chowbingo.

"More than you can ever imagine," responded Chowbingo, but only to himself, as he recalled his obligation to Schezak. His assignment now seemed to be changing from just ensuring the happiness of Angelina and Val, to that of including Yuri, Dominique and perhaps their entire village, should that be Father's wish.

"Puppy, perhaps we should have Yuri Kolvalenko and his butcher shop involved as well. After all, how else will we be able to fairly compensate you from our budding enterprise? I don't suppose that snacking on a weekly paycheck will bring you much satisfaction when you find yourself with a growling tummy?"

"No, you big dummy, it won't, but I don't choose to eat my friends either, so you can forget the butcher shop too," thought Chowbingo to himself. *"And if you would just show Father a big dose of your faith instead of running about with your own stupid ideas, perhaps we could all*

avoid these unnecessary 'trips around the mountain'. Also, maybe I would be able to return to Neveah and then I could be with MY friends."

"Look at him, Mr. Bellingeri. It almost looks like Puppy knows what you're saying."

"Well, it would certainly be nice if he understood that I also have his interest at heart. It's unfortunate that we really can't know what's actually going on in the minds of our four-footed friends."

"I certainly do wish some people actually could be a little more like them," volunteered Angelina. "You know, so innocent and faithful."

"If you only knew," thought Chowbingo. *"If only you really knew!"*

"Well, time's a-wasting," piped in Angelina.

"Val, we don't need to take up Mr. Bellingeri's valuable time as a chocolatier. You take Puppy on home now and let Dominique and I get to doing whatever it is that I'm supposed to do here about this chocolate business. Chocolatier—that is the correct title for you, isn't it Mr. Bellingeri?"

"Actually, Angelina, my candy shop, here, makes far more than just chocolates; so I might also be referred to as a confectioner. Now you, with your quick mind and abiding sense of responsibility, will soon be referred to as the chocolatier, but first we must start you out as a chocolate maker. You will begin by being the one who creates chocolate from cacao beans and other ingredients."

"What other ingredients, Dominique?"

"Angelina, please permit me to pick up from where our conversation abruptly ended last night with my inappropriate remark about 'all the boys' wanting to date you."

Angelina just smiled coyly. "Yes, Dominique, please, why don't you just continue?"

"Ah, now you are starting to delve into my world wherein lays the secret between the chocolate maker and the chocolatier. You have just arrived at my shop and already you have bypassed the chocolate maker, and I find that you are now seeking to know the art of the chocolatier. You will do well, Mrs. Patadarski, very well indeed!"

"Mr. Bellingeri, I apologize. I did not wish to be forward. I guess my student's curiosity overtook my sense of good manners. Please forgive me for my forwardness."

"That's okay, Angelina. It's because of your inquisitive mind that you are here. Now, as I was saying, a chocolatier is a person who makes confectionery using chocolate and other sugar-containing delicacies. Chocolatiers are separate from chocolate makers, the ones who create chocolate from cacao beans and other ingredients. Often the distinctions overlap but you'll catch on, so let's get started. I'm starting you out as a chocolate maker because I believe that this will soon provide you with the opportunity to work at home. At that time, you will be able to work in familiar surroundings while also making use of that copper pot that your late husband left you. I certainly wouldn't expect you to bring your precious keepsake down here to use in my store. Later, as we expand, we can move you into the work of a chocolatier and finally that of a confectioner."

"Mr. Bellingeri, I sincerely do appreciate all that you're doing for me, but could you please explain to me once again why my pot is unique, or so special, that you would choose to use it over others?"

"Your pot is special because it is first of all large and more importantly because it is copper. This permits it to maintain the constant, even heat, throughout its entire cooking surface. Angelina, the making of chocolate is fully dependent on two things, temperature and time. Your copper pot is the only one that I know to be locally available and built of a material having the capability to comply with our production needs—and also let us not forget that you, as an excellent future partner, come with it. Your attention to detail provides the other ingredient, a fine sense of attention to timing and to quality.

"I will start by showing you how to extract the ganache from the cocoa through the cocoa press. Then perhaps, we can go from there."

"The 'who' from the 'what'?"

"My cocoa press allows us to separate the cocoa butter from the cocoa beans. The remaining residue, which is left over after the butter is removed, we will refer to as the 'chocolate solids'. The solids can then be cooked, cooled, and re-cooked until our desired consistency, texture, shine, and hardness is achieved. It is in this manner that we are able to make hard chocolate for chocolate bites; cream chocolate for pie filling, and finally, a very smooth texture to complete our signature chocolate truffles."

"But how do we . . .?"

"Let me interrupt by showing you this little black book that I keep right here, in my vest pocket, next to my heart. You see, Angelina, every time I make a new batch of chocolate, I record the time, temperature, and the results so that I can duplicate it whenever I choose."

"But what about . . .?"

"Because I'm going to share the contents of my book with you, my lifetime collection as a chocolate master. Angelina, I am not very social and therefore this is all I have. It has been for more years than I care to recount that I have yearned to share the contents of my book with a willing pupil. Although perhaps trite to most, this is nonetheless my legacy, and I want to share it with a deserving, eager student. Unfortunately, candy making just doesn't seem to interest many people, despite the smiles it brings to so many faces when a well-prepared batch is consumed."

"Dominique, I must say I'm honored that you're willing to share this with me. However, I certainly can't promise this early on that I'll be your special pupil."

"Only time will tell, Angelina, so for the time being let's just get started on our new adventure together."

"Sounds like a wonderful idea, Dominique. Just tell me what I should do first."

"If you'll follow me into my kitchen, Angelina. So we'll begin with my pot and my utensils. We're going to start with the formation of a basic chocolate ganache. This is basically a mixture of 50% cream and 50% chocolate. Now, with only two ingredients, you can well understand why it is essential that we use the finest chocolate and the best heavy cream that is available. In this particular case, I've purchased only the finest cocoa beans. Conveniently, I'm able to buy my cream from Mr. Ellison's farm, which, as I'm sure you already know, is just a short walk from here."

"Ah my yes; Mr. Ellison, I know him. I haven't seen him though, since my husband's accident. How's he been?"

"Mr. Ellison's doing just fine. He's remarried since Lilly, his former wife, passed away about three years ago. He's wed now to Sandra, a really wonderful woman. Don't know where she came from, but she's certainly not a native to these parts. You can tell it immediately when you listen to her accent. She's been a real blessing to him though. Wouldn't like to see a man in his nineties running that farm without a bit of help."

"Wow, I don't know how he does it, even with Sandra."

"Well, you probably didn't know it, but he sold off most of his acreage. He just keeps a few Jersey cows now. They provide a pretty high cream content, which he sells mostly to the Loukas Ice Cream Factory, to me, and also to a couple of specialty stores throughout our region. It helps him out and I certainly do appreciate it. His cream can make our candy real smooth to the tongue."

"Puppy what are you doing here?" exclaimed Angelina, as Chowbingo sheepishly scooted out from behind the sack of cocoa beans where he had recently planted himself.

"Now I don't expect you to understand, but this is my first day on the job at Mr. Bellingeri's candy factory and you certainly aren't helping me to make a good impression! Now scoot, hurry up and get out of here—NOW!"

"Well, some appreciation I get around here," Chowbingo thought to himself, as he scampered outside, all the while uttering a couple of voluntary yelps to dramatize his exit.

". . . AND you go directly home and stay with Val, until I get there," Angelina added, as a closing afterthought.

"Yeah, I'm under orders to come down here to make you happy and this is what I get for thanks—a yelling at," thought Chowbingo, as he scampered down the pathway with a couple of exaggerated, but futile, whimpering barks.

"Oops, I'm going in the wrong direction. Oh well, might as well saunter on up to Mr. Ellison's farm and say hi to his Jersey cows. At least I can thank them for their contribution to Mr. Bellingeri's chocolates. Certainly no human can communicate with them like I can. Everyone likes to be appreciated, even cows."

Then it happened: Chowbingo's chest first became warmer and warmer, then hot, and finally unbearable, as if it were about to catch on fire. He started to twirl and spin about in an attempt to diminish the feeling from the overbearing heat. As he spun and jumped about, he began to notice that in one direction the heat intensified while in the opposite direction it cooled. Momentarily he found that he was able to acclimate himself toward a favored direction, not unlike a lost explorer trying to navigate to a compass heading. He rapidly switched to a new southeasterly direction, not because he had selected it by choice, but because it was the one direction that alleviated the intense burning pain that he was experiencing. Coincidently, the direction in which he then found himself speeding, just happened to be the same that lead to the Patadarski's cottage.

Was all this heat the work of Angelina? After all she had given specific instructions for him to go to her home and stay with Val. Chowbingo, on the other hand, had thought it more interesting visit the cows.

Slowly, and then with increasing intensity, they began to emerge. Those bland, dark shadows that were being cast to and fro by the mid-morning's rising daylight started to take on life shapes of their own. At first it was just a feeling to him, a sensation, but then Chowbingo's fur began to stand upward as if it were being sparked by electricity. His amulet, the chrysolite, began to glow increasingly brighter, until finally his furry face shone with a warm green glow from the reflection of its rays.

"Wow, that Mrs. Patadarski, she sure has a lot of power. Just about lit me on fire, and all because I wanted to go say hi to a couple of cows rather than head back to her home."

Then a spiritual voice began to call from inside of him. Somewhat like the unmistakable voice that Father reserves for when He's speaking.

The sound of the voice grew louder, darker, and more authoritative. However, listen as he might, the meaning was unfathomable to him. It touched him like the tremulous sound a deaf person might experience when vibrations and movements are felt but the ability to discern meaning remains unavailable. Yet! Yet Chowbingo found something ominous about it all. This was not Father's voice; it was the voice from the "Angel of Light"— the "Great Counterfeiter" was speaking. This was the voice of the underworld with all of its evil malevolence.

Suddenly, in overwhelming evil brilliance, he appeared whole and undiluted in all of his malfeasant power—Xeres – the Apostle of Death!

Chowbingo, witnessing an unfolding of the apparitions, froze in stark terror before the emerging shapes. First to appear was the red, three-headed dog with each head barking different curses and swearing profanely. The longer they continued, the more the meanings and understandings began to reveal themselves to Chowbingo.

"Of course, those are the sounds from the 'Great Gulf Fixed' that I'm hearing."

But then it all changed. The three-headed dog morphed into a blue, hairless monkey, with teeth of pearls. Yet the eyes, the eyes, they didn't change.

Those eyes looked at him, piercing through to his spirit, as if they were aiming to destroy something that lay far beyond.

"I know those eyes," recalled Chowbingo. *"Those are the self-same eyes that radiated evil from Xeres back*

when he had first uttered his curses and blasphemies from our Father's home."

The shadows continued to take on ghostly shapes with their commanding presence, living silhouettes, not unlike a choir behind its leader, responding to every move of the conductor's baton.

Unrelenting, they remained, right there in the light of the garden path, red dog to blue monkey, to yellow cat, to sparkling chameleon; each one louder, larger, and more intimidating than the one from before.

As the scene continued to escalate, Chowbingo's fear and panic started to give way to an ebbing curiosity. His amulet's light grew brighter. The townspeople began to assemble. First it was a trickle, then a few, then a swarm. They came. They arrived from every direction. Each villager was drawn by the green light that was now electrifying the sky about Chowbingo.

They looked, each one upon his arrival, to see a puppy standing in the center of a well-worn garden path leading to Mrs. Patadarski's humble home. There he stood, Chowbingo; his stance was unusually erect, his tiny ears pointed skyward and his muzzle was curled into a slight snarl. Those who were moved to observe sensed something ominous. It was, to them, as if this dog was aware of a presence that was far beyond their abilities to comprehend. Undecided whether to run or remain, they all stood, transfixed by the green light glowing from the amulet about Chowbingo's neck. It was a transforming light, coming from a stone that offered an energy source that appeared to be totally unrecognizable and unknown to all those villagers who stood to witness it.

Chowbingo continued to stare, transfixed perhaps, as Xeres assumed his greatest and most intimidating form. His presence, unknown to those about him, was only for Chowbingo. His height was greater than a three-story building. His arms extended full width to a reach that could encompass a city block and crush it to smithereens.

He roared, he spit, and then he hissed. He displayed his outstretched claws in threatening gestures. His spines, which led from below the back of his skull to where they terminated just a few feet before the tip of his tail, undulated with each enormous breath and served as a metronome, pacing the rhythms for his body's every move. The slit pupils of his garnet-red eyes opened to display the window to his inner-being, undiluted evil. Although Chowbingo knew that this was a spiritual encounter between just Xeres and himself, he still could not help but wonder if this gathered crowd might also, as he did, smell the foulness of Xeres' breath.

Because of the odor, familiar to Chowbingo from millennia past, he was brought to the height of his fullest senses. Prompted to act, Chowbingo in his most authoritative voice from Neveah, addressed Xeres.

"Xeres, I know you and you know me. I am Father's beloved pet from Neveah, here on assignment. You and I, we have met before. I am His comfort, here now in earthly form. I'm the self-same spirit who used to raise warnings of your arrival when you approached Father's

home. That was my assignment. I alerted all to your comings and to your goings. I'm not afraid of you. You're just continuing to be the self-same, unwelcome intruder as from before.

"So, SHUT UP!"

Then just as suddenly as it had all begun, it ended. The silhouettes returned into the trees and again became the selfsame shadows that had been from before. Instead of Xeres' imposing image there now sat, beside the road, an elderly man, conservatively dressed. One might imagine, according to the clothing, that he might be a gentleman woodsman, even to the burl walking stick that lay gently between his legs.

The man, visible now not only to Chowbingo but also to the surrounding populace, looked over and politely asked, "Could you come over and sit with me for a spell. I believe we need to talk."

"I don't think so, thank you."

The folks who gathered, by now most of the village, witnessed, except for the arrival of the country gentleman, none of the foregoing. Only the continuing glow of Chowbingo's green amulet, which by then had subsided considerably.

Meanwhile, sprinting up the path came Angelina, closely being followed by Mr. Bellingeri, huffing and puffing as he tried to catch up from behind.

"My child, my child! Where's my boy? Val, Val what's happened to Val? Is he still alive? How bad, how bad is he hurt?" Angelina continued her screaming, blinded by the tears that were beginning to well up in her eyes.

Dominique Bellingeri, now with a muscular arm about Angelina's waist, bellowed out from deep within his diaphragm. "The boy Val, is this about him?"

"No, no," came a voice responding from the crowd. "He's fine. It's about the dog in the pathway and the green light that's hanging from around his neck. We don't know how his stone stays lit, and why he just stood there, like he was talking to someone we can't see. Craziest thing we ever came across."

"Mom, Mom," yelled Val from the back of the crowd. Next, without waiting for a response, he continued to force his way toward Dominique and Angelina, pushing his way through people's legs, and bending apart their knees, he continued pressing forward, as young boys are moved to do.

"What's happening? What's going on here? Why's everybody at our house?"

Then, before he could even approach his mother's waiting arms, he heard it.

"That light, that dog's green light; it can only be for evil," someone yelled.

Then another, and another, they all began to take up the cry.

"It's evil, it's evil," they began to all chant in unison.

Even before Dominique could react, Val sensed the danger and ran to assist Chowbingo, who was standing transfixed in the middle of the path—unmoving. He knelt down beside "his dog" and wrapped his arms tightly around Chowbingo, intent upon protecting him with every fiber of his young being.

Oblivious to his surroundings, Chowbingo looked intently at the woodsman stranger and then politely but sternly inquired in his spiritual language, *"Who are you and do you speak my language?"*

"You know me as the Prince of Darkness, minister to the long dead," he replied. "And it will not serve you well to deny me an audience this time. We need to talk."

"Ah, same Xeres—different costume. No, Xeres, again the answer is no; we don't need to talk. Good has no place for evil. There will be no discussion."

"So you say now," replied Xeres. "But you will change. Time will change you just like it changes everyone. You will see.

"Look, here, at me, Chowbingo! I am a common gentleman, well able to blend with your Father's loved ones. Well able to cast deceit, suspicion, fear, inadequacy, and disbelief throughout all the land. I don't have to bring harm to your friends to fulfill my goals. No, I prefer to deceitfully lead them into accepting my thoughts as theirs. Finally, they will cause harm to themselves and to each other. I can then return to your Father's house and laugh about how His loved ones again self-destructed, just like the two of them did back during that special time that we all shared together in his garden.

" Remember, the fruit? Remember when I convinced those two 'earthlings' that they were missing out by not seeing evil? Now that was fun. I messed up the whole garden thing, remember? That was so much fun.

"See, even now His loved ones, His lost 'earthlings' standing here around you are crying out that your light is evil. Where do you think they got the idea? I gave it to them while I was sitting here waiting for you. Now they're coming for you, Chowbingo. You're just a pesky dog to them. They'll soon figure that if they just kill you, your 'evil light' goes out. It's not going to be a pretty sight when they rip you out of that stupid boy's grasp.

"Chowbingo, you'll be cursing your master when they start to tear your limbs from your puny, puppy body. Then, when He does nothing to save you, you'll scream your blasphemies, and you'll be mine FOREVER! That's when I'll ask you, 'Where's your faith?' Where will your faith be then, Chowbingo?

"Farewell for now, Chowbingo, 'fare-thee-well' till we meet again in my kingdom."

As suddenly as the woodsman had appeared he vanished, lost in the melee, the villagers later concluded. Chowbingo, free from his trance, spun around to assess the fast-approaching crowd moving toward him. Val, valiantly positioned beside him, continued to hold his puppy's mid-section.

"Kill the dog, kill the dog," came the cries from the mob's instigators.

They were almost upon him. Chowbingo remained still, more mystified by all that was happening about him than by the impending danger that was about to befall him. Val, in the interim, had begun gripping Chowbingo ever more tightly—his ashen face now a caricature of frozen fear.

Without hesitation, the maddened crowd was upon them! The green halo coalesced, translating itself from its former soft glow, into a laser ray, that created a semi-circular shield to encircle Chowbingo. Thin as a knife's edge and resplendent as an emerald beneath a jeweler's light, it encircled Chowbingo's neck,

His head protruded through it, while Val, still grasping the midsection, remained behind it. The crowd stopped. Not a word was spoken. The silence was both deafening and troublesome.

The leadership were the first to dissolve into the crowd's matrix, each making a singular effort to leave in a different direction from that of his neighbor. Perhaps this was their sheepish attempt to deny any participation in what apparently had become an embarrassing and ill-conceived maneuver.

There they remained, alone on the path, Chowbingo and Val. Following shortly behind them came Angelina and Dominique. Gathered together, not a word was spoken. The amulet below Chowbingo's neck returned to its soft glow while Val, finally standing upright, released his hold.

Dominique was the first to speak. "Shall we continue on to the Patadarski home? I believe that's where we were all headed. Thankfully, I threw the door latch at the shop when we left."

Moving forward, like locusts without a leader, they proceeded in an orderly fashion toward Angelina's doorway. Solemnly, as she unlatched the door, they entered one by one. All those except for Chowbingo, who ran in the opposite direction, as fast as his doggy legs would permit.

Immediately Val spun about prepared to follow in hot pursuit. Dominique, anticipating Val's very move, stepped into the doorway and blocked his exit.

"Val," he spoke. "Your mother has had enough excitement for this day. In fact, all of us have. I would imagine your puppy is just taking a moment to relieve himself. Perhaps you should just sit down, relax, and give him a small bit of privacy."

Chowbingo, in the interim, continued to scamper away from the cabin and into the woods to where the sun was setting. He had business to attend to, and he didn't need interference from any of these "earthlings". Didn't matter, at the moment, if they were Father's favorites or not. Chowbingo wanted answers and he was determined to get them, his way!

He headed into the first moonlit clearing that he found, skidded to a stop, sat on his haunches, and looked up through the clear full moon to a place far beyond. He then began to howl with a primordial yell. It was a sound drawn deep from the recesses of his canine ancestry's most primitive beginnings. Screaming at the top of his spiritual lungs, not an earthly sound was uttered, but all of the universes listened and heard.

Chowbingo was troubled, afraid, hurt, and confused, all at once. He wanted comfort and he wanted solace. He wanted to be home. He was tired of this journey. He felt forsaken and he most assuredly felt abandoned.

"I want my Father," he cried inwardly.

Silence! The sound of silence became deafening. It sounded to Chowbingo as if he were being drawn into a dark, black, lifeless hole. It felt as if all light had been extinguished. Doesn't a deaf person at least experience some internal sound; perhaps a slight buzzing within the ears? Chowbingo heard nothing.

"Puppy, Puppy where are you?"

It was Val; having sidestepped Dominique's grasp, he was again determined to take possession of his recently found pet.

Chowbingo heard the call as if it were coming from a pure crystal bell.

"Oh there you are," exclaimed Val as he began dragging a reluctant Chowbingo along by his forepaw. "Did you have to go 'number two'? Are you finished now?"

"Oh my golly," exclaimed Chowbingo to himself. *"Here I am stuck with these 'earthlings' and Father won't even answer my cries. Woe, woe, woe is me! Abandoned and unloved, a reject from Neveah. How can there be a plight worse than mine?"*

His tail bent down as straight as a chow might be enabled to do such a thing, and his head hung so low that the amulet's soft glow became lost between the soft fur of his neck and the dirt that he was dragging it through. Chowbingo sauntered, freed now from Val's grasp, back to the cabin. Inside, he made his way over to the hearth where he lay upon the warm stones, faced toward the flames, and attempted to erase all that had recently happened; especially where he was—and his body, and the "crazy" dog suit which he found himself inhabiting.

"What is Father's comforter, His spiritual friend, doing stuck in a fur suit, on a stone hearth, a millennial distance from Neveah," wondered Chowbingo as he slipped into a deep, dark, dreamless sleep.

Morning came soon. The sun's rays shone through the humble cabin's eastward-facing window while casting its luminous glow throughout the home's interior. Nothing escaped the warm light, especially not Chowbingo, who jumped up and off the hearth with a start.

Awake now and gathering his thoughts, Chowbingo realized that he was completely alone. Gone for the moment were Val and Angelina.

Mr. Bellingeri would have left earlier in the evening, recalled Chowbingo, knowing that it would have been inappropriate for him to remain for the night. No need to check the proximate areas for him.

"Well now," thought Chowbingo. "Here is my opportunity to escape from these 'earthlings'. I can leave now and be done with this entire sordid mess. But wait a minute, where will I go? Hmm, I certainly can't go home. No way to get there. I can't talk to Father. He just doesn't want to answer. No use in calling for Jabez or Schezak. Father's probably got a muzzle on them, especially if He won't talk to me.

"Well, that doesn't leave me with too many choices. I can spend some time with Mr. Ellison's cows or I can join up with Mr. Kolvalenko. I think I'll go join up with the cows. They seem to make more sense, even though they apparently spend their days doing nothing."

With that, Chowbingo shook himself fiercely before taking a moment to carefully stretch his legs, extending each one separately, between long languorous pauses. Then it was off to see the cows he went, while still remaining ever vigilant within his surroundings, as he made certain to circumvent those crazy villagers from the previous night.

"Hi there, cow," muttered Chowbingo, to himself, as he turned toward the first one that he encountered, quietly ambling along the fence line.

"Well a good day to you too," came a voice from the Jersey, and in a most pleasant tone at that.

Chowbingo liked to have jumped out of his fur: a talking cow? This was not the response he had anticipated from an Earth animal. This was a spiritual response such as might be expected from Khasmar, or even between Schezak, and himself, but from an earthly cow?

He recovered, paused, and then looked again at the cow. He then barked, but no reaction from the cow followed. She just continued to chew her cud, apparently electing to remain oblivious to Chowbingo.

Chowbingo then growled his fiercest growl, but still no reaction.

Separated from the cow by the fence, he apparently posed no physical threat to her other than that of being a nuisance.

"This certainly is strange," thought Chowbingo. *"I know I was spoken to, but by whom?"*

Again the same voice responded. "It's me, the cow, the one you keep trying to pester. Now please stop being rude and allow me to digest my meal."

One more time Chowbingo barked at the animal.

The cow again spoke to Chowbingo. This time Chowbingo carefully noted, however, that she still spoke in the same clear voice as before. However, no sounds came from her mouth, other than the soft sounds of her chewing cud.

"Cows can't talk," Chowbingo muttered, under his breath and mostly to himself.

"That's quite true, but I can," came the immediate and unexpected reply.

"My golly," replied Chowbingo, *"You're speaking to me in Father's language."*

"Yes, Mr. Dog, I am speaking to you in Father's language, and I am also in a 'cow suit' just as you are in a 'dog suit'.

"Like you, I may be dumb and unable to speak in an earthly manner, but I'm certainly not stupid, Mr. Dog. You can bark, roll over, and scratch for fleas, but can you eat grass and produce nutritious milk? Can you sleep while standing? Can you chew cud? You see, Mr. Dog, among the cows I run with, we think that you, and those humans you pal around with, perhaps are not the sharpest crayons in the box."

"I think I understand now," responded Chowbingo. *"But it just seemed like I was talking to myself until your voice, deep inside of me, answered—now, I know that it's really you."*

"It is. So, shall I continue to address you as Mr. Dog, or shall I call you Puppy like your young friend, Val? Perhaps you would prefer to be called by your given name?"

"My name's Chowbingo, my home is with Father in Neveah, and it's from there that I've been sent."

"Good to visit with you, Mr. Chowbingo. My name, here, is Lucy."

"Lucy, why can I talk to you but not to the others?"

"Chowbingo, you have the ability to speak our spiritual language because you are from His place, just like me. Your friend Val, and the others, are not from there, so they can't understand us. However, don't worry. There will come a time, I've been told, a special time, when not only earthlings, but even the rocks and the stars will speak our language."

"Wow! Lucy, that's very exciting. Then I'll be able to speak to Val and finally give him a piece of my mind."

"Hold on a minute, Chowbingo, it's not going to be that simple."

Lucy paused and took a moment to chew her cud for a bit before continuing.

"Chowbingo, some earthlings will die and pass from here to there, where they will acquire our gift of spiritual speech. Others will reside with Xeres and, unfortunately, they will only learn his speech."

"What about you, why is this working for us?"

"Chowbingo, you are here because you are lonely and because you're afraid. You cried to Father in faith, and He has placed me here to comfort you. Father wants you to remember that He loves you. He cares deeply about you, and He is protecting you, even now as we speak."

"Lucy, I don't understand, I don't . . . Lucy; why won't you answer me?

"Lucy, please quit chewing your cud and talk to me!

"Ok, Father, I get it—conversation over!"

With that, Chowbingo ambled back down the path from where he had first come. Perplexed and confused, he considered the day's events that had just unfolded. Why was he here, what was his purpose, and how could he help? He had faced demons, he had been accosted by villagers, he had been captured by a boy wanting a pet, and now he was being ignored by a talking cow. What would be next?

"Dominique, I mean Mr. Bellingeri, why do you call your condiments, truffles?"

"You don't need to call me Mr. Bellingeri, Angelina. In fact, I would prefer it if you would call me Dominique, or even Dom, if you like."

"Since I will be working in your store, don't you think it would be more appropriate, for the sake of your professional reputation before your customers, if I were to address you in a formal manner?"

"I can surely see your point, Angelina, but I just thought that perhaps . . ."

"Mr. Bellingeri, before you continue, let me inform you that although we are friends, I consider this to be strictly a business relationship. I would ask that we both treat it as such from the beginning."

"I fully understand, Mrs. Patadarski, and I certainly do intend to conduct myself accordingly. However, may I have permission to address you as Angelina when I find myself in your company, say away from the store?"

"Of course, Dominique," replied Angelina with a coquettish smile. "As your friend I would truly expect that and also welcome it."

"Good, now let's get back to this truffle business and why it's called a truffle. About December of 1895 the first chocolate truffles were made in Chambery, France by M. Dufour. Later, in the beginning of the 1900s, all of Europe became familiar with this delicacy. The name's origin is really quite basic. The original delicacies were shaped like the truffles of the mushroom fungus. It was from this shape that they were so named and soon afterwards they began to be distributed throughout our more modern world."

"Mr. Bellingeri, how do we make your brand of truffle?" asked Angelina, now becoming a bit miffed over hearing the details of what, to her, apparently looked to be such an easy process.

"The making of the ganache is actually quite simple. You heat heavy cream in a pot at medium heat. You then add the chocolate, which has been separated from the cocoa bean, and allow it to simmer. Finally, you add butter, if needed, and then stir it until smooth."

"Well that certainly sounds simple. I'm sure it's something I can do quite easily. Let's get started!"

"Please, not so fast, Mrs. Patadarski. The simple truth is that a six-year-old can play a piano and a seasoned maestro can play the same piano, using the same song with the same notes. The difference between the two lies in the sound and in the tonal qualities that are produced. So it is with a chocolate truffle. Whereas a maestro's music is candy to the ear, a chocolate truffle, expertly prepared, becomes a sought-after candy for the palate.

"The first thing we're going to do, Mrs. Patadarski, is to make a small, sample batch of truffle mix, using my ingredients, and according to my recipe. We'll make this batch using the pot I have here. It's approximately the same size as the copper pot at your home. Then when we're finished with this first batch, we'll make ourselves a second batch, exactly the same way."

"What's the point of two batches, Mr. Bellingeri, other than to require that we wash two pots after we finish?"

"Rather than explain it all to you, I will simply show you. Now, can we please get started?"

"Puppy, Puppy where are you?" cried a frightened Val after returning from checking his "mushroom bulbs" outside. Although he found his mother to be gone, that did not, for the moment, concern him. It was not unusual for her to be absent at mid-day; but Chowbingo, he was different. After all, hadn't they almost been inseparable since their first meeting? Chowbingo's absence was quite unusual and very troubling, especially after their run-in with those evil-intended villagers from last night.

"I should have taken Puppy outside with me. I guess this is what I get. Everyone's gone now but me. I really must find my Puppy—and right now. He'll probably be in some sort of danger if I'm not there beside him. Those people from my village, they still might want to harm him. I don't even know if his green stone will work for him again, like it did last night. I've really got to find him before those villagers do! After all, he's still just a helpless puppy. He needs me."

The more he thought about it the more distracted his mind became.

"Heck, I'm just a boy," he thought. "I need some help too.

"Mom's probably working with Mr. Bellingeri. She's certain to be mad at me if I ask her to help me find Puppy right now. I know, I'll go see Butcher Kolvalenko. He was very kind to Puppy when he first met him. I'm sure that he'll help me."

Revitalized, with a child's optimism and a new sense of purpose, Val headed toward the Yuri Kolvalenko Butcher Shop. Walking along the well-worn pathway, from his cabin to the central village, his foot stumbled upon a somewhat unique, loose stone. A stone that could only be of some particular interest to the likes of a young boy, and so it was for Val. Obviously this would be a stone, specifically purposed to kick before him, while he made his way to the butcher shop—and so he did. He kicked it and it bounced along the well-beaten path, kicked it again and lobbed it off the corner light post, kicked it a third time and it ricocheted off the masonry building walls adjacent to the pathway's left border. Deeply lost in his thoughts, he absent-mindedly kicked it once again, and was almost oblivious to the fact that he had, unwittingly, just kicked it into a seated man's lap.

"Ouch," came the unexpected response. "You'd better watch out where you're kicking your stone. It's not nice to try and hurt people."

Val, having immediately snapped out of his daydream, looked in the direction of the voice with a start. There, on a pale, weathered green bench, sat an elderly man dressed in a well-tailored suit, an outfit that one might expect a country squire to be wearing. It was slate gray in color and a mottled plaid in design. The narrow lapels and high-buttoned vest almost concealed his nattily turned ascot, which was puffed with just a bit of flair, such that it might draw a bit of reserved attention by those trained to notice such detail, but not so flagrant as to be ostentatious in its presentation. His silver lapel pin, with its centered ruby, and his high-button, well-polished dress shoes, completed his ensemble. This gentleman was definitely not one to be considered a person of the village. He was, surely, too well dressed. And the burl, walnut walking stick, which rested against the edge of the bench upon which he sat, definitely was not of a crafting that might be considered native to the region.

Val, of course, had been born in the village, never travelling further than a few miles from it. Salvio, his father, used to take him, in the family wagon, to the urban center that lay further to the west. Those trips predictably oc-curred, about once a month, before Salvio was killed in the industrial accident. Those had been wonderful trips, just Val and his dad. They would hitch up their horse to the wagon and take the ten-mile journey to the Walloon's Hardware and Feed Store. There, they would pick up the bulk supplies for Angelina and also the feed for their horse. The two milking goats, the few additional rabbits, and the chickens all seemed to multiply on their own, no matter what they ate.

That all ended on the eve of the day that Val had lost his father. Over time, the horse, the goats, and their small menagerie of animals, gradually disappeared. Even their wagon finally had to be sold. They simply did not have the money to support even the more basic of essentials. The odd jobs, her babysitting services, and the laundry intake, which Angelina contracted from the village people, al-lowed her to purchase only the most basic of foodstuffs, along with the occasional medicines required to repair the cuts and bruises which such a hard life commanded.

Following Salvio's passing, the purchase of new clothes could no longer be a consideration, nor could the purchase of the store-bought fabrics to home sew them. Through the courtesy and good will of her wash clients, Angelina learned to make do with their hand-me-downs. Many gifted her with their well-worn threads, such as should not even be considered appropriate for a scrub woman's work. Such offerings were mostly from those who expected a prompt, timely, thank you for every shredded piece that they provided. It was mostly these same villagers who expected, from Angelina, a well-displayed demeanor of humble appreciation as she accepted their rags. The others, the ones who expected no thanks whatever, were the ones who provided her with their "left-overs", which still retained sales labels of the most recent dates and just "happened" to be exact fits for Angelina and Val.

Val, who seemed to have known everyone in the village, including the history of most of their comings and goings, never enjoyed playmates from that date forward. He was friendly, and of course like any young boy, he wanted to have friends. It simply became his plight as time passed, that no one wanted to play with him, a boy who was so poor. If Val didn't make the other kids uncomfortable, then their parents most assuredly did. The dinner table conversations about that "poor widow Patadarski and her boy" soon served to sever any opportunity that Val might have had for companionship.

─────────

"Boy! You come over here," growled the man, speaking in Val's direction.

"Yes sir," answered Val, in his accustomed, meek, mild, manner, as he shuffled over to the foot of where the elder was seated.

"What caused you to kick that rock at me? You sure must be a nasty little boy. Bet your mother doesn't do a very good job of raising you."

"I'm very sorry sir, but I was just kicking the rock along. I didn't even see you until after my rock landed in your lap."

"You seem to be involved with rocks a lot. Don't you own that vicious dog that runs around here with a green rock hanging round his neck? Sure seems to be a mischievous sort," the man continued. "Saw him in the middle of the pathway the other evening. Snarling he was, as I remember."

"Well, yes sir. I guess I kind of own him. We just sort of came together, and he's been living with us ever since."

"Your mama allows that?"

"Yes sir."

"Well, your mama, she hasn't got a lick-a-brains. Just goes to show everyone why you're in the mess you're in: no money, and no friends."

"Now you just hold on, Mister! Mister?"

"Name's unimportant for you, Sonny. Just be careful what you say to me. Don't you forget, I'm your elder."

"Elder—smelter, you're just being plain rude to me. You've got no right to speak to me like you have—no matter my age. Furthermore, Mister, my mama's a very good woman. She raised me right and, if you say another bad word about her, I'm going to take that rock out of your lap and hit you on the head with it—more than once!"

"Slow down there, Sonny, don't get your knickers in a knot. I'm a lot older than you, in fact a heck of a lot older. I've seen things and know things that you can't even imagine. I know for instance that your dog's name isn't Puppy. His name is Chowbingo, and furthermore, I know where he comes from! He didn't just wander down that path to your home on his own. That was somebody else's idea."

"I've never seen you before, Mister. I've lived here my entire life. Also, I know just about everybody who does live here. You don't know anybody. In fact, you're a stranger. You don't even know Puppy," continued Val, now in a rant.

"Why ARE you here?"

"I know you don't believe me; I run into that a lot—but you soon will. So you just run along now. Oh, when you see your dog, with that stupid stone around his neck, just call him Chowbingo, and then watch how he reacts. After that, I'll bet you'll want to come back and talk to me more politely."

"Where can I find you?" asked Val, now a bit inquisitive.

"Don't worry, I'll be around. I can always find you when need be. I'm always available. That's one thing I'm really known for. I'm always available. Now you run along—go and tell your mother that she needs to teach you some manners."

———————

Chowbingo continued his walk along the less-traveled path, behind the village's main course way. He certainly didn't need another encounter, such as had just happened the previous night, especially now that he was alone. He would have preferred to have made his way over to the chocolate shop and snuggled up beside the sack of cocoa beans. Unfortunately, Val's mother would certainly squelch that idea, once again, just like before when she had shooed him away earlier.

"Might as well make my way back to the cabin," Chowbingo thought. *"I can probably find Val there. It's certainly better than watching over my shoulder for those crazy villagers.*

"Oh, no!"

Just then, here they came again—the villagers!

"Drat, why me? Where's Val, now that I need him? It's still too far for me to make it safely to the butcher shop. I guess I'll just roll over onto my back and surrender. They won't hurt me when they see that I've surrendered, I hope!"

They showed no sign of slowing. They just continued to rush him, a maddened crowd driven as if by a single mind. All of them coming together, all that was except for the one solitary, elderly man seated on the bench off to himself.

Then, without hesitation or warning, the first man to reach Chowbingo snatched him off the trail by an upstretched hind leg and snatched him skyward. Almost as quickly the green amulet about Chowbingo's neck turned a green so bright that the crowd involuntarily began to shield their eyes. Rapidly it turned into a single, searing point of light, beaming directly at the man's wrist. His hand, then completely paralyzed, loosed the grip on Chowbingo, and dropped him to the ground with a disturbing thud.

Chowbingo, finding himself prostrate on his back, rolled over while trying to regain his composure. Simultaneously, the emerald light redirected its beam, focusing it toward the foot of the lone man still seated on the bench. The acrid odor of the scorched earth began filling the villagers' nostrils, raising an uncomfortable level of uncertainty among them that soon bordered on panic. The elderly man stood, snorted, and walked away without concern. It was for him, a man well versed in un-pleasantries, not an unfamiliar occurrence.

"This is crazy," said one.

"It's supernatural," added another.

"My hand, it doesn't work," cried the one who had first rudely lifted Chowbingo by his leg.

"Does it burn?" asked another who had stood beside him.

"No, it feels like ice," was the reply.

"What are we going to do?"

"Who was that man?"

"Has anyone seen him before?"

"Where's he from?"

"Forget him! Where's that dog from?"

"Got to be a devil dog," volunteered another—and so it continued.

While the commotion continued, Chowbingo scampered just as fast as his little doggy legs could carry him. It was just a matter of minutes before, sliding on his butt with all four paws facing forward, he hit the base of the butcher shop's counter. The impact was so sudden that dislodged price tags, advertising Mr. Kolvalenko's display meats, found themselves momentarily stuck to Chowbingo's fur.

Butcher Kolvalenko, responding to the sound of Chowbingo's impact, hurried to the front of the store. There, just as suddenly, Val also entered tripping over the still bedazzled dog. "What are you both doing here? Actually, I mean why the sudden rush to get here," Yuri asked of no one in particular.

Chowbingo, of course unable to voice himself verbally, screamed inwardly, *"If you had an entire village that wanted to dissect you in the middle of the pathway, perhaps you too might come here in a bit of a hurry."*

Then it was Val's turn. "Mr. Kolvalenko, I just met a man who was very rude to me. He told me that my mama was no good and that he knew all about Puppy and where he came from."

"Well now, that's a good one," thought Chowbingo. *"And where does he think he's from, Neveah?*

"Father, please, why won't you let me talk? You know, speak to them in their earth language."

Philip I. Amos

Chapter 8

Certainly Un-neighborly

O kay Mrs. Patadarski, we have now completely cooked two batches using similar ingredients. We have measured each batch exactly, heated them both for the same amount of time, and maintained the stove setting at the same temperature. We've even timed the cooling period before we set the pots in ice to stop the cooking process.

"Now in answer to your earlier question, I will show you why we have cooked two identical sample batches. Here's a spoon. I want you to first eat this piece of bland cheese to cleanse your palate and then taste and savor from our first batch."

"It's delicious. Now I understand why you take such pride in your product."

"Thank you, but now take another piece of cheese, repeat the process, and sample the second batch."

"Umm, it's also quite good but why does it taste so different?"

"Don't worry, you'll get the hang of it.

"Anyway, as I was about to say, for someone new to the industry, you have an exquisite palate. Most people can't pick up the difference, and that's what it's all about. The two batches taste different because of the material composition of the pots from which they were each separately cooked. Although quite satisfactory as a product for my store's candy counter, my current chocolate processing equipment is, unfortunately, unacceptable for commercial distribution. There, quality control is more often determined by machines than by personal taste.

"Perhaps now you understand why your copper pot will be so necessary for our success. I want our ganache and our truffles to be of the highest quality, and without peer. Mrs. Patadarski, the highest grade chocolates are sought, by name, throughout the world. We want that name to be become ours, 'Bellingeri & Patadarski'— chocolatiers to the world. Doesn't that sound rich, expensive—just like the finest chocolates?"

"Mr. Bellingeri, I certainly have come to admire your vision, but we must also use with it our faith, or your vision will perish. And I'm afraid that real faith is something that was stripped from me long ago."

"Val, is your mother at home?"

"No sir, I believe she is over at Mr. Bellingeri's store learning how to make chocolate."

"Well that's just around the corner. Tell you what, it's almost closing time. Half hour shouldn't make much difference. I'll grab a piece of meat for your mother, we'll lock up here, and then I can walk over there with the two of you. Now sit with your dog, over there in the corner for a minute, while I wrap this cut of beef.

"Ready? Okay, let's go.

"Ah, there you are Angelina," exclaimed Butcher Kolvalenko glancing through the window, prior to all of them entering.

"I've picked up a couple of strays along the way. Looks to me like they might have needed rescuing. Wouldn't you agree?

"Why don't you come on in, Val? Puppy, you might as well follow. I really don 't think Mr. Bellingeri will mind. After all, it's almost closing time for him, too.

"Oh and here's a peace offering on their behalf, a nice piece of meat. I hope you'll all be able to enjoy it."

"What's happening?" asked a slightly bewildered Dominique, as he emerged from the rear cooking area to join Angelina, at her side.

"I have here with me, an upset dog that can only pant and whimper, and a boy who is upset over a man who spoke harshly to him, one whom he has never seen before," replied Butcher Yuri, with a slightly mischievous grin.

"Yeah, well don't forget Lucy, the talking cow, and your neighbors who tried to kill me," reflected Chowbingo to himself.

"Would you look at the size of this piece of meat that Yuri has brought us," piped up Angelina, as she tried to redirect the discussion away from what was starting to become a topic of nervous excitement, an emotion that was contrary to her normal, emotional comfort.

Dominque, quickly catching Angelina's uneasiness, added, "And let me add a few ounces of mixed candies for dessert. In fact, I'm also going to add some milk, from Mr. Ellison's dairy, so you can make hot chocolate before you, Val, and his puppy, all retire for the evening."

"There, now that's all settled," quipped Dominique, as he executed the authority, while adopting the countenance of an accomplished peacemaker.

"Not quite so sudden," exclaimed Angelina, as she looked directly toward Mr. Bellingeri with a gaze that one might reserve for an errant school child. "It's not settled! Not that is until both you and Mr. Kolvalenko agree to join Val and me for dinner this evening."

"And what about me, spirit-in-a-dog-suit?" thought Chowbingo to himself, as he shot visual daggers toward Angelina's direction. *"Don't I count for anything?"*

"Oh, I'm sorry, I almost forgot—and Puppy too."

"Nothing like a little 'spiritual inducement' when you need to get your message across," reflected Chowbingo, with a bit of self-satisfaction. *"Father's probably going to get me for this one, but we can settle up when I next see Him, I hope."*

The more immediate issues having been seemingly quashed, the little group began their trek toward Angelina's cabin.

"There's that confounded devil mutt again," resonated a familiar voice from one of the village passageways.

"Who are you, don't I know you?" queried Yuri, with a quickened response.

Another voice piped in, "It doesn't matter whether you know us or not. We're here to make sure that your satanic dog is either dead or out of our village. Yuri, we're here to protect our families. Come on now, guys, you know the plan—just like we rehearsed."

Shadows began to cast their silhouettes over the village square, pushed forward by the mob approaching from behind. The noise increased proportionately, as they approached, coming from every direction.

Chowbingo stopped in mid-step, his tail pointed down and his ears cocked forward, frozen in fear. Dominique instinctively placed his arm about Angelina's waist, while Yuri took a defensive position at the front of the group, not realizing that the forces already had them surrounded and were now approaching from all directions.

Val, as he had done before, knelt down beside Chowbingo, wrapped his arms around his dog's midsection and softly whispered, "Don't worry Puppy, I'm here. I'll protect you!"

Not for a moment did he consider how he, a small boy, might accomplish such a task.

Then rapidly they began to appear, not as a force intent upon attacking, but rather as a mob seeking to escape, a mob in a panic. Run, and run they did, in as many directions as they could, while trying to escape the pushing and stampeding of the Jersey cows that appeared to be prodding them from every direction.

Chaos!

Suddenly it seemed that every man and boy in the village was running in a different direction, confused as to whether they were pursuing, or being pursued. The former authoritative cries of leadership were systematically being replaced by the mooing of cows, followed by the boyish outbursts of grown men, as they were being bounced off the sides of structures, or rolled like logs, through the dirt and gravel of flower beds and pathways.

"Sorry I couldn't get here sooner," bellowed Lucy to Chowbingo, as she passed him, while smartly bouncing the buttocks of an errant villager with her stubby horns. "It took me a while to convince my sisters, from the neighboring farms, to join me; but as you can see, they're certainly all about it now, and having a wonderful time at that!"

"I, I just don't know how to begin to thank you, Lucy," replied Chowbingo, as he slowly began to regain his composure.

"Well, you can start by getting that kid to turn you loose. Then you can act like a cattle dog and round us all up."

"What's a cattle dog? I don't understand."

"Sorry, I forgot, they don't have rodeos where you come from. Look, just run around us and bark and nip at our ankles. Then you can just go about letting us do the rest."

"All right, but I don't get it."

"Listen, many humans think that cows are stupid, just because we stop and think situations through before we go off and do dumb things. If they knew we were smart, then they would have us doing all sorts of unnecessary human things. This way we just walk from our fields, down to the stalls twice a day, and give milk. In exchange for which they give us feed and shelter. Gives us a lot more time to think and discuss philosophy with one another.

"Your job is to pretend that you are directing us back to our farms. That's one of the assignments for a cattle dog. Humans think we're too dumb to know where to go. Therefore, they have dogs, like you, who they think are smarter than us. They're trained to direct us where to go by barking and nipping at our hooves.

"Now please get started before they actually figure out that I was the one who arranged this stampede in order to save your sorry butt . . . C'mon Chowbingo, get with the program. I'm getting tired of this. I'm just not in shape to be running around here butting heads. Start acting like a cattle dog and get us back home so we can return to doing a little quiet grazing."

Chowbingo, not wanting to be yelled at twice, especially by someone as big as Lucy, gave a mighty, squirming, twist and was out of Val's grip before he could recover. He then responded, exactly as he thought Lucy had instructed. First he barked, then he growled, then he began running in every direction, behaving just as he thought a cattle dog should behave. He ran to and fro. Then he ran left and right. Then he ran in left circles. Finally, he ran in right circles. The cows, who were now beginning to observe his behavior, began to run in the opposite direction, anything to avoid this crazy animal.

"Lucy, what's going on," bellowed Maria, the neighboring cow, from the pasture adjacent to Lucy's.

"Girls, girls," Lucy mooed in their language. "Chowbingo's trying to be a cattle dog but he doesn't really know what to do. Just follow me back to our pastures."

The cows, after a brief lapse and a bit of confusion, began following Lucy's lead as she moved away from the village and headed up the trail toward their familiar pasture land. Chowbingo, still intent upon fulfilling his part, followed right behind them barking, growling, and running crazy patterns as he went.

The villagers, running about in pandemonium, began to realize that the cows, rather than chasing them, were now following behind Lucy and returning back to their respective grazing lands. Perhaps, even more important, was their realization that chasing them, from behind, was Chowbingo.

Mr. Emerson, the sometime self-appointed village governor, and otherwise village green grocer, watched in awe as the cows, in perfect formation, peacefully headed away from his village.

"Well I'll be," exhorted Sam Emerson. "That kid's dog is marching them cows out of here like a marine drill sergeant."

"No telling what might have happened to us if it hadn't been for that mutt," exclaimed another.

"That crazy dog probably saved our lives," volunteered a third.

"You ever see anything so crazy," softly mooed Maria to Lucy, as they ambled up the path, side by side. "We first get ourselves a bedazzled dog doing pirouettes in the dirt, and now here come those nitwit villagers who think that we're going to kill them."

"Yes, I know. And they think we need watching because we chew our cud and discuss a little philosophy amongst ourselves. Do you think this is all because of those two crazy humans who went and got themselves all messed up in His garden?"

"I'm not sure, but it's a thought. I heard that He was pretty upset about the whole thing."

"Word is He still hasn't gotten over it."

"If only they had just done as they were told . . ."

"Val, Angelina, Dominique, I want you to all get over here beside me."

"Okay, but maybe we should continue over to my house instead. After all, that's where we were headed, and besides I'm even more frightened now than before," answered Angelina.

"Val, where are you headed?"

"I've got to go get my puppy!"

"You come right back here—it's too dangerous for you to follow him now."

"I'll be right back, Mom," yelled Val over his shoulder, unintentionally ignoring his mother as he ran in the direction of the pasture land where he quickly found himself, following directly behind the sauntering cows.

"I don't know what I'm going to do with that headstrong son of mine," she muttered. Angelina's face, now distorted from the emotions welling up from within, displayed her unabashed frustration as she witnessed Val disappearing behind the path's curves. Despite her continued pleadings for him to stop, he remained intent upon continuing to his intended destination, even to the point of disobeying his mother's fervent calls.

"Where you headed now, Sonny?"

"Who's asking?" responded Val, now a bit breathless from running up the hill toward the pasture lands.

"Over here," responded the elderly gentlemen.

"Oh, it's you!"

"Never mind the smart remarks. Did you call that dog by his real name yet—Chowbingo?"

"No! And why should you care?"

"When you finally do what I ask, then you'll know."

"You've got to give me a better answer than that."

The old man just stared at Val, refusing to answer. Val waited a moment for a reply and then, as impetuous boys are inclined to do, he merely continued on his way.

"Puppy, Puppy where are you? C'mon, I can't spend much longer looking for you. I'm already in trouble with Mama because of you.

"Oh, there you are," exclaimed Val, as he caught sight of Chowbingo's tail-fluff rounding the corner up ahead of him.

"Puppy, there you are. I can see you. Come here—RIGHT NOW," yelled the now frustrated Val, who at the moment, felt he had certainly succeeded in stretching the upper limits of his vocal chords.

But his yelling was to no avail. Chowbingo was not to be deterred from his cattle dog assignment. Not before, that is, personally being dismissed by Lucy. It had been a nice respite for him to have been able to communicate with someone in his familiar language, for a change. He was not, for the moment, inclined to dismiss it in exchange for the ramblings of a ten-year-old earthling.

"Chowbingo, you come back here right now," screamed Val, again yelling from the top of his lungs. He was feeling the emotional presence of his mother's command to return, and this tacit refusal to comply was beginning to unnerve him.

Time froze for Val and Chowbingo, as each halted in their tracks, neither moving! The first to speak was Chowbingo.

"HOW DID YOU KNOW MY NAME?" he demanded.

"That nasty old man on the bench, he told it to me," Val responded, without even realizing, in the excitement, that he was talking to a dog.

"Well, come on up here," answered Chowbingo. "I have to catch up with Lucy so I can talk with her, AND NOW YOU!"

"Who's Lucy?"

"The cow who just saved you. Now hurry, come on along, and catch up with me."

"Wait up a minute, will you? I don't have four legs like you, so can you slow up a bit?"

"I'm sorry! Okay, I'll slow down, but you have to hurry it up.

"Hey Lucy, we're almost there. Do you still need for me to be a cattle dog?"

"No, your assignment is complete, Chowbingo, and you did a wonderful job. Anyway, that's what the humans will think. Now the girls, they'll just continue thinking it was funny. It'll keep them off their philosophy kick for a few days while they have fun discussing your antics."

"Philosophy, antics, cattle dog? What's this all about?"

"Oh, oh! Lucy, can you hold up for a bit? I think I have some explaining to do and I believe that I'm going to need your help.

"Val, I think I'm going to need you to sit down for a moment. Let's set ourselves over here, next to this tree, close to Lucy."

"Lucy, who is Lucy? OH MY GOLLY! Puppy, your mouth, it isn't even moving, yet you've been talking to me. AND . . . and, I can even understand you! What's going on here?"

"Like I said, Val, you need to sit down. This is going to take a moment, I believe."

"Okay, I'm sitting down, and I'm scared. Now where is Lucy?"

"I'm right here. Nice to make your acquaintance, Val."

"Oh, my golly! A talking cow?"

"Now, what's wrong with that, Val? We've been talking longer than you've been alive. Had some pretty enlightening conversations, I must say. Certainly more interesting than a lot of the human babble your adults insist on speaking. We just try to have peaceful days, and that's what we often have to tolerate; especially during milking time, when they all seem to crowd in."

"But, but—you're talking to me. I understand you and your mouth, again, it isn't even moving."

"Val, that's why I asked you to sit down so that we could talk to you," interrupted Chowbingo.

"You see, Val, we're not speaking in the worldly language that you know. You're communicating with us in Father's spirit language."

"What do you mean by 'spirit' language?"

"Val, I am speaking to you, now, about the language of creation. This is the language that you knew and understood from the time of your beginning. Your spirit language was with you before you were first in your mother's womb. It still remains with you, even though you are now here, on Earth. It is that 'still small voice' that occasionally speaks to you from deep within."

"What! What are you talking about—you're both crazy!

"Mama, Mama," Val cried, as he took off in a spirited run.

"Whoa, now wait just a minute" cried Chowbingo, as he took off after him. *"Stop! Val, I know you can hear me. Please, stop and let me explain.*

"Thanks! This is actually all very natural, certainly not something that should cause you any reason for fear."

. . . and off Val went again, panicked.

"Hang in there, Lucy. I'm really going to need your help for me to explain all of this to our crazy friend; that is as soon as I can catch him, again. I don't know why Father didn't give me some longer legs. Golly, that kid can run!"

Val, now gaining speed on his downhill sprint tried leaning into the corner as he prepared to skirt alongside the upcoming building. Instead he lost his footing and slid on the sand-coated surface before coming to a final rest, planted flat on his back, with his feet pointed upward, firmly set against the building's plaster wall.

Sitting nearby on the bench, and peering directly into Val's eyes, sat the old man.

Dazed at first, Val's eyes did not make any connection, not until his gaze crossed that of the elderly man. It was then, for the first time, that he understood the attraction. The man's pupils were scarlet red. Not red, like one's eyes might become from being rubbed too hard, but rather a deep garnet red, as if two rubies had artificially been planted deep into the orbital recesses of the elderly man's skull.

Val jumped up with a start, just in time for Chowbingo to round the corner on all fours and hit him right at the kneecaps. Down he went, for the second time, whereupon he found himself staring up into the drooling muzzle of Chowbingo, who was then poised directly above him.

"Get off of me, you crazy dog," muttered Val, as he wrestled out from under Chowbingo. He then found himself more intent upon escaping Chowbingo's unintended muzzle shower than attending to any other concern.

It was then that Chowbingo also caught sight of the old man sitting on the bench chuckling to himself; the man that he knew as Xeres.

"So, it's from you that Val has learned my name. What purpose have you here now with us?" challenged Chowbingo.

Before Xeres could answer, Lucy rounded the corner in her own uncontrolled four-legged slide, straightened herself just enough to redirect her horns into Xeres' backside, and launch him, sending him airborne.

There stood the three of them, Val in absolute amazement, Chowbingo with a certain sense of expectation, and Lucy with a look of peaceful satisfaction as the old man flew through the air, before disappearing from them, in a cloud of red vapor.

"Oh, I've been waiting such a long time for the opportunity to do that," muttered Lucy, in her very polite, cultured voice.

"Lucy, I didn't know you had it in you," remarked Chowbingo, with a bit of astonishment.

"Oh Chowbingo, you only know me as the quiet grazing cow who loves philosophy. Well let me share, with the two of you, a little of my genealogy. My father was one of the bulls who ran at Pamplona, Spain. The humans killed him in the bull ring, of course, just like they do to all of them every year. Nonetheless, he died a hero's death. My earthly father was a brave bull. He didn't want to fight but when called upon he arose to the occasion. Just like me, I guess.

"Val, I suppose you might as well know, now, rather than later, that there is a lot that happens in your world that comes from forces that you cannot see, nor hear, solely because you are an earthling. It was in just such an incident that Xeres caused one of my friend's children to die from a horrific accident. There Xeres looked at me and laughed. When I asked him why, he said it was because he was showing one of his minions how to have fun.

"I know that butting him in the backsides isn't my finest moment, but, nonetheless, it feels quite satisfying."

"Lucy, I guess you also know that what you did wasn't very wise. You're supposed to leave revenge to Father. Remember, only he knows all the details, the whole story, we might say."

"You're right, you're right," replied Lucy, in the most loving, soothing, spiritual voice that she could muster.

Chapter 9

Another Realm

What ARE you two talking about?" interjected Val, almost hysterical now. "I just don't understand!"

Val's shouts were, by now, reduced to whispering sobs.

"Well, you just sit yourself down, and we'll explain it all to you. Won't you, Lucy?" Chowbingo then chuckled aloud as much as any spirit, captured in a dog's anatomy, might be able to laugh. *"I'll just sit over here and take it all in while our great philosopher, Lucy, waxes elegant and extolls her wisdom."*

"Can't do it," yelled Val, as he jumped up and started to run again. "My mom must be going crazy by now. I can't just leave her wondering what I'm doing. It's just not fair to her."

"Come back here," coaxed Lucy, in soft measured tones.

The voice resonated in Val's inner self, whereupon he stopped, turned, and returned to the two of them, not quite understanding why.

"Okay, okay, I'm here, Miss Lucy, but what about my mom? I've never disobeyed her and ignored her calls like this before. I don't want her to panic. I know that I'm all she's got."

"Val, here is your first lesson. When you speak or hear in your spiritual language you will need to remember that the sense of timing will be different from that to which you are normally accustomed."

"What do you mean, 'different from that to which I am accustomed'?"

"Okay, let's assume you want to read a book to me that has three hundred pages in it. That would certainly take you a few hours to complete. And, if I wanted to listen to you read it all to me, perhaps I should first find a nice cool shade tree. Can we agree to that?"

"Yes, I guess so."

"Well, using our spiritual language, you can transmit that same three hundred pages to me in far less than one minute.

"Val, you will come to learn that, in our 'spirit-world', a second is as years and years are as forever or, just as simply, vice-versa. So, please don't be concerned about your mother's expectations. We will do nothing to give that woman fear or concern. Isn't that true, Chowbingo?"

"Speak for yourself, Lucy," said Chowbingo, expressing a hint of laughter in his reply.

"Now as we said before," continued Lucy, "this is the first language of your creation. From this language came the first words that Father spoke, softly to you, as you matured within your mother's womb. Also, from there, came the careful words that He spoke while preparing you for your adventure, into this land, that you call Earth."

"Where you are now," added Chowbingo.

"Those were creation words," continued Lucy, raising her voice over Chowbingo's unappreciated interruption.

"This was the language Father gave to you so that you could understand the words that your mother first spoke to you. This was your language, to use, before you were first able to understand human sounds."

"How did I understand those first words if I didn't yet know words?" asked Val.

"Your very first spiritual word was 'love'. Father gave you full and unconditional love. That became your first word."

"Where is 'love' now?"

"It is still right where it has always been, inside of you. It has never left you."

"So, you're telling me that I have two languages, my world language and my spirit language. If the very first word of my spiritual language is 'love' and that word has been given to me by Father, then what is the first word of my earth language and where did that come from?"

"Val, Father gave you your spiritual language and with it the ability to understand all of the world's languages. It was your mother who taught you her particular language, Walloon I believe you call it, through her patience and her love."

"So I thank Father for my spiritual language and Mama for my worldly language?"

"You got it," popped in Chowbingo. "Now we can all get going."

"Not so fast," interjected Lucy. "Chowbingo, you've lived with this a long time. I believe that the youth might have a couple more questions."

"You bet. How come all of a sudden I can speak and hear so clearly in this spiritual language?"

"Simple: you called me by my Neveah name and that's all it took. Now let's get going."

"Wrong, Chowbingo."

Lucy again spoke up. "Val, this has all been set up by Father in Neveah. Once the tranquility of His garden had been upset by Xeres' misdeeds, Father's desire has been to restore it to its former state. Unfortunately, He could not re-visit it. As the 'Spirit of Perfection' He could not go into an imperfect garden."

"Who exactly is Xeres, and why did he mess it up?"

"Xeres ruined it because that's his nature. He wants to be the greatest, and he just can't accept that he isn't. Therefore, whenever he tries to be what he never can be, he just causes trouble for all of us; especially for himself."

"Where is Xeres? Now I want to meet him. I'll tell him to stop causing trouble. I know that my mother would never accept that kind of behavior from me. Maybe I could ask her to talk to him."

"Val, you already have met him. He's the elderly man you recently encountered, dressed as a country gentleman. The one who I just butted into the next world."

"I'm afraid he is a little beyond your league at this time," added Chowbingo.

"I'm still confused. Why me? What do I have to do with this?"

"Val, you're still just a little boy."

"I am not. I'm a man and responsible for my mother's well-being," retorted Val, as he expressed what he thought to be appropriate indignation, not in his recently acquired spiritual voice but rather loudly in his earthly language, to which he was the more accustomed.

"Yes Val, we hear you," responded Lucy, again speaking in her soft, measured, spiritual tones. "Shall we just say that you are a young man? Now, can we please get on with the explanation at hand?"

"Very well," asserted Val, feeling cautiously confident for the moment, in his own self-centered sense of maturity.

"Val, it's now time for me to ask you a question. Where did you learn that your puppy's real name is Chowbingo?"

"The old man! He told me that my puppy's name was Chowbingo, when he spoke to me from the bench, where he was seated."

"Just before I butted him into the air?"

"No, the time before, when he scared me and said hurtful things about my mother."

"So, you've met him before now?"

"Yes I have."

"When, exactly, was that?"

"It was before all the people in my village decided that they wanted to hurt Puppy, I mean Chowbingo. I believe that was a little bit before you came here, with your other cow friends, and helped us."

"So, did you believe, then, that your puppy's real name was Chowbingo?"

"No."

"Then why did you call him Chowbingo?"

"I was mad at him because he was following you to the pasture. He should have been coming back to me when I called him, so that we could go. I just wanted to get him and return to my mother before she became angrier with me.

"Miss Lucy, I've answered all your questions. Now will you please tell me what this is all about?"

"Val, remember, I told you about Father's garden being disturbed?"

"Yes Ma'am, I mean yes, Miss Lucy."

"Well, it has caused a lot of discussion in Neveah. Do you remember that part I told you about, the part where Father, in His perfection, wouldn't go into an imperfect garden?"

"Yes, you taught me that perfection could not exist with imperfection. So, what happened?"

"There was a council meeting and everyone decided that one of us would have to get down there and fix it for Father."

"So who's coming?"

"He's already here, and he's Chowbingo."

"Whaaat!" exclaimed Chowbingo.

"Yes, Chowbingo, that's actually the fullness of the story."

"Why me?"

"Actually, Chowbingo, if you must know, it's because you are a companion spirit, whereas we, who were in the meeting, are exalted spirits of Neveah."

"So you just picked me because I'm His servant spirit, and you probably just didn't want to go yourselves?"

"Well, yes and yes. We picked you because we didn't want to go and we also picked you because we know how much Father loves and trusts you."

"So Lucy, were you at the meeting?"

"Ah, uh."

"Lucy, there are no cows in Neveah."

"Ok, ok, so I'm not a cow. I'm actually Esau, your good friend from Neveah."

"And what's this about you being a cow here? How do you explain that one?"

"Well, Chowbingo, if you can be a dog then I can be a cow."

"Esau, I can only imagine you falling through space as a cow. That most certainly must have been some humorous sight."

"Let me tell you, Chowbingo, there was nothing funny about it when my udder hit the Earth's atmosphere. That was pretty painful, and I can't wait to register a complaint with Father when I next see Him."

"And Maria?"

"Oh, say hello to Khasmar when you see 'her'. He wanted to come along to keep me company and to help if need be. You know, just to get personally involved for a time, but he'll be going back in the not-too-distant future. By the way, we thought the way we became females— you know, 'cows'—was pretty clever. We figured that might keep you guessing for a while. And, it appears, we were right."

"Okay, your antics are all very funny, but how did Val get brought into this, and most importantly, why? I believe we would both like to know the answer to that, wouldn't we, Val?"

"Chowbingo, Father sent you to Earth on a special assignment."

"What special assignment?"

"If you don't interrupt I'll continue."

"Sorry."

"Your specific assignment was to redeem Father's chosen people from the evil that Xeres caused through his mischief in His garden."

"What do you mean my assignment 'was'?"

"Chowbingo, everyone's plans can change, even Father's, especially when one very particular thing happens."

"What's the one very special thing that you're talking about?"

"When man elects to exercise his own free will."

"I don't think I understand."

"Chowbingo, none of the three of us were born here on Earth, you, Khasmar, or myself. We, all three, came here directly from our home, which we call Neveah. We tend to view things from a universal viewpoint. Everything, for us, is captured at once. Like looking at a picture. Earthlings, however, gather their information sequentially, like reading a book, one word at a time. Now that you understand the differences, please model your behavior to better adapt to their ways. It will better please Father. He created humans, similar to Himself, so that He might have fellowship with them.

"You have friends, Chowbingo. Don't you want your friends to be able to express their thoughts and ideas as their own?"

"Of course I do. If not, I wouldn't have a friend, I would just have a 'yes' person, right?"

"Right, you would just have a robot for a friend, which is just the same as not having a friend."

"A what?"

"Never mind, Val can explain it to you later; he's human, he'll understand. Now, as I was saying, Father sent you on an assignment to redeem His chosen people from Xeres' evil. For you to do that, He intended for you to have a human partner."

"Thanks, now I understand. When do I meet my partner?"

"You actually already have."

"Now I'm totally confused."

"Don't be. Val's now your human partner."

"Val? Has Father gone off the deep end?"

"You better hope Father forgives you for that one! No, Father did not make a mistake. Val is now your Earth partner because Xeres has once again been up to his mischief."

It was, Val felt, once again his turn to engage in the discussion, so he blurted out in his earthly voice, "What mischief?"

"Xeres has the freedom to move to and fro about Neveah, as he pleases. He also can travel about his own personal kingdom, or throughout Earth, as he freely wishes."

"Why can he do that?"

"I'm sorry, but I don't have the answer for that one. Actually I find it quite puzzling myself. You'll have to ask Father why.

"Anyway, Father always wanted Chowbingo to connect with a special Earth partner upon his arrival here, but that partner was never intended to be you, Val."

"Why not? I'm perfectly capable; you can ask my mother. She'll tell you that I'm very responsible, and a hard worker; well, maybe up until now."

"Val, it's not about your capability. This just wasn't supposed to be your assignment."

"So why is he my partner then? Explain that to me."

"Because he called you by your Neveah name," responded Lucy.

"So what, what's that mean, how's that important?" asked Val.

"Hold on, hold on, just a minute—give me a chance to explain. Chowbingo, yours was the name Father had ordered to be spoken into Earth. That spoken word was meant to establish a partnership uniting Neveah and Earth, to re-establish His fruits for the people."

"I'm sorry but I'm still very confused."

"Okay, Chowbingo, you were sent here because of a meeting that I had with Father and a couple of others. You were to join up with one special human here from Earth. That connection was to be made when he called you by your real name."

"Well, Val called me by my Neveah name. So now what?"

"That's just the point, or I mean the problem. Val's not the one who He had planned for you to join. Val doesn't even know Father's chosen people. Now everything is just all mixed up."

"What caused the mix up?"

"The question should be, who caused the mix up, and the answer to that question is Xeres. He undoubtedly knew of Father's plan from the very moment that you left Neveah. He had probably been here scheming, about how he might ruin Father's plan, ever since you arrived. And now we know that he finally settled on providing your name to Val."

"What did that accomplish," asked Val.

"When you spoke his name, you became Chowbingo's Earth partner."

"Does it have to stay that way?"

"Once Father's word is spoken, it cannot return void. There is nothing that can be done to change that.

"Well, it's been a busy six seconds and I'm sure that you and your puppy, or should I say Chowbingo, have a lot to discuss about your new partnership. Also, I want to catch Maria, I mean Khasmar, and say goodbye to him before he leaves and returns to Neveah."

"How's he going to get up that ladder? I didn't know cows could climb ladders."

"That's very funny, Chowbingo—and I'm sure that since you also know that Neveah doesn't have cows, you know that Khasmar will also be returned to his former self, just as you will, when, or should I add to that, IF you ever finish your assignment."

"That's just great," interrupted Chowbingo. *"And what am I supposed to do now?"*

"You're a smart puppy. You'll figure it out, my good friend," responded Esau, with a hint of laughter in his voice. "Now you two better get moving. We can visit later. I hear Mrs. Patadarski calling now for Val."

Chapter 10

The Partnership

Lucy turned about and began to sashay up the hill, in a steady gait, tail swishing, as if to the steady cadence of a metronome, all the while ignoring the succeeding remarks of protest that followed from both Chowbingo and Val.

"Come on, Puppy, we better get going. We don't want to be in any more trouble with Mama than we already are."

"Don't 'Puppy' me," responded Chowbingo. "Don't forget, we can converse with each other now. Therefore, from this point forward, I'm no longer going to allow you to consider me as some sort of a pet dog. And, if anyone's going to be in trouble with your mother, it's going to be *you, not 'we'. We're partners remember? And now we have an assignment to complete."*

"Well, that all sounds like a great adventure, Chowbingo, so what's our assignment?"

Actually Val, right now I'm a bit embarrassed to say to you, really, I don't know."

———————

"There you are, Val. I've been calling your name for at least five minutes. Have you just recently decided to become deaf?"

"I'm sorry, Mother. Puppy, here, got involved with a couple of cows and I had to separate them so I could bring him back."

"Nice cover story, Partner."

" C'mon, Val, let's head toward your home. No sense in giving your mother any more reason for concern. It looks to me like she may have had enough for one day."

"Val, you really had your mother quite concerned."

"I'm very sorry, Mr. Bellingeri, but I got into a conversation with Puppy, and it took longer than I expected."

"What do you mean, you got in a conversation with your puppy?" inquired Angelina. "I'm beginning to think you're a little addled in the head, Son."

Then Val heard a cautionary warning from deep within his heart. *"I suggest you change this subject before you get both of us into any more trouble."*

Val turned his gaze toward Chowbingo only to be met with a stare that could melt ice. Val, now frozen between the chastisement of Dominique and the stare of Chow-bingo, decided that perhaps his best course of action might be to direct his complete interest solely in the direction of the path that lay before him.

The five of them, Mr. Bellingeri, Mr. Kolvalenko, Mrs. Patadarski, Val, and Chowbingo, continued down the well-trodden path in uncomfortable silence. No sooner had the quiet encompassed them, with a feeling of peace and tranquility, then their serenity was once again ripped apart from an unexpected sound coming up from behind.

"Hey you, wait up! Mrs. Patadarski, Mrs. Patadarski—please hold up a moment!"

"Isn't that Sam Emerson calling?" inquired Yuri Kolvalenko, to no one in particular.

"Yes it is. Wonder what he wants?" added Dominique.

"Wasn't he just yelling before that he wanted to kill Val's puppy? Something about a 'devil dog'. I'm afraid of that man. Val, you and your puppy go and run along ahead of us, toward the cabin, and make sure you . . ."

"Mrs. Patadarski, I'm so happy I was able to catch all of you. I've so wanted to thank you—and especially your dog, for saving all of us the way he did—never saw anything like it before in all my born days."

"Sam Emerson, what in the heck are you talking about?" asked Yuri, who by then had come to the point where he had exhausted all of his patience toward Sam and his antics. "First you call the kid's puppy a 'devil dog' and then you organize our village to scare the boy half to death while you're trying to kill his dog. Now you want to come over here and thank them. What's got into you?"

"I'm sorry, I'm really very, very, sorry. I was misinformed. Then—and then Val's dog went and chased all those cows back up the hill. Those stampeding cows were surely going to kill us. Val's dog, he certainly saved our lives; yes, no doubt about it, he certainly did!"

"You mean the very same puppy that you were going to kill," added Dominique, reaching deep within to avail himself of all of the sarcasm that he could possibly muster.

"I know it really looks bad, and I'm truly sorry for my part, but that stranger put us up to all that happened."

"What stranger?" asked Angelina, now more curious than miffed or afraid.

"The old man who walked into my store and purchased three of each kind of red-colored fruit that I had. Six different kinds in all. Never saw anything like it. I looked into his eyes when he went to pay for it. They were both red. Must have been some form of new-fangled lens. Never know what those citified doctors will come up with next. Anyway, then he went and paid for it all with silver coins— nothing else. Haven't seen that type of money in these parts in—I don't know for how long."

"Wow, this sounds exactly like the same man who said unkind things to me about my mother," added Val who, along with Chowbingo, had worked his way back to where the conversation was taking place.

"What did he say about my son, or this puppy, that would cause you to think about harming either one of them?" voiced Angelina, with her mother's concern.

"Yeah, Sam, you better start explaining yourself, quickly, before I decide to do to you what you tried to start on this harmless puppy."

"Now I'm really starting to enjoy this," Chowbingo intimated to Val. *"Now just pay attention and watch what I'm going to do."*

With that, Chowbingo's dark purple gums rolled back and his teeth were exposed to a length and a brightness of porcelain white that could not have previously been imagined by the group—especially by Mr. Emerson. Chowbingo purposefully turned his attention directly to a spot within Sam's soft inner thigh, all the while yelping with the ferocity of a half-starved timber wolf.

Sam Emerson, overcome with fear, fell in a helpless heap before the feet of Angelina, begging her to save him from the apparent ravages that were about to befall him.

"Pretty cool, huh," exclaimed Chowbingo to Val, as he settled back down on his haunches and allowed his receding gums to return to normal and restore his features to the countenance of a calm, loving, puppy.

Before anyone could react, it was over, and Sam was sheepishly pulling himself up to his knees.

"I'm really sorry for all the trouble I've caused, but that stranger really set me up. You all have known me since grammar school. Please, you know that's not the way I am."

"Mr. Emerson, we all have known you for many years. None of us have any reason to disbelieve you. We would certainly like to hear what the stranger told you, but the middle of this path is not a proper place for you to share your information. We were just on the way to my house to have dinner. Why don't you join us?"

"I would love to but not unless I can stop by my grocery store and pick up some fruit and vegetables to add to the meal. I absolutely cannot allow myself to attend empty-handed, especially after all the trouble that I just recently caused."

"Shall we just say that it was 'excitement' rather than trouble," quipped Angelina, with a welcoming smile.

"I see that Yuri has the meat and that Dominique is adding the sweets and milk," he added, while politely dismissing Angelina's latest remarks. "Really, I can't even think of arriving empty-handed. Please allow me just twenty minutes extra, and I will be delighted to join you."

———————

"Val." It was Chowbingo speaking to him. *"Ask your mother if we can take a quick trip back to the pasture to be sure that you have locked Mr. Ellison's gate. I need to see Lucy for a moment."*

"Not Lucy the cow but rather Esau, the cow—right?"

"You're pretty bright for an earthling. Yes, it actually is Esau, my friend from Neveah, who I must see. Also, you might as well know that the other cow who was leaving is actually Khasmar, Father's special messenger."

"Aren't those boy's names?"

"Well yes and no. Where I come from there are no boys or girls or men or women. Everyone is the same."

"Since I can speak your language now, does that mean they can be my friends too?"

"Well, I guess so, Val. Why not? Besides, we're part-ners now."

"Mom, while Mr. Emerson goes for the groceries, can Puppy and I go check Mr. Ellison's gate? I may have left it unlocked."

"I guess it will be okay, Val, now that all this is settling down, but I don't want you to dawdle there. You've already given me enough fright for this day."

"You be sure to mind your Mama," added Dominique, with additional urgings from Yuri.

"Just what we need—a committee," interjected Chow-bingo, as Val was thanking his mother for granting him permission.

"Lucy, Lucy where are you? We need to talk!"

"I'm right over here, and please call me Esau. I'm really getting tired of this cow suit, and I feel that I need to prac-tice being who I really am. I sure hope Father will bail me out of here soon.

"Excuse me Val, Chowbingo. I'm sorry for my ram-blings, just now. It was all personal and very selfish of me. Now what was it that you wanted to talk to me about?"

"Esau, who was supposed to be my partner, before Xeres enticed Val into calling me by my Neveah name, and changed everyone's plans?"

"That person you are asking about would have been George Ellison."

"George Ellison, the dairy farmer, here?"

"Yep, one and the same. The one who owns the pasture where we presently find ourselves standing. Father recognizes that George is a man who, for years, has led a humble life. He has, accordingly, been rewarded with wisdom, knowledge, faith, discernment, and the recognition of our spiritual language. Father chose these very pasture lands, from all the others available on Earth, for us to graze. That is how much he appreciates Mr. Ellison."

"Can Mr. Ellison understand spiritual conversations like we're having now?"

"No, he can't understand direct subject-to-subject communication like you can, with us, now. However, Mr. Ellison does recognize that such a form of communication exists. Also, through his humility, and through his faith, he can, within his own quiet spirit, understand the will of Father."

"Do I have any of those gifts?"

"Val, the answer is yes and no. You have some but not others. For instance, you now have the gift of speaking in our Neveah language. Mr. Ellison, as you are now learning, does not."

"And I can certainly say that you haven't mastered the wisdom one yet," added Chowbingo.

"How do I get that one?"

"You be quiet, then you be still, and finally you will learn how to listen for that still, quiet, voice of direction that will come to you from Father."

"How can I do that if I've never met Him?"

"All you need to know is that He's met you."

"Now that's crazy. How can I even know that He exists? What if He's a phony, like all those people who pretended to be my friend before Papa died, and then never spoke to me again?"

"I know that you are very hurt, and rightfully so. That is why we have been sent here to represent Him. We're here to show you that Father loves you and that He cares for you. All will be made right, believe us. Now have faith."

"What's 'faith'?"

"That's where you have an acceptance that something exists, and you believe it to be real without any doubt, but you can't see it, or feel it, or touch it."

"Why can't I see it?"

"Because then it wouldn't be faith, silly."

"I don't understand!"

"You think I understand why I'm walking around here, stuck on Earth, in this dog suit? Do you realize I can't even teleport; I have to walk to everywhere that I wish to be. Can you even begin to understand how frustrating that makes things for me? How do you think Esau feels, walking around in his cow suit, or standing under a tree, all day?"

"Hey, hold on for a minute. I've made some nice friends under these trees, and we do enjoy our philosophy."

"What's 'teleport'?"

"It's psychokinesis. It's how we travel; you know, walk, ride, get about—move!"

"What . . .?"

"Oh, never mind. Val. I was about to conclude, we've adjusted to your world and now you should try adjusting to ours. Obviously, now that we've been joined together, we have a mission to complete."

"Esau, that brings me to my real question. What's my assignment, here? Now that Xeres has caused his damage. You know, now that Val's in and George Ellison is out."

"I'm sorry, Chowbingo, but that one's above my Neveah hierarchy platform. I was in for the original plan but now that it has been altered, I really don't know too much more than you."

"Well then, do you know who does?"

"That person would be Khasmar. I'll ask him to get in touch with you just as soon as Father brings me home. Remember, I just said goodbye to him as Maria. Too bad we didn't think to ask him sooner, while he was here."

"Can't you speak to him anyway, in our 'spiritual' language?"

"Val, Father in His infinite wisdom, set up a communication shield between Neveah and Earth. He also wisely included Lambda and Strakula in that separation. It just stops a lot of unnecessary chatter."

"Thank you, Esau, or is it Lucy to whom I am again speaking?"

"Come on, Val, before I'm in trouble with your mom again."

"I'm on my way, Chowbingo. Please have a nice night, Lucy."

"Hey Puppy, now that we can speak to one another, what do you think about what we're going to have for dinner?"

"Well, I know that you earthlings like your meat, but I kind of have mixed feelings about it."

"What do you mean, you have mixed feelings? I don't understand."

"Well, your mom is going to cook Yuri's roast, and that is definitely part of an animal. Now, home in Neveah, animals and beings, we exist, side by side. We try not to harm one another, ever!"

"Yes, but here you are a dog, and here dogs are supposed to eat meat."

"Val, I just can't believe that every dog here eats meat. I may like the taste of meat because of this confounded dog suit, but I still have to be considerate toward Lucy's, I mean Esau's, new friends."

"Well then, what are you going to do for supper?"

"I'll just eat some vegetables, mushrooms, and roots, thank you. Maybe I can coax you to prepare or cook something from the ground. Is that a possibility—partner? Maybe I can even run off again and start digging up some more of those herbs—and then you can try to find me again—sound like fun? Possibly there is something edible growing from the 'bulbs' you planted alongside your home. Or . . ."

"Or, maybe you can just eat some roast and avoid all the confusion. How does that sound?"

"Val, as you well know, we can communicate with one another now. Just think, I can keep you up all night with incessant jabbering if I choose."

"Okay, okay, I get it. Garden goodies it may be for you, but it's still going to be a nice slice of roast for me."

"Val, please don't forget Lucy, Maria, and all the others who saved you from your neighbors."

"You know, Chowbingo, you can be a very troubling puppy at times."

"I've had that trait attributed to me before. I first learned it while performing my work assignment back home in Neveah."

"Assignment? What assignment? Do people work there?"

"Well, technically, no, but in a broader sense, yes."

"Now I'm confused, please explain."

"Val, we don't really work, as you understand it. We serve. Our work, in Neveah, is to serve one another. Then everyone can live in increasing happiness. Here, on Earth, many only work for their own selfish achievement. Here humans selfishly work to have more and better things. There they work so that others can have greater and greater happiness."

"What if someone cheats?"

"Val, no one cheats in Neveah. It's Father's home."

"Okay, you can go sniff up some of those fancy bulbs if you like. I'll go on home and make peace with Mom and the others. Afterwards, I'll come out in the woods and help you haul back your treasure. So listen for my call, or shall I whistle?"

"Whistle.

"Okay, I'm turning here and I'm off into the woods. I'll listen for your whistle."

"Hi Mama, Mr. Bellingeri, Mr. Kolvalenko. Where's Mr. Emerson? I thought he said he was coming too."

"I know, Val, that's what he said all right. Remember, he left us along the walkway because he insisted that he wanted to stop by his store and collect some additional groceries for our dinner. I really thought he'd be here by now."

"Val, you've hardly been gone for any time at all."

"Your mother's right. Did you even remember to check the gate lock when you were over there at Mr. Ellison's?"

"You can't ignore that," piped in Dominique. "Remember, Mr. Ellison's definitely too old now to be chasing loose cows all over the countryside."

"Don't worry, everyone. I promise you the gate is locked. You can even see it for yourselves. Anyone can see the lock from the bottom of the hill. No need to even walk that far if it's already been locked."

"Only if you're still young and have children's eyes," murmured Yuri, half to himself.

"Speaking of missing people, where's that dog of yours? Don't tell me we're going to have to go chase him down again and get me worried all over again. Besides, my stomach can't take it again. It's starting to get really settled in for a taste of that roast."

"He said that he wanted to go collect root balls, Mother."

"He SAID?"

"Well, actually, just before getting here, he darted off to the left and scampered into the woods. I caught a glow from his stone and followed it. There he was, with his nose stuck down by a large tree, digging for something. I tried to pull him away, but he really acted like he didn't want to come. It's not far from our house so I just left him there to his business. He can come home when he's ready, or I can just go and get him when I finish my chores here."

"Val, that's not what you said to me the first time. Are you starting to lie to me?"

"No mother, it's kind of like both. When I saw his actions it was kind of like he was talking to me."

"Okay Val, I think perhaps that I understand now."

"Thank goodness," thought Val. "I didn't think that I would ever be able to explain my 'other' language to her."

"Now what about the chores that you're talking about? I don't remember asking you to do any chores recently."

"Oh, these are my own chores. I want Chowbingo, I mean Puppy, to help me get some herbs for our dinner. Remember what a nice flavor they added last time?"

"Okay, go help your puppy get the herbs. Have you renamed him Chowbingo now?"

"Well, I just think it's a better name than 'Puppy', don't you?"

"Dear, if you like it then I like it. Run along now and find your herbs while I get Yuri's roast started. It's going to take a while, considering its size and all.

"Now Mr. Kolvalenko, why don't you and Mr. Bellingeri just sit down and relax for a few minutes while I go ahead and get this roast started?"

"Not until I help you get it ready for the spit," replied Yuri.

"And I'll help by getting the fire started," added Dominique, not wishing to appear as the only slacker in the room.

"When Mr. Emerson arrives, I believe I'm going to feel like a queen. I haven't had this much attention since before my Salvio passed away."

With that remark, tears welled up in her eyes. Yuri and Dominique quietly turned away, allowing Angelina her moment of quiet mourning.

The forest seemed to reverberate from the shrill whistle of Val calling for Chowbingo. First in his natural way he whistled, two fingers stuck between his lips as he gently pressed against the roof of his mouth. Then he tried whistling in his newfound language, the one he had been introduced to by Chowbingo and Esau. Still there was no reply.

He considered. Did he have to learn some particular new way of whistling to be heard in this new language? Did he have to form some particular shape with his mouth or would it just burst forth as a communication, from his inner-being, as had his other thoughts?

Again he tried to whistle in the natural way. Then he alternated from the physical and tried to draw down deep from within his inner self to bring forth a whistle that would transfer itself directly to the innards of Chowbingo's very self. Unfortunately, the harder he tried, the more foolish he felt. It was only but a short time before he found himself seemingly out of breath and beginning a headache. Finally, his stomach was starting to feel sore from the strain of doing the things that, he finally concluded, either failed to make sense, or definitely had proven to be beyond his ability to accomplish.

Tired now, and feeling as though he was almost out of breath, he found the nearest tree, sat down, placed his head between his legs, and just quietly hoped that perhaps he might experience a bit of temporary inner comfort. Without his "friend" he was feeling a type of loneliness unlike any he had ever before experienced since the loss of Salvio, his father—and best friend.

Chowbingo, on the other hand, seriously intent on his truffle search, pushed his nose further and further into the root bed, near the large tree looming above him. The odor, although faint, was recognizable; Xeres, the master counterfeiter, had again demonstrated his skills. Perhaps, Chowbingo thought, with some more digging and an added bit of perseverance, he would be rewarded with his prize. Instead, unexpectedly and without warning, Chowbingo found himself stuck inside a hole beneath the same tree where he had just been digging.

Although certainly ample in size for Chowbingo's girth, it was, nonetheless, restrictive in design. Chowbingo definitely wouldn't be leaving without a struggle. Perhaps, he thought, if he continued to move forward she might be able to adjust his body and circumvent the restrictive maze to permit himself an alternate exit. Finally, moving forward became his decision, but it certainly was not his choice. To turn around, toward the light, which he knew he would find behind him, was unfortunately unworkable. His plump, furry body was doing an absolutely perfect job of blocking all possibilities for turning about at that point.

Sensing that he was proceeding in error, nonetheless he moved forward. The idea of any chow dog successfully backing out of this hole, with its bushy undercoat, would be akin to that of a porcupine attempting to back out of a briar patch; possible, of course, but not very likely. The further forward he moved, the more that the gray darkness before him relinquished itself, to the consuming black abyss, towards where he was inching himself.

Philip I. Amos

Chapter 11

A Sudden Drop

In a most untimely manner, Chowbingo's passageway went from a tight, restrictive crawlway, to a downward, deep-dropping, chute; and down Chowbingo plummeted. His stubby, stout legs, inadvertently shot outward in all four directions, as he desperately attempted to gather traction, to slow himself down, to break his fall—anything!

Gravel, sand, pebbles, dry leaves? He wasn't sure what it was that he felt beneath him but it certainly was not firm. It offered no traction, no stability. He was out of control. It was dark, it was black, and Chowbingo was, if nothing else, scared.

Splash! It ended, and he was wet. Chowbingo was in over his head. Furry dogs with thick undercoats don't float. They sink. Chowbingo was going to sink. He felt it and, furthermore, he knew it!

Silently, a net wrapped him within its unforgiving grip, as it steadily tugged against his water-soaked body. Chowbingo found himself fighting against a force he could not see. It continued to drag him. He felt himself being pulled through the water until he hit sand and the dragging ceased. Yes, it was sand, for sure. He knew the feeling. It was soft, and it was warm, just like in Neveah, where he enjoyed idyllic times in his neveahnite body.

There he lay, on unknown sand, in an unknown place. He tried to gather his thoughts. What was happening?

Slowly, very slowly, his stone began its soft illumination. The color, which he had oftentimes seen before, began to glow from below his neck. Feeling a bit more comfortable, as he paused to rest in the warm glow of his now familiar stone, he stopped and took a brief look about his surroundings.

It was certainly all there in plain view. The glow of the stone made it all clear, especially the waters where he had almost drowned. It appeared to be a stream, coming from a distance far beyond, and continuing past him, in the same measure to which it had first arrived. Its breadth was reasonable for its travel, about one hundred and fifty feet, and it was fresh. This he could tell from its smell, fresh and sweet. There had to be both a source and an exit, for this was certainly not stale water.

The place, where he found himself seated, shone as if it were emerald dust. The color, he readily understood, actually was a reflection of his stone's light. This place, where he now unwittingly found himself planted, might appropriately be defined as a riverfront beach. Not large, but adequate enough for the moment to fulfill his needs—a place to sit, to rest, and to regroup. The water's edges gave way, at each of its opposing sides, to a curved ceiling of stalagmites which reflected vibrant, multifaceted greens, emanating from his stone. A beautiful, un-restricted discordance of colored hues, exceeding all earthly description.

"Well I'm here and it doesn't look like I'm about to be too soon in getting out. Help! Esau, Esau—help, Esau!

"Schezak, Schezak can you hear me," he hoarsely whispered in a pleading, spiritual, soulful cry.

Chowbingo began to hear a distant lapping, of the quietly moving water, as it passed before him. Upstream there appeared to be a barge, a very small one, drifting toward his direction. He couldn't tell, from his vantage point, if it was actually a crafted vessel or just some flotsam. It was still too far away, but it moved as if it were adrift. This, he finally decided, was definitely not going to be of any help to him, even if he were able to reach it.

Chowbingo returned to sitting on his haunches, and he was about to resign himself to his untenable plight, when the vessel unexpectedly executed a perfect ninety-degree turn, from cardinal point to cardinal point, and headed directly toward him. It moved, with purpose and directional control, before finally settling its prow upon the bank, a mere six feet from where Chowbingo had elected to sit.

The vessel seemed, to Chowbingo, to settle itself reluctantly into the sand, where its stern sashayed gently, allowing it to lightly respond to the river's minimal currents. Chowbingo jumped to his feet in wonderment and curiosity. The barge had come without oars, motor, or sail; but come it had. This, assuredly, must have been the work of Schezak, on assignment from Father.

He surely was in trouble now!

"Why couldn't it have been Khasmar, rather than his high priest who came to bail me out? Khasmar and I could have just kept this between ourselves. That Schezak, he blabs EVERYTHING!

"I guess, perhaps, I better be grateful that I can even get out of here. I really should be worried about facing Father later."

Chowbingo gingerly stepped up and onto the magnificently crafted vessel, which, before he could settle in with proper footing, lurched from the shoreline and rapidly began moving toward the river's center. All last-minute thoughts, which Chowbingo might have had to abort this trip, were brief and quickly set aside.

The barge, and it was a barge, appeared to be no longer than eight meters from prow to stern and a bit less than half across its beam. It had a raised bow while its stern gracefully rolled toward the trailing water. The side rails only slightly cleared the water's surface. Its freeboard was purposely set low, not unlike that of a Rhine riverboat plying its trade.

Chowbingo could easily have stepped off from any direction but he resigned himself to go wherever he was taken. Had he not recently been reminded that his abundant fur coat would surely make short work of him. The fullness of his coat would sink him no matter the shorelines proximity.

Settling in for the ride, Chowbingo turned from his own doubts, concerns, and fears to that of surveying the barge, which was apparently taking him to a destination that he did not know.

Schezak had that way about him: secrets.

The barge, he noted, was strikingly beautiful and certainly well-crafted, now that he took the time to look. However, it was not of the colors that he might have expected. The hull, from the waterline to her stanchions, was ebony black of the finest hue. The decking was of a satin-coated blonde cedar. Its small raised deck, at the prow, was plated with solid silver. There were six stanchions on the leeward side, six stanchions on the windward side, and six stanchions at the stern. Each of the eighteen stanchions was capped with a red ruby, not less than the size of an average man's fist.

The bow rail was low, set to the foredeck, and common in appearance except for the angel mounted at its fore post with outstretched wings. It was alabaster colored and of the same hue and patina as the barge itself. Quite unremarkable, were it not for the red rubies recessed into its eyes' sockets, and the knowledge that it had actually become a life-breathing entity, in his very presence.

The motion began to trouble Chowbingo as the barge's movement increased to an alarming speed. It soon barreled along, under the stalagmites, which appeared to be transforming from cones, to blurs, and finally to flowing colors. The barge's acceleration carried Chowbingo to a state, which he later described to me, as one of "controllable panic," as it continued to increase its speed, ever more.

The green glow from Chowbingo's stone quietly gave way to that of a red hue, which encompassed his entire locale. His view of stalagmites fell away, and the quiet waters silently disappeared, as the barge became airborne. Behind him now were the stalagmites, while below appeared the stalactites, quickly replacing the ceiling that had recently appeared above them.

The head of the angel spun about a full one hundred and eighty degrees. The ruby eyes looked at Chowbingo as if it were about to pierce his inner being.

"Bite one of the rails and hold on. We're going to be flying for a while."

The alabaster angel returned to facing forward, just as the barge started downward, settling into a fifteen-degree descent. Chowbingo braced himself, as he set upon his haunches and bit down hard on the barge's starboard railing, using all of the power that his jaws could muster.

The barge turned with a perfectly coordinated thirty-degree bank to the right and continued its downward path. Spiraling, in perfect symmetry, it corkscrewed toward the roiling waters that waited far below. As the barge settled into a perfect rate of roll and descent the resultant balance between lift and gravity provided Chowbingo with a very comfortable ride. Surprisingly, he found that not only was he able to release his bite from the railing, but that he was also able to relax the muscle tension that he had been exerting in his futile attempt to cement himself to the barge's deck.

Downward, downward they descended. It was as if one might be trying to glide through the center of a human artery, riding a stream of host fluids through the twists and turns of an anatomy.

There was, next, a sudden sense of speed, a rush you might call it. That was, until the sounds began. Sounds of wailing. Forlorn sounds, cascading across the deck of the barge. There were rumbling sounds, piercing sounds, and finally just the sounds of desperation. Although different, they nonetheless all shared a common sameness about them, gut-wrenching cries of hopelessness! These were not just human sounds, these were also the sounds of animals, the sounds of times past, and the sounds of future times still yet to become. Even the rocks were making sounds. At the time, according to Chowbingo, it seemed especially to be from the rocks.

They were all around him as he traveled past them at blinding speed. They groaned, they creaked, and they yelled in their unabashed misery while they were cracking and splitting at his passing.

"Stop, stop," came the yells, as he passed. "You don't know where you're going. No one ever returns. Stop, stop we beseech you!"

All the rock surfaces cracked and broke, split and screamed. Yes, they could scream, each with its own independent thought as it might wish, but none were permitted to move from their appointed places.

Then again came the yelling, of the humans and of the animals.

"Hurry, hurry, pass here if you must, but do so quickly and then please leave, please leave!"

"Why?" asked Chowbingo, now totally confused.

"Because you are awakening the rocks, and they are cutting and scraping us. We have no peace here, and your passing is making it worse for us. Please, please hurry and move on."

"I'm sorry, but I'm not in charge. I'm not driving. I don't know why I'm here, and I surely don't know where I'm going!"

The alabaster angel spun around and faced Chowbingo. "You are going to the center of Earth. You have an appointment."

Just as suddenly, the alabaster angel returned to his original position; not another word did it speak.

"Mr. Emerson, please come in. We've been waiting for you."

"Thank you, Mrs. Patadarski."

"Dominique, Yuri, could you please help Mr. Emerson with his groceries. I don't even know how the poor man got them here. Look at all that he's just brought."

"Can we just consider this as my humble peace offering to all of you for my earlier series of misjudgments?"

"Now Mr. Emerson, that was all settled out on the pathway earlier. You are my guest, here in my home, and all past mistakes are not only forgiven, but also forgotten."

"Thank you again. Now will all of you please call me Sam like when we were all friends?"

"Sure, but will you also please remember that I'm Dominique, he's Yuri, and she's Angelina, if that's all right with you, Mrs. Patadarski?"

"It certainly is, Dominique, provided that you remember to call me Mrs. Patadarski during our business hours, for professional reasons.

"Now that Yuri has helped me to prepare our roast for cooking, and Dominique has been kind enough to start the fire, maybe now we might have a few minutes to visit before Val and his puppy return.

"Mr. Emerson, I mean Sam, perhaps we can start with you. The rest of us have had a bit of time to reacquaint ourselves, so maybe you might like to bring us up to speed on your activities."

"Normally I would be more than happy to, but I just heard you speak of a 'professional relationship' between you and Dominique."

———————

The screams intensified and the scene before him became brighter, but brighter in reddish-yellow tones only. The speed increased, again, to the point where all that Chowbingo remembered was the dizzy, blinding sweep of color, in motion. Down, down they continued to drop, while he found himself focusing completely on the statuary angel planted at the barge's bow. He remembers finding it difficult to stabilize himself and to overcome the spinning, careening, gravitational forces that had begun to press his innards to a point of unconsciousness.

Seconds, then minutes continued to pass, until it seemed that they had travelled for hours. All the while, just as old age crawls upon youth, the lights' dim glow imperceptibly continued to increase until, finally, Chowbingo found himself immersed in the brightness of a red, so brilliant that it felt to be almost beyond his ability to withstand.

Just as we all feel drawn to look toward that which we often fear most, Chowbingo found himself glancing down over the railing, downward toward an abyss that seemed to be diabolically welcoming him, beckoning him from far below.

There it was, Earth's boiling, churning, inferno. The source of all the light. It looked not unlike a great ocean having been set afire. The waves were tumultuous, roaring and hissing, as if each capped crest, having its own mind, was engaged in an angry debate with its neighbor.

He spotted it, the attraction, a great calm resting within the epicenter. An area about five miles in diameter where the water was smooth as glass and calm as a warm summer day. It was there that the barge appeared to have been preparing for its landing.

Like a pilot preparing his passengers for touchdown, the alabaster angel, transformed from a statuary fixture to a living being, dutifully announced landing instructions. This monologue of instructions was summarily dismissed by Chowbingo as all of his attention had been drawn to the sights unfolding before him.

Never before, in Neveah, Earth, or beyond, had Chowbingo ever witnessed such an orchestrated display of misery, loathing, pride, and envy.

The fortress, where they apparently were destined to land, was magnificent in its structure and architecture, yet foreboding and perhaps as unwelcome an edifice as one might be capable of crafting. It sat upon an elliptical island whose edges were defined by a beach of black onyx sand, and diamond dust. The encircling translucent red pond, which formed its setting, was protected from the roaring waves of Earth's tumultuous core, by the outer edge of a reef line, set approximately five hundred yards offshore.

Equally distant, about its perimeter, Chowbingo found there to be twelve structures, no one greater or lesser than its neighbor. In type, each held the image of a mausoleum, but in purpose I would guess them more to be dwellings.

All appeared to have the look of sameness about them, except for the embossed signatures, mounted above each of their individual entrances. Each was different as follows: the first showed, emblazoned on black marble in "bas relief", a hooded cobra. The cobra was followed in counterclockwise direction by the spider, the lizard, the scorpion, the fire ant, the tarantula, the cockroach, the rat, the boa constrictor, the nutria, the flea, and finally the grasshopper.

Located exactly thirteen meters from the structures' frontal line of demarcation, and sitting upon a pedestal exactly eighteen feet above their base elevation, were set individual thrones, upon which were seated each of the "twelve". All, therefore, were identified by their own crest. Each, when seated upon its respective throne, reached nine feet in height and possessed similar eyes of ruby red. And it was from here that their similarities ended. All twelve were individualistic in thought and nature, except for their one common bond, EVIL—they all enthusiastically shared it.

They were each, unto themselves awesome and, most assuredly, fearsome to behold. They all resolutely shouted their obscene orders, in a continuing and non-ceasing cacophony of irreverent expletives, lending to a chaos that only they seemed able to decipher.

Chowbingo could not help but feel the evil majesty of his surroundings as he absorbed the unrequited sounds of misery. Fitfully, as he tried to reconcile the totality of it all to his understanding, he was interrupted by a sudden bump, which abruptly returned him to his prior state of overwhelming confusion.

The alabaster angel again repeating its one-hundred-and-eighty-degree shift announced, "We have landed." This was immediately followed by its return to a position of statuary immobility.

No amount of prompting or questioning by Chowbingo served to extract any further response from the stone angel.

Perplexed, scared, and still in a quandary, Chowbingo gingerly stepped off of the barge and onto the smooth glass surface where he found the forward portion of the barge resting. Unfamiliar with the nature of this untested landscape, Chowbingo took extra care to assure himself of its ability to properly support him. Beautiful though it may appear, quicksand, nonetheless, it could be. Slowly, continuing to test the surface upon which he found himself, he began to inch forwards toward the diamond-encrusted beachfront. Moving slowly with cautious determination, he paused intermittently to grasp with his teeth the side rails of the barge which, for security, he continued to keep alongside him.

Moving gingerly, he cautiously permitted his weight to settle until, finally, he became confident that this strange surface would support his weight.

"Now where do you think you're going?"

Chowbingo stopped, frozen in his tracks by the unexpected suddenness of the voice. Taken aback, he turned to see a most handsome man. He was about seventy years of age. And dressed, he was, in a splendidly tailored black vicuña suit, sporting red lapels, and finished at its waist pockets, in red piping. His soft graying hair, could mostly be overlooked, from the piercing glare of the ruby-red eyes.

"Follow me!"

Without another word spoken, he turned on his heels and walked directly away from Chowbingo, toward the building. This was the same building that Chowbingo had observed from the barge, as it was reducing its speed for their final descent to landing.

The first thing that Chowbingo focused upon was a suspended clock, mounted as if in pure air above the island's castle, which told the tale. Every fifteen minutes the mighty clock would rotate ninety degrees and stop at the next cardinal point.

After a few paces the man stopped and turned back toward Chowbingo. He spoke, without emotion, as if he were directly responding to Chowbingo's unspoken question. "Every six minutes, from each of the twelve dwellings on those further shores, a serf will be pulled from my worker ranks and summarily executed in the manner prescribed for that fiefdom. Twelve executions every six minutes. This is done, most assuredly, to encourage fear in its most absolute form.

"Every eighteen minutes a captain officer will also be exterminated. These captains, while still alive, will often be cannibalized by their serfs. The continuation of retribution and revenge is hereby assured and populated.

"Now please follow me inside."

"*I know you! Those eyes, your voice. You're Xeres. You are that same rude old man from Val's village. It's just your face that's different now.*"

"Yes, and I am also the same one who destroyed Father's garden, I am proud to say."

"You're also the very same one whose scales were left behind at Father's tree, the same location where good and evil was first displayed."

"Yep, you're certainly correct with that one. That was, most assuredly, me! I did a pretty good job of 'remodeling' the place, wouldn't you agree? Kind of ruined the party, you might say."

"Why did you hurt Father like that? What purpose was served?"

"He hurt me when He kicked me out. You know He did that just because I was better looking and smarter than Him. Now that wasn't very nice of Him, was it?"

"That's a lie! You're not better looking and you surely aren't smarter. I really think that your mind must be twisted. You've caused a lot of trouble, especially for yourself."

"So you say! Follow me up onto the parapet. There, now take a look over this sea to that shoreline beyond. I'm going to show you who has the problem now."

Chowbingo adjusted his eyes to the distance, before focusing on the events, which he began to see unfolding before him.

"Take a slow, close look, Chowbingo. See what is happening. Look at my fiefdoms, twelve in all. Don't dare to overlook even one."

Chowbingo obediently directed his attention toward each of the twelve, while slowly continuing his rotation, in a counter-clockwise direction. Each overseer was seen to be directing orders to its own cortege of captains, minions, and serfs. There was a sense of oneness, such as might be expected from an assembly trained in the art of military precision. The unique difference remained that each leader applied its own unique skill-set to enforce compliance. The cobra, spider, scorpion, and tarantula forced horrific deaths upon their chosen underlings through the use of poisonous venoms. The lizard, fire ant, and nutria resorted to contaminating bites. The boa constrictor utilized suffocation. The rat, the flea, and the grasshopper utilized asphyxia by multiplying themselves and swarming their victims.

Their actions were not executed to maim or to kill for any purpose other than for gratuitous sport. However, they did guarantee, through fear, a continuing compliance to the rules set forth within each of Xeres' twelve fiefdoms.

"Chowbingo, look now. Look there at my worm."

"What worm are you talking about? I don't see any worm."

"Look over there, just to the edge of the lake's shoreline. There she is lying in front of my fiefdoms, comfortably along the water's edge. One very important purpose for my twelve fiefdoms, is the continuous caring and feeding of my worm.

"Father has a son who had twelve assistants. And I have my twelve fiefdoms and the worm. Don't you just love the genius of it?"

"You're actually very, very sick, aren't you? Schezak once shared with me that there are those who call you the 'Great Counterfeiter' yet you can't actually get that right, *can you? Every time you try to copy what Father creates, you fail."*

Then he saw it, Xeres' worm. It circled the shoreline of the entire lake, opposite from where he stood. This massive creature, immobilized by her own fertility and too large to move, resembled a queen bee captured within the confines of her hive. The worm's only movement appeared to be the undulation of her enormous diaphragm as she swallowed and processed a seemingly unending intake of digestible solids. This consumption, which regurgitated through her bowels, continued to be meticulously transformed into nourishing life-giving fluids, as it flowed beneath her translucent skin. The entire transmutation, clearly visible to Chowbingo, he found to be both repulsive to observe and disgusting to consider.

"She's my darling, Chowbingo. Isn't she beautiful? I raised her myself. She is my special project, incorporating my very finest evil."

"That's your purest evil? A bloated, oversized worm that just sits there and belches?"

"No, no, you don't understand. It's not what she is, but it's what she does, that makes her so very beautiful."

"Okay, so what does she do?" asked Chowbingo, as he settled a bit into the unfamiliar environment in which he found himself.

"She consumes the unwanted. She freezes their very beings, and then their spirits become mine."

"She freezes whom?"

"Babies . . . Never mind, that's a topic for later. Take a moment and come with me inside my dwelling. What would Father's people call this? A 'summer cabin' I would certainly guess. Now that's funny. Think of it. I have, here, a cabin, that one might imagine stays warm every day. How many do you know, besides me, who have a cabin next to a lake of fire?"

"Just you. Now how about showing me the way out of here, and I'll just return to that rabbit hole from where I first came, and then I can be on my way? I will be out of your hair, or should I say out of your scales, and you and Father will be free to settle your differences without me."

"Oh, that's really quite good, Mr. Chowbingo. Actually, the reality of it all is that you're not leaving here. Therefore, I strongly suggest that you take advantage of my hospitality before I assign one of my assistants to show you to your quarters."

"What quarters?"

"Your new home, Chowbingo. Where you will be spending all of eternity—forever and ever, of course."

"ETERNITY!"

The sudden realization of what had just been said sent a shock through his body, like a severe but unexpected jolt of high-voltage electricity. One that was high in voltage but low in amperage. Although it didn't kill him it surely did get his attention.

"How do you expect to keep me here for eternity? Where is your right to do such a thing?" demanded Chowbingo, as he began to feverishly search for some viable exit strategy.

"My right? My right is by contract, Chowbingo. No, it's more than that. It's by a covenant with Father; and a covenant is something that He never will break. Anyone who doesn't accept His kid doesn't get to go to His place; so once you're not accepted there, I'm all that's left. That's pretty simple, isn't it? Now you come on along with me. I want to show you the interior of this, my second home. I designed it for myself, and I'm very proud of it. Actually I'm very proud of everything about me. Yep, very proud indeed.

"I don't get a chance to have many visitors. Matter of fact, to the best of my recollection, you're only the second one to 'drop-in' since I was reassigned."

"Who was the first?"

"Oh Him! It was just Father's kid. He came down here unannounced and started messing around with my operation. Parents should have better control over their kids."

"What was His son's name, if you know?"

"Doesn't matter. I'm so mad at that brat that I won't even allow His name to be spoken down here. He's actually nothing but a thief. He went so far as to steal my keys before He just took off without any warning. Not even so much as a good-bye. I haven't been able to get a second set from Father, and I'm just plain tired of asking."

"What did Father say when you asked that the keys be returned?"

"Last time, when I was up there and asked Him for them, He suggested that I take it up with His son. He mentioned something about everything passing through His son."

"Well, I guess that settles it then."

"Not according to my ledger," replied Xeres, who was suddenly taken by the assurance that was proffered through Chowbingo's last remark.

"Enough of this nonsense, Chowbingo. Come on inside; I'm going to show you some of my furnishings."

Reluctantly, but obediently, Chowbingo followed Xeres into his dwelling. There, upon entering, Chowbingo found himself shocked by the unrelenting cold that permeated its interior. It was surely unlike the cold that he had experienced when he had been inside of Angelina Patadarski's home. This was a "spiritual" cold. It permeated his entire being; body, mind, and spirit.

Notwithstanding the unwelcome cold coursing through him, he could not help but admire the opulent interior that he found unfolding before him, almost as if counterfeited from another place. Distinctly beautiful it was, but original it clearly was not.

The dwelling was filled with statuary, stoneware of the finest detailing, and fanciful tchotchkes beyond any worldly comparison. Noteworthy was the fact that all the colors reflected only coldness and somberness. Colors and displays of warmth were conspicuously absent. There were no fabrics or coverings to portray even a sense of warmth. These colors were in the hues and tones of deep red, mustard yellow, and black, and they included somber earth tones of the most foreboding sort. Chilling might properly describe them. Even the mirrors, of which there was a sufficiency, failed to reflect images.

Chowbingo's natural inclination was to look toward the first mirror to capture his attention, expecting a vision of his image. Yes, the mirrors were present, the reflective glass was in place, but his countenance was nowhere to be captured. Momentarily transfixed by this oddity, he paused to inquire of Xeres the meaning of such an anomaly.

"Chowbingo," replied Xeres, "you must understand that here resides death, of which I am the undisputed master. It is my kingdom and it is my realm. There is no life that exists here. Therefore, there remains nothing of life's reflection for you to view."

"Except for the digestive system of your stupid worm and . . ."

"Now, now—please, let's continue without any further interruption. I would like to start by taking you to see my wardrobe closet for which I am particularly proud. Actually, I am personally very proud, and take great delight, in all that I have and all that I do—but that is also a matter for another time.

"Ah, here we are. Now look! Isn't it absolutely splendid? Over here to my left, it's my first garment. This is the one that Father gave to me. I call this one my 'Splendiferous Outfit'. You have to admit that He does have good taste, for an egomaniac. Whenever I wore it, all of creation 'OOH and AWED' me. However, unfortunately, He really just didn't understand. He failed to recognize that the greatness of this costume came from more than just His handiwork. It was actually me, through my magnificent presence, who made this costume splendiferous. I was the 'wow', the 'zing', and the 'zip' that provided the real 'ah ha' factor.

"Now take a look over there. See my serpent suit. I designed that one myself for that time when I visited His garden. I surely ruined His day there. You'll recall, Chowbingo, I had a bit of a wardrobe malfunction at the time. When you were sent there I'm sure you found a few of my scales lying about, right? Look, you can see, there along the tail, where they're still missing from my outfit. However, it doesn't really matter because I don't plan on wearing it again, soon.

"Father only has to speak something into existence. I, on the other hand, have to fabricate whatever it is that I want. Unfortunately, this just doesn't leave me with enough time for making new scales, especially not with all the evil that still remains for me to accomplish. Perhaps it will be more valuable if it remains just the way it is, without any repairs. What do you think?

"I really do want to preserve it as a memento, a visual testimony you might say, to my greatest singular triumph, the day I turned Father's creation against Him.

"I still remember that day, a very fine day it was. I looked absolutely splendid in my outfit. When I strolled into His garden, my head was held high, and my wings were outstretched to their fullest span. Fourteen feet tall, I measured, and the ground behind me glistened with golden dandruff from my scales. My tail carved a trail in the ground behind me, my signature mark you might call it. You noticed it, when you were there too, Chowbingo. You saw my trail and you knew that I had been there.

There I was, at the pinnacle of my glory, when He intervened. I don't know how He knew what I had intended to do, but He did. It was at that exact moment, at the height of my pride, when suddenly, without warning, I found my mouth in the dirt, legless, wingless, and armless. The only way I could then move was by twisting and turning my tail through the dirt. But I persevered, Chowbingo. Yes, I persevered—and ultimately, I won!"

"Your wings were gone, your legs were gone, your arms were gone, and you were groveling in the dirt—and you won? How do you call that winning?"

"I won because Father gave His creation their very own free will. He actually had given them the opportunity to choose for themselves, without His interference. Can you even begin to believe such nonsense? He has some crazy notion that without free choice there cannot be a true relationship and love cannot manifest. Have you ever heard of anything so completely, absolutely, stupid?"

"I think it's a very good plan. He gives us His love freely, and therefore we are able to give it freely to others. It's a very beautiful plan."

"It's really stupid, Chowbingo! What's love got to do with it? I offered them a plan, a better plan."

"What was your plan, Xeres?"

"Turn against Father's instructions, eat from the tree of 'Good and Evil', and you will then know everything that Father knows and you will be equal to Him."

"How does that work?"

"It doesn't work. I lied and those stupid humans believed me."

"They didn't know that you lied?"

"Of course not. Before I came up with the idea, there were no lies. Remember, I am the one who invented the lie. I am now known as the 'Father of Lies', of which I am very, very proud. It is an excellent accomplishment? Don't you agree?"

"Okay, you did your evil, and you turned Father's creation against Him, and now here you stand. Doesn't look like much of a win to me. So what about your suit? I notice that it still has wings, arms, and legs, but now it's all dull and dark. What about this gold and glisten stuff?"

"I see that you doubt me, so let me finish this episode for you. Once I finished, in the garden, and had successfully turned humanity against Him, Father then became so distraught that He brought one of His 'hit men' down to clean His garden out. That guy immediately threw all of the humans out, left some of the animals behind, and then told me to leave also. It was kind of funny, in a stupid way, since at the time I had neither, arms, legs, or wings. Well, that surely stopped the show. Anyway, after some discussion between the two of them, Father decided that He had to restore my limbs so I would leave. Then there was the part about my personal glory, now, that seemed to really bother Him. He remained absolutely adamant about 'no color'. So now you know the story of my suit and why it is black. I love it because black just happens to be one of my favorite colors. And, as you can see, I snuck in just a little dark red to see if He would say anything.

"Did you know that the color black is actually the incorporation of all colors? You see, Chowbingo, I got Him again. He dresses in white, which is the absence of color, whereas I dress in black, which is the inclusion of all color. Therefore, it is I who remains the colorful one, not Him. I just continue to be awe struck and overwhelmed with my beauty, my intelligence, and my choice of colors. Vanity, vanity, it's all for me; don't you agree, Chowbingo?"

"You are actually a very trying personality, Xeres. All I know is that there's a lie in your explanation somewhere. That, unfortunately, just continues to be who you are."

"So be it, Chowbingo. Now let's move to my 'Executive Suit'. Here it is, in its special space, Chowbingo; right at the center of my wardrobe, in a place of honor as is only befitting."

"Where is it? All I see is an empty niche with nothing in it."

"Obviously that's because I'm wearing it. I felt I should put on my 'best' to welcome you, upon your arrival—as any gracious host would be expected to do.

"Next to it please find my 'Angel of Light' ensemble; suit, shoes, tie, and cuff links, all in white. You see, Father stripped me of color, but nonetheless I found myself enough fabric and leather to make this outfit."

"Where did you get the white materials?"

"Stole them, of course, just like everything else I get. Picked it all up in Neveah the last time I stopped by to harass Father. I wonder if that solider, of His, misses it yet. I think he was the same one who threw me out of the garden that day; if so, it serves him right."

"And what's so important about the suit? Seems to me like you went through a lot of trouble just for one outfit."

"This is where I am able to portray myself as the 'Angel of Light', a perfect counterfeit portrayal of Father, Himself."

"And?"

"And when I present myself as Father, to unsuspecting humans, I can deflect them from Father's will to mine."

"Now really, I may just be Father's pet, but even I'm not going to fall for that."

"You hold your tongue there, Chowbingo. Remember, I'm the accuser here, not you! Besides, it's amazing what I can accomplish when I pump one of them up with some false pride, envy, or avarice. It simply works wonders. I save this outfit for the brainy 'know-it-alls'. It doesn't seem to work as well for children of innocent virtue or even for those of humble spirits. For them I find using the 'clown suit' to be the most effective."

"Clown suit?"

"Yes, the one I have mounted over there to the right."

"That's just a plain old 'devil suit', tail, horns, and all. Where's your pitchfork?"

"Oh, that's over in my hand weapons section, at the armory. It's located just down the hallway to our left."

"So, why do you call it a 'clown suit'?"

"Because it's funny looking, obviously."

". . . and the purpose?"

"Remember, I mentioned the humble of heart and the children?"

"Yes?"

"Well, I just scare them into fearful submission. I know it doesn't necessarily get them to my place, like my white suit, but I sure have fun watching them. Besides, it sets them up for later."

"Then, of course, there's your 'everyday suit'?"

"Yes, the one I wear for inauspicious occasions when I'm just traveling about. It's just like the dog suit that you're wearing now. These allow both of us to wander about the Earth 'to and fro' without a lot of notice or interruption, don't you think?"

"Okay, I think I've seen enough of your home. Can we go back outside now?"

"I didn't think you cared for my outside operations. I was trying to be a cordial host by bringing you inside."

"It's freezing in there. At least the Lake of Fire provides heat.

"Xeres, what's the point of all of this?"

"Remember the garden? My victory there was satisfying for the moment, but that moment passed so long ago."

"Can't you just rest in that?"

"I want more! I need more, and I deserve more, always. Yes, I successfully thwarted Father's desire to visit with His creation, but that isn't enough. Vanity must always be mine. Therein lies the real purpose for my everyday suit. It allows me to wander among the humans, to plot and to plan whom I will devour next."

"How do you 'devour' them, Xeres?"

"Simple, I just trick them into violating the rules of love that were set forth for behavior in Neveah."

"How does that happen?"

"Just substitute faith, hope, and charity for fear, hopelessness, and covetousness."

"Is that it?"

"No, finally there comes my master plan where I convince humanity to turn against itself and destroy its own."

"How do you do that?"

"I seek out the unborn, mistaken, and denied children of the Earth. Beloved of the Father, yet despised and abandoned by their own. Their unwanted are my prey. They cry for help, but they have no advocate. They do not speak because there is no one to hear."

"They aren't your prey. You can't get to them. You've been banished to the underworld. I witnessed it; I was there when it all happened."

"True, I was banished to the underworld, but my travel rights were not taken away. I travel freely from here to my mansion below the seventh foundation of Neveah. That's where I was when I watched you travel through space, on your rather unceremonious journey to Earth, a furry little fireball as I remember you. Actually, I also travel to see Father quite often, just to remind Him of my presence and His mistake; the 'Great Accuser', some call me. However, now I spend most of my time travelling about Earth in search of new acquisitions for my worm. In fact, it was because of your most recent assignment that I first decided to take an interest in Valentino and his mother—my next acquisitions.

"Thank you for that lead by the way.

"Tell me, Chowbingo, what can you think of that could possibly be more fun than to take Father's own creation, His beloved, those uncared for and abandoned by their own, and feed them to my worm? My beloved worm, that lowly caretaker of Earth's foundation? Earth to earth, so to speak. Ah, revenge can be so sweet."

"Xeres, is there anything about you that is not evil?"

"Nope!"

"Well, I'll be leaving then."

"Chowbingo, you can't leave. You know that once you arrive here there is no returning. The Father set it up that way, and He can't renounce His own word. So here you stay."

"So what do you have planned for me, Xeres?"

"Since you are Father's personal pet, I have devised for you evil such as has never before been contemplated, either in Neveah or here."

". . . and what might that be, Xeres?"

"Chowbingo, I was going to provide you with an offer but due to your condescending, smug, attitude I'm going to withhold it at this time.

"Ah, here is my barge again, just on time. I just love that little statue; it's always on time and it has absolutely no feelings whatever. I just couldn't ask for a better associate."

As Chowbingo glanced over his left shoulder, there it came again, the same barge that had originally transported him to the island. The difference was that now, disembarking from it, were two cotillions of creatures marching toward him with military precision. Each one was led by its own separate leader, one by a scorpion and the other by a rat.

"Who will have him?" asked Xeres.

Immediately, as if on command, the rat began to re-
gurgitate from its mouth swarms of rodents, hundreds by
count. Seemingly without a leader, yet with a common
purpose, they swarmed the scorpion cotillion, smothering
and consuming it down to the final insect. All that was except for the scorpion leader, who by then vanquished,
was the first to return to the barge. This was a scenario
that appeared to Chowbingo to have been played out
many times before.

"As you can see, Chowbingo, whenever my forces
travel, they do so in pairs. Two go out but only one returns. Keeps the spirit of competition at a peak, wouldn't
you say?"

"You're insane!"

"Actually, to the contrary, Chowbingo, I am just fulfilling
my assignment to supreme perfection, and with delightful,
unabashed relish, I might add.

"Unfortunately, Chowbingo, my hospitality toward you
must come to an end here. You will now leave to live for
a time and a while with my rat commander and my victor
for the moment. So, tarry not, hurry! Hurry now, and follow
him to his castle. I suggest that you don't resist, or it will
be all the worse for you. Oh, and I further highly recommend that you be most careful to keep a safe distance
from my rat's face. His breath is really quite horrific, even
for us down here.

"Remember, Chowbingo, should you have a change
of attitude, I may be willing to reconstitute my prior offer;
an offer that will surely appeal to you later, if not now."

"And so what might that be?" queried Chowbingo, as he watched the barge begin to pull away from the shoreline.

"Renounce Father and I will appoint you my second in command."

"I think not," responded Chowbingo, without hesitation.

"You are about to spend your eternity here, in darkness, in pain, in agony, and in loneliness; and that begins only after you first spend a thousand years as a guest of Mr. Rat, standing here beside you. Now what say you, Mr. Chowbingo?"

Chowbingo, shouting above the tumultuous waves crashing against the barge responded in his loudest voice, *"I will never betray Father. Do with me what you will, Xeres."*

Before Xeres could respond Chowbingo's chrysolite stone began to glow, dimly at first, but soon the entire area was bathed in a warm, green glow.

"You can't do that," screamed Xeres. "He's mine. You promised me!"

The glow methodically turned to a knife-edge ray of green that cut through the center of the lake, splitting the waves, some to the left, the others to the right.

"No, no," cried Xeres, in a piercing wail. "You did that before. Chowbingo is mine. He's no longer yours. I got him here, fair and square. He's mine now and I get to keep him."

A golden light, bright like the sunlight travelling from beyond their view, moved toward them. The lake's void, opened by the chrysolite ray, filled with a comforting warmth.

Before anyone could respond there came from the distance a coach drawn by seven white horses. Six were paired side by side. The seventh, leading from the front, but also in traces, appeared not to be pulling any weight. It became quickly clear to all that its sole purpose was to lead.

The voice came from everywhere: "Xeres, Chowbingo is not a creature born of Earth. He is mine!"

The coach came into full view, led by the single white stallion. It pulled up onto the shoreline, directly at the entrance to Xeres' castle, whereupon its door opened. Inside sat a solitary man. He was dressed in white linen. His hair was white and curly as sheep's wool. His complexion was ruddy like the color of a man of all nationalities. His eyes blazed with the color of blue, a blue that a Polynesian tribesman might see while gazing across the ocean's surface on a crystal-clear day.

"Chowbingo."

"Yes?"

"Get in!"

"Yes, Father."

Chapter 12

The Dinner

Chowbingo, Chowbingo! Puppy, Puppy, where are you?"

Chowbingo stretched and awakened from his slumber, snuggled amongst the leaves, where he lay against the tree.

"Thank goodness, there you are. I've been looking all over for you. You had me really worried. You've been gone for almost half an hour now, and Mom's going to be wondering why we're not back. Where did you go, anyway?"

Chowbingo pondered the recent events for a brief moment. *"Nope, Val definitely wasn't going to believe this one, not even with his limited understanding of our Neveah language. I'm not so sure I wasn't dreaming this one myself, hmm?*

"Uh, I was sleeping."

"Sleeping. How could you be sleeping out here in the middle of the day?"

"Dogs do that a lot, Val. I'm sorry. Do you want me to follow you to your house before I cause any more trouble?"

"Yeah, I mean, sure—thanks!"

"Okay, but remember we can't communicate using our spiritual language in their presence. That would require more explaining than the two of us can muster."

"Well, I can see you weren't sleeping too long. This bunch of herbs you've collected is really going to please Mama and the others."

"Oh yeah, yeah—sure," commented Chowbingo, as he looked about to see what it was that Val was talking about.

The soil, recently turned, had unearthed kilos of the most succulent white truffles that ever could have been imagined. These were ones that would impress even an experienced, well-trained connoisseur possessing the most discerning of palates.

Neither Val nor Chowbingo were then sufficiently skilled to appreciate the riches that presently lay before them. But that was soon to change. In fact, their lives, as I would learn, were soon to be radically altered.

"C'mon Chowbingo, let's get back to the house before we get into some real trouble."

"Val, how are we going to get all this stuff back to the house? It's too much for you to carry, and I can't be of much help with just my mouth to carry it in."

"Tell you what, Chowbingo, we'll just leave it here and when we get to the house we can get some sacks, and then maybe some of the others might be willing to help us."

"Sure, so long as they're not mad at us for being late."

"You're right, Chowbingo, so maybe we better get to running. Remember, you've got four legs so be sure and slow it down a bit for me."

"Okay," replied Chowbingo, as he immediately took off with all of the speed he could possibly muster.

———

"What I actually mean, Dominique, is that Mr. Bellingeri recently invited me to participate in his candy-making business, isn't that right?" She then involuntarily glanced toward Mr. Bellingeri, unwittingly seeking his affirmation.

"Well, actually it is a bit more than that," volunteered Dominique. "I had wished, for a long time, to increase the production of my business from one of a small entrepreneurial shop to that of a boutique manufacturing plant.

"Reluctantly, oftentimes I have felt that people really don't care what I do with my life or with my dreams. I've always known that good looks, appropriate mannerisms, and a sprinkling of athletic ability, would probably assure me the prettiest girl for the dance and a guaranteed advantage within the business community. Unfortunately, I never possessed any of those attributes. Therefore, as the acknowledged overlooked mouse in the corner, I found that my road would be longer and perhaps more arduous than it might be for others.

"Silently, for years, I have prepared for the fulfillment of my dream. However, it was not until Mrs. Patadarski's availability that I ever felt I had met someone who displayed the necessary grit for my vision to manifest successfully. You know, anyone can shine during the good times, but it takes someone with the resolve of Angelina to carry through during the hard times. We all know that she displays that rare ability. And I commend her for persevering during her personal journey. This has not been an easy journey for her, or for her son."

"Here, here," added Yuri Kolvalenko rising up from the fireplace hearth with his fist upraised. "She's there to help you with your business, Dominique, and we all know that she's the prettiest one at the 'dance'. Oops, I'm sorry. Got a little emotional there for a moment, it being so true and all."

"Why, thank you, Yuri. I guess you did get a bit enthusiastic, but nevertheless I am extremely flattered and therefore wish to take this moment to say again, thank you. I guess I have had a few hard spells. Nonetheless, I have always just tried to 'move ahead' in the best ways that I know how."

"Mrs. Patadarski, please don't ever feel that way again," added Sam. "I know that I'm new to your little gathering, but I want you to know how much I've admired you from afar; ever since the passing of Salvio, your wonderful husband. He was a man whose memory continues to be respected and admired by each of us, I'm sure.

"I'm so honored to be invited to your dinner, and I want you to know that I've taken extra care to select some of the finest offerings from my humble grocery. In fact, I've even included two ounces of fresh, select, imported truffles, from one of my French sources to add that special 'oomph' to our meal."

"Oh, Mr. Emerson," exhorted Angelina with a chuckle, "that is exactly what Mr. Bellingeri is teaching me to make in his candy store."

"I'm sorry for not being clear," responded Sam.

"What he means," interrupted Dominique, "is that the truffles that he brings here tonight are an edible fungi found under the root of trees whereas my truffles are manufactured from chocolate and derive their name from their similarity, in shape, to Mr. Emerson's fungi.

"Do I have it right, Sam?"

"Absolutely, in fact the two that I have brought with me tonight are known as Black Perigord Truffles. They derive the name from their place of origin, which is located in southwestern France. I'm sorry I couldn't bring more but, with black truffles, just a few shavings can cost hundreds of dollars when served in fine Parisian restaurants."

"They're even sometimes referred to as 'black diamonds'. I understand," added Dominique.

"Yes, that's because when they're harvested they have little 'diamond points' on their surfaces," responded Sam.

"There are also white truffles, which mostly come from Italy. Those can cost three times the price of the black ones. Obviously, those are not the ones that I can afford to carry in my market. My customers, your friends and neighbors, would never pay the required price for such an extravagance. This has always been, after all, a humble community."

"I guess 'white diamonds' are what you would call them," added Yuri.

He then started to chuckle aloud as he began to consider it nonsense that people would actually pay such extravagant prices for "bulbs" coming out of the ground.

"No you don't," responded Sam, with his correcting laugh. "Those are just too expensive to be diamonds."

"Why the expense?" inquired Dominique, reservedly expressing his businessman's interest.

Sam, seizing the moment to act professorial and also perhaps to impress Angelina, jumped right in. "Truffles, the natural ones, are rare and cannot be cultivated in growing rooms or even in a greenhouse. There is a symbiotic relationship that exists between a host tree and the truffle. Truffles live partly in the soil and partly on the tree's roots. The tree provides sugar to the truffle, and the truffle provides mineral salts to the tree. Since they are extremely rare, the more they are harvested, the less there are, and then the more expensive they become. Finally, like elephants' ivory, rhinoceros' tusks, and diamonds, artificial pricing is also applied to truffles thereby serving to assure their value."

"Well thank you for that fine explanation, Mr. Emerson. I feel just like I am right back in the classroom," Angelina volunteered with her whimsical smile.

Sam, realizing that his overstated attempt to impress didn't quite hit the mark found himself, emotionally, for the moment, shrinking quietly into the shadows.

Dominique, wishing to rescue his friend from a social "faux pas", picked up the conversation. "Truffles are a fancy, edible delicacy. They are referred to as an aphrodisiac and are indisputably, ounce for ounce, the most expensive food in the world. I have found, through reasonable inquiry, that truffles are also counterfeited, trafficked like drugs, and readily stolen."

Sam, grateful to have been rescued by Dominique, for his faux pas, re-entered the dialogue: "I actually do inventory a small amount for my few, more discerning customers, but that is known only to them. My other customers would not even be expected to know their value. Were my store actually situated in a large, or more cosmopolitan city, I would still be unable to actually display them, unmonitored, for fear of theft."

CRASH: the door flew open, as Chowbingo came sliding in on his haunches, while unsuccessfully attempting to backpedal with his front paws.

"Now that's what I call an entrance," remarked Yuri, somewhat taken back by Chowbingo's unexpected entrance.

"He'd be looking like one of those pug dogs if the door hadn't been unlatched," added Dominique, jokingly.

Next it was Val, huffing and puffing, as he followed about thirty seconds behind.

"What's with you two?" asked Angelina. "Why all the speed and commotion?"

"We were afraid that we'd be late and then you'd get mad," muttered Val, now half doubled over, trying to catch his breath.

"Well, fortunately for the two of you, Mr. Bellingeri, Mr. Emerson, Mr. Kolvalenko, and I were enjoying a little 'adult time', so I guess you're off the hook."

"See there, Chowbingo, your stupid race was all for nothing. I even told you that it wasn't fair because you have four legs and I only have two, remember?"

"Now that's quite a funny conversation that you're having with that dog of yours," Yuri exclaimed between giggles. "Remember, you are talking to a dog. He can't tell two legs from four. He was just running because that's what dogs do."

"Don't you even think about letting on," Chowbingo admonished Val, while looking at him with his most soulful puppy dog stare.

"See, I told you," cautioned Yuri. "Look at those eyes. He doesn't have a clue what you're talking about."

"Val, what have you and your puppy actually been up to? You've been gone for much more time than was needed."

"Just tell her about gathering the roots," offered Chowbingo. *"Don't get into the part where you were afraid I was missing for that period of time. Also, keep your gaze away from me when talking. That is a tell-tale sign that we are having a conversation. I love your mom, and her friends,*

and would like to be able to include them in our spirit language, but they just wouldn't understand it any more than they would understand this stone tied to my neck."

"Speaking of your stone, what IS the deal with that?"

"We don't have time to go into that right now. Remember, you are having a conversation with your mother that I am not supposed to understand."

"Yes but . . .!"

"No buts. I'll explain at the appropriate time, I promise."

"Double promise?"

"Yep—now back to your mom."

"Mama, remember when we had our roast beef dinner last time due to the kindness of Mr. Kolvalenko?"

"Of course Val, how could I forget," she replied, while directing an admiring glance toward Yuri.

"And remember, I brought those roots, from the forest, to add flavor to our meal?"

"Yes, Val, I most surely do."

"Well, Chowbingo uncovered a whole bunch, somewhat like them, again; but he now has so many that we can't carry them without the use of a container."

"So, do you need some help?"

"Yes, Mama, we do, and perhaps something, from you, to carry them in also."

"Will one of my empty flour sacks do? I'm sorry that they're so small, but I've never been able to afford to buy the larger sacks of flour since . . ."

"They would be great, Mama."

"They?"

"Yes, we will need three or four sacks to start. Do you have that many, for us to use, or must we make more than one trip to gather it all?"

"Well, if needed, I suppose you can also take the ones that you and I have been using for pillow cases. I believe I can always wash them after you're done. You will be returning them, won't you?

"On second thought, Val, what are we going to do with all that you have collected? I can only use the smallest amount in preparation for a dinner, such as this, and I just can't see how we can even begin to store the rest."

"What kind of herbs or mushrooms do you think that you and Chowbingo have actually collected?" asked Sam, as he settled into what obviously had been Salvio's easy chair.

"I believe we have truffles," responded Val.

"Well, Val, I don't want to ruin your dream, but what you probably have there are mushrooms, and maybe even poisonous ones at that. I've brought some nice greens, which I know will complement this lovely roast. Furthermore, we certainly have enough to eat when we include all that is here. I believe, now that we have everything that is needed, we should all sit down to a great meal, with dear friends, and celebrate our blessings."

"All right, Mr. Emerson, but will it still be okay if Mama uses some of my mushrooms too, the ones that I collected for our last meal? The one that we shared with Mr. Bellingeri?"

"I'm so sorry, Val, but I believe those are probably too old and more than likely not usable, or safe, by now. However, you can certainly look for yourself, if you like. I left the remainder of them wrapped in some tin foil. I believe they're still over there behind the pantry, immediately to the left of your tired old plant, which you obviously forgot to water one more time. I must confess, I forgot your 'mushrooms', just like you forgot your plant."

"Ah, here they are," exclaimed Val, as he began to unwrap the foil from around them. "Sorry about the plant, Mama. I'll give it a little water before I sit down to eat."

"You can forget it if you like, Val. Probably too late for that plant. It's what happens to life when you don't care for it." Taking a bit of personal glee from the "teaching moment" that she had just proffered upon her son, she glanced over her shoulder with a knowing smile to catch his reaction.

"Let me take a look," offered Mr. Emerson, as he walked toward Val and the package that he was carefully beginning to unfold.

"Hmm," sniffed Sam. "Unfortunately these actually aren't truffles, just a close appearing counterfeit, I'm afraid. Yes, I can tell by the texture and the smell. No doubt about it. These are just some form of, what those in the trade call, 'false truffles'. Sometimes you can occasionally find ones that are tasty, but unfortunately they may also be poisonous. They certainly can never become a replacement for actual truffles. Fortunately, you must not have used enough in your former meal to hurt you.

"Val!" exclaimed Sam with a heightened voice. "Are those 'truffles', the ones waiting for us in the field, just like the false truffles that I am looking at here?"

"No Sir, they are quite different than these."

"Okay," replied Sam, with an air of reserved hopefulness in his voice. "Then the ones you left in the field could still actually be something."

Yuri, feeling this subject was perhaps moving toward foolishness, decided to break in. "Perhaps we could eat our supper now, if you're ready, Mrs. Patadarski."

"All right, Yuri, that sounds like a fine idea to me. Please, perhaps we can all be seated now," Angelina announced, as she exercised her gentlest demeanor. "I recall questioning Val before our last dinner, which we shared with Dominique. I expressed those same concerns back then. Isn't that right, Dominique?"

"I do believe that you did make some mention, back then, about the source of Val's findings. But we were having such a good time, I believe we just simply let it pass."

The probability for disappointment on Sam's face was apparent and transparent to all of them. However, these were folks who lived a hard life, in an unforgiving area. Disappointment was the norm for them and the few gains that they encountered were taken as precious jewels to be cherished and protected. This, however, was not to be one of those times—or was it?

"The ones we have in the forest now, they could really be truffles though," offered Val, with a youngster's unbridled and uncompromising enthusiasm.

"Val, why don't you seat your mother. You're certainly old enough to be the head of your household," volunteered Yuri, as he attempted to shift a dark cloud of possible disappointment to that of a more uplifting moment.

"Hey, that's a great idea," interjected Dominique. "I'll pull the roast off the spit and place it here on this platter beside me, if that's all right Mrs. Patadarski?"

"Oh, Dominique, you're so cute. It's perfectly okay to call me Angelina for now, or even Angie, if you like. We're here, right in my home. We're certainly not at work now. At least, I hope not!"

"Thanks Angie. And don't worry, I'll get the hang of it. Just a little slow sometimes, I guess."

"You're not slow, Dominique. You're a sweet, considerate friend, and I so appreciate you for all that you do. You have certainly brought great hope and a ray of light, into the lives of Val and myself. The first one, I might say, since the death of Salvio. Don't you agree, Val?"

"Uh, hmm, ah," stuttered Val. "Yes, Mr. Bellingeri is a nice man," reflected Val to himself, "but he isn't my father. Surely, my mother can't be comparing this man to my father, or can she?"

Val turned toward the direction of Chowbingo, whom, he felt, was now speaking to him.

"Just say yes," Chowbingo commanded Val, using a voice that rang through Val's innards with the unmistakable clarity of a crystal bell.

"Yes," replied Val, in a clear, uncompromising voice that shocked even him, upon his hearing it.

"Well, that certainly was nicely answered," acknowledged Angelina.

"See, Dominique, even my son agrees."

"I'll add to that," recited Yuri.

"And an Amen from me too," spoke up Sam.

"Well, Dominique, you seem to be pretty popular for the moment," commented Angelina, a bit flustered.

"Just because Angelina said it, don't let it go to your head," chided Yuri. "Now let's concentrate on getting dinner ready for the table."

"Look everyone, I'm going to set the roast here on the sideboard to breathe for about fifteen minutes. That should give us some time to finish preparing this nice salad using the greens Sam has brought; and thank you again, Sam."

"You're welcome, Dominique. And while I'm here taking up space, perhaps I can complete the salad preparation, since that is somewhat my specialty."

"Well that leaves me with nothing to do. How about I carve the roast when it's ready? After all I am the butcher."

"Great idea, Yuri. Now everyone has a part to play, except for me."

"Oh, you have a part to play," offered Dominique. "You're the hostess."

"Oh Dominique, thank you. You're so sweet."

"Hey, what's my part, and what about my pal, Chowbingo? What's his part?"

"You're the man of the house, remember," added Yuri, restating his earlier remarks.

"Leave me out of this, or we'll both have too much explaining to do," added Chowbingo, as he directed a searing look toward Val.

"Okay now, I'll start fixing the salad," offered Sam. "It'll take a few minutes to get prepared. Val, would you like to help me wash the greens? Perhaps, you can wash them and then I'll pat them dry, here on the drain board."

"Do you want to try some of my mushrooms?" persisted Val. "They still might just work."

"Val, I'm sorry but I really don't think we should try them, considering the time that they've been sitting. Notice how much different they appear when we compare them to the few slices that I've brought from my store. I really don't think it would be wise for us to chance it. Since they've been wrapped up, and in storage for so long, we just can't tell. Might even be that they're poisonous mushrooms!

"Now, then, those 'mushrooms' that you and Chowbingo have gathered, tell me a little more about them. Let's try to think a moment and be sure that they're something we really want to collect after dinner. Remember, once you have a full stomach, going back for them might not seem quite so appealing."

"Val, your mother's friends here, they just don't seem to show any faith. Nothing but doubt, doubt, doubt!"

"What are you trying to tell me, Chowbingo?"

"What I'm trying to tell you, Val, is that if you, your mother, and her friends can't begin to see yourselves in

happier, more successful, circumstances, then it's never going to happen."

"Well, when can something like that happen?"

"Right now!"

"How?"

"Truffles."

"What truffles?"

"The one's that I left under the tree."

"But Sam really believes that they aren't truffles, and I think he's an expert."

"Why do you think he's an 'expert'?"

"Because he told me, when we were standing over by the drain board, that truffles don't grow in this area. Furthermore, he said that it takes a different type of tree than the ones that live here for truffles to be able to survive."

"So, that makes him an 'expert'?"

'Yep, I guess he figures that they are just more false truffles, like the ones he thinks I brought home for the last meal we had with Mr. Bellingeri."

"Val, now you listen to me, and you listen very carefully to what I am about to say. What is waiting for you out in the field, which I left behind, are not only truffles, they are very, very, expensive white truffles."

"How can you be so sure that you're right? After all, Mr. Sam said . . ."

"Val, look at me! I am talking to you, and my lips aren't moving. Remember, I'm communicating with you according to your own understanding. I'm, for all appearances, a common, everyday chow puppy. Take a look at me. I

have an amulet around my neck, and it has certainly gotten us out of more than one jamb, right? Well, where do you think one gets a stone like this, buys it at Sam Emerson's store, from the 'expert'?

"I am here to tell you that there remains behind, uncovered where I left them, kilos of 'mushrooms'. Those 'mushrooms', as you choose to call them are, in truth, expensive, white truffles.

Should I be correct, and I am, you and your mother can have a life more materially abundant than you will ever imagine. If I'm wrong, you'll have many kilograms of product that Mr. Emerson can sell at his market which will still serve to improve your sorry lot.

Val, you've been given Father's gift of a 'free will'. The choice is yours. I have been forbidden from making this choice for you. This is your choice. What do you want to do?"

"Val, Val come back here! Now where is my son off to this time? This just isn't like Val—especially with dinner almost being on the table. Look, he hasn't even closed the door. My goodness, Chowbingo has more sense than this foolish boy. Man of the house, humph! The boy actually has no more sense than a crazy toad.

"Oh my goodness! Now there goes Chowbingo. It's almost as if those two can talk to one another."

"Just hold the dinner a bit," yelled Dominique, on his way out the door. "I'll see if I can redirect their exuberance back toward the dinner table."

"Hold up, Dominique, I'm right behind you," yelled Yuri, trying to catch up to the longer-legged man.

"Darn it, Yuri, I just can't see them anywhere. This forest gets so dense, so quick. We're probably going to lose each other if we're not more careful."

"Let's just go on back. They're sure to return when they're finished with their mischief. I'm certain that Angelina will be well able to handle the matter when Val finally decides to return."

"Yep! Mothers seem to have a special gift when it comes to handling their children. I remember, all that it took from my mother was that one special look. Probably could still freeze me in my tracks right now, were she still alive, God rest her soul!"

Chapter 13

Out to the Woods

Who's asking?"

"Come, come now, Chowbingo. I thought we would be good friends, by now, for as long as we've known each other. Remember, you were even my personal guest at the retreat before you just upped and took off with Him. Very rude on your part, I must say. How quickly you forget my hospitality."

"Who are you talking to anyway?" asked Val, his spiritual ear now attuned to the conversation that was taking place.

"It's me, Mr. Valentino. Surely you must recall me from my visit to your village. Remember, I was that dithering, senile, old man who was seated on the park bench near the corner of the building; the edge with the trailing ivy growing along its eaves."

"Oh gosh, my, is it really you? You look so very different standing here."

"Don't let him fool you, Val. This is Xeres, a spirit of no good. In fact, let me rephrase that, THE spirit of no good."

"So, what do you want with us now, Mr. Xeres?"

"Nothing, my boy, absolutely nothing. I was just enjoying the wonderment of nature here, by this lovely tree, and suddenly the two of you appear. Strange coincidence, wouldn't you say?"

"No coincidence at all, Xeres. You just absolutely never rest from your evil deeds. The only reason that you're here now is because you heard that the fortunes of Val and his mother were about to change, and you can't stand to see goodness prevail."

"Chowbingo, don't you ever dare to use that word 'goodness' in my presence again."

"Well, why not? It's a word my mother uses very often. In fact, her face lights up a little whenever she says it. It's just great to see Mama whenever she has even the slightest look of a smile. She's not smiled ever since . . ."

"This is not the time for that, Val."

"Why not? Heck, I remember when . . ."

"I'll explain later," answered Chowbingo. *"Too much history to go into it all right now."*

"You're quite right, Chowbingo, too much history. And that's the way that it's going to stay. I know about your truffles. I also know what you want to do for Mrs. Patadarski and especially for your friend, the brat, here."

"I'm not a brat! You quit calling me that, or . . ."

"I'll handle things from here. Thank you very much, Val. Xeres and I are old acquaintances from times long past. Aren't we, Xeres?"

"Yes we are, Chowbingo. And therefore I'm certain you will recall that this realm is mine, under covenant from Father. Also, as part of that promise, Mrs. Patadarski, the youth here, and their village are mine; a village filled with people who have spent their lives in unrequited labor, just the way I want it, and just the way it's going to remain—a village filled with people mired in indebted servitude."

"What is servitude, Chowbingo?"

"Servitude, hmm? I like that word. I have lots of earthlings who are in servitude, to me, and will be for all of time. That is after they are finally transferred to me.

The wonderful part of it is, I don't even have to work for them—all because they chose not to join his son's club.

Now this brat here and his stupid mother, they seem to be different—a bit more of a challenge. I thought Mrs. Patadarski would turn to me when I arranged for the demise of Salvio. I thought she would give up her faith and turn away from Father's son, but no, she's a stubborn one. She just keeps holding on—and holding on. That's going to change. They're going to be mine, and I'm starting with the brat, now."

"What do 'demise' and 'servitude' mean," asked Val.

"Soon as he loses his faith, he'll be mine. Then, after I have him, his mother will fold, of that you can be sure."

Chowbingo quickly jumped in with a response to short circuit what he knew would be coming. *"It's not important, Val. I'll explain it all to you later."*

The conversation continued.

"No, they won't, Xeres. They absolutely will not be subjected to you. I was there, beside Him, when He set forth His plan and banished you. You've manipulated circumstances and brought about events that have caused hurt and despair. Father, on the other hand, set forth His events to be righteous and orderly. You have counterfeited them and brought about nothing but evil, hurt, and pain."

"And I might say, Chowbingo, I've done an absolutely awesome job of it!"

"Yes you have, Xeres, and it's because of your actions that I've been sent here. We, from Neveah, speak of servitude in the sense of serving, not of slavery. There beyond the trees of this forest lies a village filled with good people. Those who selflessly serve one another. They are not there to provide you entertainment through their sacrifices, diligence, and hard work. Now that I have been placed here, on assignment from Father, there will be corrections!"

"Chowbingo, hear me and hear me clearly. That is never going to happen! You have my personal assurance regarding the matter. Be assured that so long as I'm here, Earth remains my realm! Did you not forget, or were you asleep, at Father's meeting, when He assigned all of Earth to me?"

"What are the two of you talking about? Now, you're really starting to scare me."

"Scared, I'll show you the real meaning of scared, you insolent, little waif."

"C'mon Val, we don't need to continue this conversation any longer. Let's go get the truffles and be done with Xeres' nonsense."

"What's a 'waif'?"

"Nonsense you say . . ."

"Chowbingo look! The trees, they're moving."

"Trees always move, Val. in fact that's what they do during most of their day. They move their branches to and fro. They just sway in the breeze."

"No, no I mean their trunks and their roots. They don't do that! They're moving into new positions."

"Yes, my impertinent friends, the trees, my trees you might call them, are in fact moving. They are now moving into a phalanx. I believe, Mr. Valentino, that such a maneuver is what you earthlings would call a military formation."

"What's he doing?"

"Be quiet now, Val. This is getting serious."

"Xeres, are you about to start another one of your failed power plays or can we just pass in peace?"

"Peace?"

"Come along, Val. Let's be on our way."

"Chowbingo, I can't move."

"What do you mean, you can't move?"

"I'm, I'm sinking. My body is sinking into the ground!"

"Quicksand!"

"Quicksand, what's quicksand?"

"Xeres! You behind this?"

"Who, me? I'm just a curious observer. Anything I can do to help? Help the boy sink, that is.

"Chowbingo, this is going to be interesting to watch when you try to convey, to Mrs. Patadarski, your explanation of how her son died in a mud hole while running around in the woods with you, a stupid dog. Wonder which of my costumes I'll don to listen to that explanation; you barking, yelping, and rolling around in antics while she tries to figure out why Val hasn't come home?

"Yep, Father's really going to hurt over this one. Just like when He was back in the garden. It's about time for a little more fun. I did it to Father back then and now I'm going to do it to Him again. He'll think twice about keeping me out of Neveah after this one. I was really starting to become bored with my same old, same old.

You know, for an occasion like this, I might just have to spend a little extra time and design myself an entire new outfit."

"Just shut up, you cruddy old man!"

"Hold on for a minute, Val, I'll get you out of this."

"How?" yelled Val, frightened and starting to sob. "How?"

"You know what I like about Father more than anything," Xeres addressed, to no one in particular. "He cares for one just as much as He cares for all. Makes it so much easier to hurt Him. That really makes my day, so to speak. Revenge, it's such a useful tool."

"Val, grab my collar and hold on tight while I pull you out."

"Hey, you stupid mutt. You're not going to get that kid out of there. He's going to go down. Shall I have the river boat skipper ready to pick him up from down below? You remember, he's the one who gave you your ride."

"Xeres, please be quiet and for goodness sake if you're not going to help, please quit standing over me."

"No, I will not be quiet, Chowbingo and don't you ever use the word 'goodness' in my presence again.

"Don't you remember that, with Val, there'll be no returning him? Unlike us, he's an Earth creation. If I get him, he's mine to keep, FOREVER! How are you going to save him, Chowbingo? Pull him out with your body? Val's twice your size, he's firmly stuck in the quicksand, and he's going down.

"Looks like you're about to become mine, you little brat, FOREVER! In a few moments you can even meet my pet worm. Handsome fellow, wouldn't you say, Chowbingo?"

"Help, help me, Chowbingo, please!"

———————

Imperceptibly, during Xeres' unbridled laughter and Val's screams of panic, it began. The amulet, around Chowbingo's neck, began to radiate a dark green, emerald glow. The translucent light began to focus into a beam, brighter and tighter, with each second's passing. There, as if directed by an invisible hand, its emerald beam fell upon the stately Sequoia. The tree, as its position unmistakably revealed, was the undisputed centerpoint for Xeres' phalanx.

It began and, then just as quickly, it was over. The tree, with a flash of blinding light, was separated from its roots as it began its forward fall toward Val and Chowbingo. Within the split second before its final crash all the salient portions of Val's young life flashed before him: His happy childhood with his father. Then came Salvio's death; the loss of his friends, loneliness, and finally his mother's continuing grief.

That would be the hardest, his mother's grief. How would be able to cope without him?

It was not until after the sounds of the final crash had finally subsided that Val realized the tree, which had just landed less than a foot from him, had left him totally unharmed. Even then, the final cracking and snapping of the residual twigs and limbs continued to startle him, so great had been the impact.

Xeres, from the first glowing of the amulet, recognized the trouble that it meant for him and had hightailed it to parts unknown. Chowbingo, as he shook the dust from his fur, looked at Val and began to survey what had just happened. He knew immediately from where his help had come. It had come from Father!

"Val, are you going to sit in that mud bath all day or do you intend to grab hold of that tree and crawl out of your predicament? We still have some truffles to get, that is if you haven't forgotten?"

Still shaken, disoriented, and confused, Val glanced toward Chowbingo, shook his head, and blindly began to follow his friend's suggestion.

"Where did you leave them?" Val asked, as the fog began to lift from his senses.

"*Over there. Just follow me,*" replied Chowbingo, as he began to work his way deeper into the forest.

"*Val, look at those trees. Don't they still seem to be moving closer together?*"

"I can't really be quite sure. The sound of the crash from this falling tree, it probably knocked us both a little silly."

"*Yeah, I suppose you're right. C'mon, let's speed it up a bit. We have to try and get back before dark, otherwise your mom is going to have it out for both of us—and I don't want to have to listen to that again!*"

The wind began to blow. Slowly it began as it moved through the upper reaches of the trees. Not settling to the ground, it remained above the noticeable reaches of Val and Chowbingo.

The trees, however, easily felt the breeze gently wafting through their topmost branches. First it carefully stroked their most fragile branches as a masseuse might gently caress one's fingers or toes. Manipulating, pulling, and kneading with relaxing, yet controlled strokes, the process continued. Methodically the wind increased, moving from singular directional breezes to minor cyclical vortices, they began to circle even the sturdiest of limbs.

Then it changed direction as if it had been coached by a guiding intelligence. Ever so skillfully it blew, as it began to intertwine the lighter branches, like a skilled mat weaver executing his craft. The trees were moving now, as if they were also being controlled by some external force. A force that was individually pulling on each of their limbs, reaching out and intertwining them, one after another, with those of their neighbors. Solitary trees began to join in, limb to limb, until the entire grove, like a jellyfish, coalesced into one singular colony. The wind persisted. Tighter and tighter the encircling vortex spun, causing the trees to move closer and closer together. The dirt reluctantly began to release its tenuous hold, as it began to make way for the movement of the roots, allowing the trees, imperceptibly, to begin drawing together.

Soon the wall would be completed, an unbroken semicircle, moving forward under Xeres' authority. The symphony had begun under the control of the unseen maestro. Soil continued to give way to the roots, as the trees prodded through the forgiving soil Their prescribed paths defined, they advanced slowly and methodically, united in purpose. They moved forward in preparation for the fulfillment of their common destiny—the encircling of Val and Chowbingo.

Certainly the two would remain unaware. Their interest, that of Chowbingo and Val, would remain with the fungi and the money which they would be expecting to receive.

Val was soon to learn, freedom from Xeres' tyranny was to be short lived.

He would finally have him. Such rewards, materialistic as truffles or even diamonds for that matter, would not accompany Val to where Xeres was going to take him. Xeres was, if nothing else, a formidable opponent. Although he had disappeared, following the fall of his lead Sequoia, it was only momentary. He was back. After all, was it not his very nature to return with stealth and cunning? And so he had.

Chowbingo, now he would escape. He was not born of the Earth. Father would probably bail him out again, activating that miserable green light about his neck, but Val; Val would be his for eternity. After all, wasn't that the covenant promise between Father and himself? He, Xeres, would reign over Earth's realm for the specified time and season.

Xeres knew there would be no escaping his plan. Father, Xeres was confident, would absolutely not violate His own word. Once Xeres got Val to his place, it would be there that Val would remain.

Sure, his phalanx maneuver had been interrupted by the amulet's destruction of his lead Sequoia. However, with the encircling maneuver of his remaining trees, victory was still his to grasp.

"Chowbingo, where did you leave those truffles? Everything is starting to look the same here. This is not the forest that I remember. Things are different now and now in different places. The trees, the bushes, the trails—

they're all different. The entire forest, it's been rear-
ranged, right here in front of us. Somehow it all seems so
very different, every last part. It's even darker than usual
for this time of day. It must be because the trees are now
closer together. Look, they're starting to block what's remaining of the sun's light."

*"You just stay, here, close behind me, Val. I'm going
to try and keep following the scent back to where I left
them. One of the advantages, of this constraining dog
suit, is I can smell pretty well. Kind of a 'perk' I guess you
might call it."*

"Chowbingo, I'm not so sure that I trust your sense of
smell, especially since you're new to being a dog. Now I
really think we're lost. I grew up in this forest and this is
no longer the place that I remember."

"Ah, I've got the scent now. This way, Val."

"But, wait just a minute. Now here we are up against a
hedgerow. There's never been one here, in this part of
the forest, before. There are some around a few houses.
There's one along the main road. It leads out of our village
toward the town where Dad and I used to go, in our
wagon, to get supplies for Mom."

*"That's all well and fine but there's one here now, Val,
So, I'm just going to scamper under it, through this hole
here, near the ground. You can either follow me or climb
over it, but either way, hurry. Like you said, soon it's going
to get dark."*

Without further hesitation, Chowbingo dropped to his
belly, pushed forward with his hind legs, and forced his
way through the few remaining branches still impeding

his progress. No sooner had he cleared the restrictive foliage than he let out a series of yelps, earthly in nature, before scampering out from beneath whatever it was that had suddenly assaulted him.

"I'm sorry, I'm sorry, I'm so sorry, Chowbingo! I guess I kind of landed on top of you. I tried to crawl through the upper opening and the branches; they just wouldn't hold me."

"Kind of, kind of? You almost broke my back, besides scaring the daylights out of me. I didn't know what had attacked me. Thank goodness, it was only you. I thought that Xeres was up to another one of his tricks."

"Who me?" smirked Xeres to himself, as he watched the comedy of errors from a close distance. "Heck, they managed that one all by themselves. I'm always getting the blame for things I didn't do. I guess it just goes with my job description."

"C'mon Val, I got the scent and I don't want to lose it with another wind shift. Like you mentioned, I'm still not very experienced with this smell thing. So, let's just get going, before we really become lost. Just watch your surroundings and follow me. We can always sort out the rest of this later. Right now we need to avoid the coming darkness as much as possible."

"But!"

It was less than three minutes and they were upon the pile of truffles, now almost completely hidden beneath the windblown leaves.

"Ah, here they are, just where I left them."

Philip I. Amos

Chapter 14

Something Strange This Way

Happens

Where are those crazy two? It's been more than an hour and we still haven't seen hide nor hair of them."

Angelina, somewhat shaken now by Dominique's sudden outburst, awakened from her momentary daydream. "You're right, this is not like Val. He's an obedient, caring son. He wouldn't just wander away for such a time as this."

"Remember, Val said they were on their way to recover truffles. Or shall we say to pick up some 'mushrooms', which they claimed had been collected and were waiting for them."

"Okay Sam, but what about something to carry them in? I don't remember that they left with any of the sacks that Val wanted so badly."

"You're absolutely right, Yuri. Now, please, it's starting to get dark, so can we just go find them? You know how quickly the sun sets in this valley. Within a short time. it will be too dark for us to even see ourselves."

"Now now, Angelina, there's no need to panic," reassured Dominique, seeking to take control of the matter. "Do you happen to have any flashlights handy?"

"Actually, I have three of them. They each have fresh batteries, or at least they haven't been used since I last put them in."

"How long ago was that, Angie?" asked Sam.

"It was about six months ago, I believe. You know that night, about six months ago, when our weather radio announced the last violent storm? Mr. Greenberg had stopped by, before the storm, and provided me with about ten fresh type C batteries. I do washing and some cleaning for Mrs. Greenberg. He said that she was worried about Val and myself possibly being left in the dark should the storm became violent. Really nice people. Sometimes she gives me 'hand-me-downs', for Val. Real nice of them, especially since they don't have any sons in their family. Once a label was still on the pants."

"You mean the storm that never came? I sure do remember that time. I especially recall my labor costs and the time it took to secure all the vegetables and goods in the open areas of my store."

"Yeah, well what would it have cost all of us if it had actually come? Okay, let's get started before it gets too dark. Mrs. Patadarski, will you gather up your sacks, or some kind of boxes, that we can use to collect the boy's truffles, should there be any?"

"Dominique," said Angelina smiling sweetly, "these aren't working hours, remember. You can still call me by my first name."

"Angelina, please give Sam your two empty flour sacks there by the stove, and I'll take one of your flashlights, if I may? Also, if you all don't mind, I'll lead the way. I grew up playing in these parts. Once upon a time I knew every tree within a mile of here. I suppose they've all grown up now and even had a few trees of their own. Nevertheless, the basic pattern should, hopefully, remain unchanged."

"Probably, it will have changed quite a bit, but it's still all right with me if you lead, Yuri. This way I've got someone else to blame, for when we get lost, other than myself."

"That's not a very positive attitude, Dominique."

"Just trying to add a little humor, Angelina."

"Not now please. It soon will get dark and I am really becoming very worried about Val. Mother's concern, you know. Just something that's birthed into women, I suppose."

"And a good thing that it is," said Sam, with his very engaging smile.

"Okay now, I want everyone to bunch up tight behind me and follow in a single file please," intoned Yuri, to no one in particular. "It's going to become dark pretty soon and don't want anyone wandering off, or falling against some low hanging branch. Now I'll start by pointing my light in the direction we're going to be walking. The rest of you, please point the other two lights toward the ground so we can minimize the chances of any tripping accidents. We can't afford any broken bones."

The small group moved forward, towards the darkening forest, united in lockstep. After a time of increasingly uncomfortable quiet had passed, Sam finally asked, "Yuri, do you have any idea where it actually is that you're going?"

"I do remember, as a young boy, that this direction offered the pathway of least resistance, which is why I'm taking it."

"Yes, but how do you know that this is the direction that Val and the dog took?"

"Actually, I don't."

"We have to do something. We can't just leave them out here," pleaded Angelina.

"Well, it was kind of my intention to walk us into a sparse area where we might be able to stand still, be quiet, and listen for some familiar sound; hopefully some sounds that we might recognize as coming from Val or his puppy. That hopefully might give us a clue as to their whereabouts. You know, at night sounds from wooded areas can certainly carry a long way, and that might help also."

"Makes sense to me. It's your plan, Yuri, and we certainly don't have a better one. As far as I'm concerned, carry on."

"Thanks for your vote of confidence, Sam."

"Chowbingo, I can hardly see! You've blocking my view like you're some kind of a bush. Will you please step to the side, just a bit?"

Moving away to allow Val to view the truffles, Chowbingo turned to see a sixty-foot horizontal line of stately Sequoia trees joining together, limb to limb. They were moving toward them, inch by inch; not too slow and not too fast. They proceeded with a quiet, determined stealth; yet held back, seemingly prepared to envelope them upon the receipt of some, yet unknown, order.

Before Chowbingo could gather his thoughts, Val was lying beside him. In the darkening shadows, Val had just tripped over a rambling vine. He found himself positioned partially upon Chowbingo and partially in an entanglement of roots, leaving both of them intertwined in one unceremonious heap.

"Get off me quick. We've got a problem here," yelled Chowbingo to Val, as he simultaneously bared his teeth and began snarling toward the direction of the approaching trees.

"What's wrong, Chowbingo, what are you doing? I've never heard you snarl like that before. You're beginning to scare me."

"Well, take a look behind you, Val. Do you see it? There's our problem."

"What problem? I don't see anything except that row of trees. We're in the forest. What do you expect for us to be looking at, wooden chairs?"

"Val, those trees, I think they're moving. And the truffles, they're not truffles. Those are the same false truffles that we gathered last time!"

"But?"

"Sorry what I said about truffles. I told you before that I was still getting used to my nose. Anyway, we don't have time to talk about truffles right now. We have more immediate problems now. Val, the tree's roots; they're actually moving, THROUGH THE GROUND!"

"Oh—ah, so what's really going on here, Chowbingo?"

"Xeres! This is all the work of Xeres."

"And what's he got to do with us?"

"There's no time to explain."

"What are we going to do now?"

––––––––––

"Yuri, what's the sound I'm hearing that's coming from over there? It sounds, to me, like the sound of tree branches crackling. Maybe it's Val and his dog trying to make a pathway."

"It's almost dark now, Dominique. I can't imagine that they'll be able to see after the next few minutes. They didn't even bring a flashlight with them. Let's just start going toward the sound and hope it's them. If that doesn't work, we will be pretty much out of ideas until morning; that is, with the darkness fast approaching."

"Sounds like a decent plan, Angelina, but let's not forget that maybe they are planning on just hunkering down in the darkness. Please remember, Val's not a stranger to these woods, and he's been playing in them, and around them, all of his life. And, also, I believe, he may have picked up some basic survival tips from Salvio when he was a little boy."

"You may be right, Yuri, but nonetheless, we still have to try. We can't just make some assumptions, and leave them out here by themselves, and do nothing."

"All right, Angelina, I'm turning toward the sound, but we still have to be careful about where we walk. Let's not forget to direct our flashlights, like I first asked everyone; one light ahead and two to survey the ground for tripping hazards."

"We're right here behind you, Yuri. You keep on leading us and I'll just keep on pushing, volunteered Sam from his position at the rear of the little entourage.

"Hey, what's that in the sky?"

"Where are you looking, Dominique?"

"Right over there in the direction of the noise, see! Doesn't it look just like a big blue-white star?"

"Oh yeah, I can see it now too. Looks to me like some man made object. Certainly too low to be a star."

"Well, it certainly can't be a comet, Sam," responded Yuri. "Comets aren't stationary. They move across the sky. This one's standing still right now. It's directly over where we appear to be headed—and it's definitely not moving. We can see that."

"I'm starting to become a little nervous, in fact I'm actually becoming quite worried," cried Angelina. "I hope those two are still all right."

"You mean Val," corrected Dominique.

"No, Dominique. I mean both of them. There's something special about that animal. A lot has changed since his arrival. He's family now!"

"What are you going to do now, Chowbingo?"

"Who's that?" Val cried out, but this time he cried to no one in particular.

"It's me, your sometimes friendly, and then again your sometimes not, 'dirty old man', your friend from the town square, you insolent little brat. You're almost mine now. Just as soon as my trees complete their coming together they will capture you in their limbs, and then they will begin to squeeze the life out of you. And I, at the same time, will relax right over there in the branch of that tree, while I watch with glee, as they prepare you for your final trip to my home."

"Xeres, you've been trying different tricks to scare people, especially children, since before time began here on Earth. Now why don't you just go away?"

"No, not this time. This kid is mine. I want him, and I'm about to take him now, with a little help from my botanical assistants.

You must admit, they're a gnarly looking group, aren't they?"

"Xeres, listen to me . . ."

Silence. Xeres was not to be heard from. Just the rustling of the trees from within an otherwise eerie silence.

"What's going on, Chowbingo?"

"Hey, what's happening? What's that noise I'm hearing from over there?"

"From over where?" replied Sam, suddenly awakened from his meandering thoughts.

"From over there, under that blue light, which appears to be shining downward from the sky."

"Angelina, I hear it now, too. Sounds to me like it's a bulldozer."

"Yeah, Dominique, but a bulldozer without an engine," responded Yuri. "I can hear the dirt being moved but I don't hear the sound of an engine."

"Let's head over toward that direction. Perhaps Val and Chowbingo are in some difficulty," muttered Angelina, half to herself, as she unexpectedly found herself stumbling over an errant limb lying across her pathway.

"Either that or just plain trouble," added Dominique to Angelina's observations.

"I don't know for sure, Val, but there is one thing that I can assure you. If Xeres is involved in any of this, it isn't going to turn out for good."

The trees, continuing to march directly toward them, began to adjust their course. Methodically they adjusted their movements to change from their V-line phalanx formation to that of a semicircle.

Before, they had barely been noticeable, but now they were moving through the soil with deliberation and purpose. Their roots lifted upwards, through the forest crust, before plunging deeply downwards, as if engaged in a military march. Each tree advanced forward, relying it seemed, upon its own intellectually prescribed cadence.

The uniform, choreographed, beat escalated with the cadence of the marching roots—THUMP, THUMP, THUMP. Val, terrified, began running in ceaseless, nonsensical patterns, tripping and then regaining his stance only to repeat the process time and time again. Although Chowbingo repeatedly tried, there was to be no calming of Val.

Unlike before, rather than directing Chowbingo's piercing laser light toward a favored direction, this time it became, instead, a soft warming light that bathed the approaching trees in its encompassing green glow. It rendered them ghostly and ghastly to behold. However, the soft, spreading light's illumination defined the forest's every action and afforded, for Chowbingo and Val, an opportunity for observation to the minutest detail.

Trunks expanded and contracted with their every movement like the torsos of athletes as they each reached their height of competition. Their limbs expanded and flexed, rippling in a way that well-developed muscles would be expected to perform. The tiniest of branches, even those flexed and relaxed, as they appeared to imitate the fingers and toes of those under the stress of athletic competition, counterfeit, some might call it.

THUMP, THUMP, THUMP. The trees continued to march. They stirred and uprooted the soil, like the discs of farm tractors plowing through their fields, moving side to side under the deft control of their operators.

All fright, for the moment, seemed to have left Val, who stood transfixed, as he watched, with awe, all that was unfolding before him. The green amulet, it had saved him before and he was confident that it was about to do it again, or so he hoped. Certainly, it could be trusted. Chowbingo could be trusted. Everything was certain to be okay, or so he thought!

"The amulet, it's going to do its work again, Chowbingo. Look, look at the light. The glow, it's turning back into that narrow beam again, just like the times before. It's going to cut those trees down now, while they're still on the move—you just watch."

Chowbingo, he didn't say a word. He was, after all, experienced in these matters, and his concerns were different from Val's. Xeres, a formidable adversary, was not to be taken lightly.

Chowbingo, while they were illuminated, had taken careful note of the trees, their breathing trunks, and the muscular limbs undulating under their skins of bark. These were not ordinary trees!

———————

Xeres, the great counterfeiter, he had been behind all of this, and he was about to do it again. Chowbingo had been lured here, in his dog suit, with Val. Esau was still back at Mr. Ellison's pasture outfitted in his "Lucy the Cow" suit, while Xeres had brought his underlings to the gathering suited as trees. Chowbingo could see that this was not going to be fun for either Val, or for himself.

They were already greatly outnumbered. A spiritual battle was about to begin, with each side outfitted in earthly outfits. This was not going to be a spiritual battle fought in the heavens. This battle was going to be fought in Earth's heartland, a low-lying scrub forest, Val's homeland. Here was to be the battle for the soul of young Valentino Patadarski, and both Xeres and Chowbingo knew it.

"I never get invited to the really nice parties."

"Where did that voice come from?"

"Xeres?"

"Yes, Chowbingo, it's me, Xeres. And this time I have come prepared to lay my wrath upon you and take the boy."

No further words were spoken. The forest area turned blood red from the reflection of Xeres' red laser light passing through the trees. That was before its course inverted. As its direction reversed, it pointed downward. Downward it traveled, riding atop the amulet's green beam to its very core. The point of interception occurred so quickly that it might have been counted as timeless. Upon impact, Chowbingo's trusted green amulet was shattered into fragments too numerous to count. His precious stone fell, broken, to the forest floor. Tiny remnants spread themselves through the early evening mist as tiny green sparkles, before finally coming to rest, as black flint fragments, dormant and dead.

Chowbingo, dazed and momentarily disoriented, picked himself up from among the forest debris and hesitantly staggered to his legs, still wobbling from the shock of the laser's impact. Val stood off to the side, in silent wonderment, still stunned from witnessing the violent laser collision which had temporarily blinded him.

Val and Chowbingo gathered their senses. Almost simultaneously, Val's eyesight was returning, as Chowbingo's limbs again began to support him.

"Your green stone," cried out Val, his voice filling with tones of fright, expressed the degree of his deep despair. "What are we going to do now, Chowbingo? Your stone, it's shattered and gone. Now we don't have any protection, at all, from this evil old man."

"What do you mean, the stone is gone? It's still around my neck."

"No it isn't. Now it just looks like a bit of shattered glass hanging from a cord around your neck. Mostly, it's broken and scattered all about us. I saw it all happen, just before I was blinded by the explosion."

"Are you sure it's gone, Val? I can't see under my neck and I'm still dizzy from that flash of light."

"That explosion you felt, it was the stone under your neck being shattered. What are we going to do now, Chowbingo? You heard him say that he wanted me. Now that you've just lost your green stone, you can't really protect me, can you? Heck, I'm just a kid. I can't fight against what I just saw. There's really no hope for me! I'm never going to see Mama again. And what's she going to do when she learns that I'm gone? What's death feel like, Chowbingo? Does it hurt for a very long time? What do you see when you're dead? Is it really scary?"

"Val, where there's life, there's always hope, and presently you appear to me, to be very much alive."

"So you say, Doggy," came the crotchety old voice, from just to the left of both of them.

Chowbingo, with his canine reflexes being quicker, and therefore the first to respond, turned immediately toward the sound's direction and found himself glaring directly into the garnet red eyes of Xeres.

"So, I see that the unclean spirit returns."

"Chowbingo, it must be obvious even to you, outfitted as a stupid dog, that I have won. Now, just hand the brat over to me and we'll both be gone. I might even let you come and visit again, after we've settled down and Val becomes acclimated to his new misery; oops, I mean mansion. However, upon your next visit, you'll have to promise me that you'll stay a little longer, like ETERNITY! Now give me the little brat. I've spent enough time with the both of you," screamed the suddenly over-emotional Xeres."

He then reached over and grasped Val's wrist in a grip that, although not excessively tight, was nonetheless one from which it was impossible for Val to free himself.

"Chowbingo, he's taking me and without your stone, you can't save me. I told you that there is no hope for me. You can't help me now. He's so much bigger, and he's stronger than you! — Where are you taking me, you big oaf?

"Where is he taking me?

"Let me go . . ."

"To my home to play with my pet worm," interrupted Xeres, as he interjected himself into the conversation, amidst his rolling outbursts of unrequited laughter.

Lost for a proper worldly answer, as he watched his friend being carted away from before his eyes, Chowbingo cried out the most primal response that he knew: *"Have faith Val, PLEASE - have lots of faith."*

"Faith, what's faith? What's faith got to do with it," screamed Val, as he was being dragged through the dirt by Xeres' superhuman strength. Even Val's refusal to walk did nothing to restrict Xeres' progress or his purpose.

"Val, you will learn that faith is the substance of things that are hoped for, and it is also the evidence of things that you have not yet seen! Clutch hold of your evidence. It is your future. Hold on to it until your freedom comes."

"Whaaat? What are you talking about? Are you going crazy on me? I need you now, not some silly speech!"

"Faith replaces what you hope for until such time that you get it."

"You mean like my freedom—right now?"

"Yes."

"Forget it, Val. That's just one of Father's trite sayings. Pay it no mind. It won't work for you and it certainly can't save you," interjected Xeres.

"Never mind, Val, just believe and remember that where there is life there is hope. Have faith. Use your faith. And believe! Xeres is wrong. Your faith is your assurance that you will win and that Xeres is guaranteed to lose."

Xeres reached the edge of the advancing tree line as it began to encircle the clearing. He touched the bark-covered trunk of the first tree he encountered. The tree shivered like a human whose back had just been touched, unexpectedly, by a frigid hand.

The sturdy trunk reverently bowed, in submission to Xeres' touch, like a young sapling succumbing to the wind. Its topmost branches dipped toward Earth's floor, in a show of homage, that would belie any duplication that the winds might afford. It performed, in a show of perfect harmony, with the others. It was as if it were singularly being led through an orchestrated dress rehearsal by a concert master. And, in orderly procession, the remaining grove of trees followed suit.

Val reached out with both arms, extending them to their utmost, snagging and grabbing the nearest available limbs, in a final desperate attempt to prevent Xeres from dragging him deep into the forest. His feeble attempts, however, were short lived. No sooner did he feel that he had a firm grasp on a limb then, as if possessed with its own intelligence and knowledge, the tree would wrestle itself from his grip.

Val continued, as would any panic-stricken boy, to repeat his same efforts again and again. And, as would be expected, he found himself continuing to meet with the same vain, futile, results.

Chowbingo, in a heroic moment of valor as might be expected of him, gathered together all of his doggy initiative, and in one bounding burst of energy, made a fervent dash to save his friend, Val. Through the forest's trampled undergrowth, toward Xeres' clearly marked passageway, he ran.

Marking Val's way were the trail's fresh drag marks which served to highlight his continuing resistance. Unfortunately, Chowbingo's fervent attempt to foil Xeres' plan, just like Val's before him, quickly turned hopeless. The surrounding trees rapidly intertwined their lower limbs together, forming nets, to prevent any further passage.

Chowbingo, devoid of Val's impetuous whims of youth, quickly realized the folly of any further attempts to follow and wisely turned about in retreat. He intuitively realized his progress was being permanently thwarted and that he was about to become fully immobilized by the knitted vines shrinking, ever tighter, about him.

Chowbingo, in a moment would be unable to help anyone and, as he was soon to discover, would be going nowhere! Val, meanwhile was being dragged, kicking, screaming, and yelling to a place he surely didn't want to go.

Philip I. Amos

Chapter 15

The Winds This Way Blow

Dominique, is that Val I hear screaming from over there by that forest grove? There, next to the clearing—over that way, slightly to the left of us."

"You must be mistaken, Angelina. The only sound I can hear is the wind we're all hearing. Up there, the wind whistling through those tree tops."

"Don't be too sure of yourself, Dominique. Remember, a mother can hear her child's voice through the sounds of even the noisiest of crowds. A mother's gift, you might call it, remember?"

"I'm not so sure you would call it a gift," chided Sam, "but at least it's an instinct nonetheless."

"Well, I don't know if it's Val's voice, the wind, Angelina's instinct, a mother's gift, or just plain nonsense; but at least it's a direction, and it gives us purpose. We will use it as our first sense of direction. After all, we can't just continue to wander about, while this darkness starts to close in on us, without having a hint of any purpose at all. So, I'm going to begin to move us in that same direction. Any objections?"

"No, it sounds good to me, Yuri. A mother's instinct, for the well-being of a child, it often bears fruit; so I'm definitely with you guys," added Dominique.

"Let's try to steady the flashlights," cautioned Angelina. "We can't see as well as we might, with them bouncing about in every direction."

Val accelerated his screaming to the point where his cries turned to such a piercing wail that even Xeres found himself moved to respond.

"Listen you little brat, all that racket may bring sympathy and attention from where you come, but from my land, your screams of fear and angst are sounds of joy and delight to the senses of my minions. Your cries are the sounds of pain and suffering to them; and my twelve disciples, well they'll just love it.

"Ah, what a time it's going to be, when all of you finally meet.

"First came your erratic upstart yelling, but now I find myself privileged to hear a continuum of your non-ceasing outcries. Your wailings, they are now beginning to surpass even my more favored form of enjoyment, attending the instrument tuning for earthly symphonies.

"So please, just keep on with your screaming; it so contributes to my relaxation, almost as much as when I hear musicians drag their bows across their out-of-tune instruments. An anthem to my kingdom. A theme to discordance, I so appreciate those sounds, they reach to the very pinnacle of my enjoyment. Disharmony, It's actually the central reasons that I attend. Ah, but I digress.

"Now, back to business. Mr. Valentino, as we travel this path together please understand that you won't be going anywhere, except with me, forever. Therefore, my little trophy, I mean friend, wail away; keep me entertained, you just keep on with the screeching.

"Oh, and before I forget, Mr. Patadarski, do you really know how long forever is? Let me remind you, my little trophy, it's forever; HA, HA, HA!"

"How do you know my real name?"

"Oh Mr. Valentino, or should I call you Val like all the others? I've known you from before you were created for Earth. I've been waiting patiently for the opportunity to add you to my collection, from a time before there was time. Nothing like a fine strapping youth for my minions to fight over. You're certain to make for jolly sport back home."

"Where are you really taking me, or I should say dragging me, you dirty old man?"

Val was beginning to feel the cuts and bruises from his knees and legs now that his pants were sufficiently worn through to expose his tender flesh to the forest's unforgiving mantle.

"Soon you will be playing with my worm, or should I say that soon she could be trying to consume you while you, in turn, will be pleading with me to save you."

"What do you mean, 'worm'? Where is this worm of yours and why should I even care about your silly worm? I collected a bunch of worms once. I used them for fishing. Papa taught me how to collect them and then how to put them on a fishing hook for bait. I kept them in a glass jar with some cornmeal so they could eat. I even punched some holes in the top with a nail and a hammer so they could breathe. Let me play with your worm. Then afterwards, I can just put it in a jar like I did the others. And if it's really yours, well then maybe I'll just leave the corn-meal out."

"You can ask your friend Chowbingo about my worm, wise guy . . . when, or should I say . . . if you ever see him again."

"Where is he now? Where's Chowbingo . . . and how about you quit dragging me behind you. It's really starting to hurt, and you're really starting to make me very angry!"

"Let me think. Now where is your friend Chowbingo?" Xeres paused for a moment, as if to add drama, before responding to his own remark. "Oh yes! I recall now, your friend Chowbingo, if memory serves me correctly, is presently all tied up."

"What do you mean, all tied up? He's coming after you, and he's going to get me out of this. You just wait and see," exclaimed Val, with a half-hearted declaration of hope.

"Mr. Valentino, he's not coming after you and he's not going to help you, because he can't."

It was with the finality of this declaration that the trees of the forest shook in accord, one with the other. The rustle of their leaves and the scraping of their bark resounded as if it were a crowd unreservedly applauding, in unison, to a statesman's polished delivery. The enthusiasm of their response accelerated until, in conclusion, it sounded like the din of a massive auditorium expressing an unrestricted roar of glee and hilarity.

"Why are these trees shaking? There isn't any wind, not even a breeze," remarked Val, partially to his own wonderment, as well as for Xeres' hearing—not that he expected an answer.

"They're shaking because they're laughing with glee and delight, knowing that you will soon be one with them. If you didn't already know, misery truly does love company. Now, if you'll behave, I'll let you walk behind me rather than continuing to drag you along, like some dead animal. What is your preference, Mr. Valentino?"

"I'll promise to follow behind, just as you ask," uttered Val, quickly realizing that his opportunity for escape could be measurably increased with such an agreement.

"Mr. Valentino, I cannot accept your covenant as a valid agreement, since all that you and your fellow humans ever do is to break your promises."

"How about I just lie to you whenever you ask me about anything? My mother says that you are the 'Father of Lies'. Will that better suit you?"

"Just behave and address me as Mr. Xeres whenever you speak to me. It will be good practice for you before you actually arrive at your new dwelling. Yes, do practice; it will be well for both of us."

"Alright, Mr. Xeres it is," answered Val, hoping for the moment that his opportunity to escape had just increased measurably, due to his condescending response. His confidence was then accelerated even further as Xeres selected that same moment to seemingly loosen his grip.

Val, then brazenly figured freedom was his for the taking. After all, he figured with a sense of certainty, he could surely run faster than this crazy old man, even if his name was Xeres.

"Mr. Valentino, should you choose, you may address me by my better known name, which may be more convenient for you . . . and, in return, may I also address you by your informal name?"

"Certainly, you can call me Val. Everyone else does," responded Val, slyly figuring that the more he could cozy up to this ancient old fool, the better.

"Please, what is this informal name that you are now permitting me to call you, Mr. Xeres," responded Val, in the most pleasing, juicy-sweet, condescending voice that he could muster, considering his circumstances.

"Val, you may refer to me as The Exalted Seraph when you are speaking of me, or just simply Owari, whenever you are speaking directly to me. 'Owari', you should practice saying it when we get to my summer home. You'll be amazed at how easily it will start to roll off your tongue, with just a bit of practice."

"Does 'Owari' have some special meaning, or do you just like to collect names?"

"For you, you might just think of it as an ending."

Before Val could even comprehend the seemingly foolishness of the old man's remarks there appeared before him a magnificently scaled serpent, standing erect. Xeres suddenly possessed arms, legs, and four gloriously draped wings, rising from his back to just above his head, and draping to within mere inches of the forest floor. Exclusive of his tail, which extended to a minimum of one half the length of his torso, Xeres stood, at a considered minimum, four times Val's height. The expression of decisiveness, emitting from his garnet-red eyes, instantly bespoke the authority that he commanded—and confirmed that this dragon and the addled old man were one and the same.

There would be no escaping this monster's grasp!

"You know, Val, it's truly a shame that Chowbingo did not take me up on my earlier invitation. He so missed out on the opportunity to see me, once again, in my serpent attire, which I'm now allowing you to witness. He only saw this, as a suit, in my wardrobe closet. Clothing looks so much more 'alive' when it's on, don't you think?

"Did you know that Father actually designed this serpent attire just for me? One of a kind, I think you humans call it. He and I have certainly shared our differences throughout time, but I have to hand it to Him; He is a very fine clothing designer. Almost as good as I would be, were I given the opportunity."

Surprisingly, Xeres' voice was soft and gentle, almost paternal. Certainly not what might be expected from a dominating serpent.

Val, recalling all that had occurred between him and Chowbingo, his encounter with Esau suited as Lucy, and his introduction to spiritual discernment, found himself to be acutely more inquisitive than actually frightened, following this, the latest of Xeres' revelations.

"Mr. Owari, or whatever you wish to be called, Mama told me about you. She said you liked everything dark, evil, and dead. You just spoke of your serpent clothing looking 'alive' on you. I don't understand."

"Val, Father took all that is alive away from me. That leaves me the king of all that is dead, and such is my lot for the moment. However, be assured, I will get it all back!"

"My mother says that you are a liar, in fact she called you the 'Father of Lies'. She said that you can't be believed, and furthermore she says that nothing you say will ever come to be true."

"Okay Val, where is your mother now? Where is your friend Chowbingo? Where is the Father. Where are any of your friends? Where is just one individual who might save you, from me? It's just you and me, Val. Look about you. Take a moment and look carefully around. See, even the trees do my bidding. You're all mine, Val. No one is here to save you, Mr. Valentino. Now THAT is truth!"

"Where are we now?"

"You were starting to make me look bad, and I finally just became impatient with the thought of again having to drag you through the dirt like a rag doll. So I have just transported you. What if my friends were to see me soiling one of my outfits, while dragging you through the dirt, my little trophy? They might begin to think that I wasn't in charge. Not only would that make me look bad, but it would also besmirch my reputation. Now that definitely wouldn't be good for business, don't you agree?"

"Seraph, or Owari or whatever you wish . . . you don't have any friends. All you ever have are victims."

"For the moment I will just attribute your remark to immaturity and set it aside. You asked me where we are going. Unlike you, I will provide a civil answer. Oh and, by the way, you are to refer to me as The Magnificent Seraph—not just Seraph.

"Now in answer to your question, the location where we are presently going is the same place where Chowbingo found himself when he unwittingly began his trip to my cabin. It's also where Father's son entered when He came and disrupted my malevolent home. The rascal—He even stole my house keys—He did. And there is where you will soon begin your journey to everlasting—and where you will be able to better understand my name, Owari."

"You don't have a home; you only have a dwelling! So, what now?" Val asked, suddenly shivering and shaking uncontrollably.

"Why you poor child," Xeres offered in his most solicitous demeanor, having now returned to the body of an elderly man. "It must have been my reptile suit that caused you such unease. Although I do look quite glorious in that state of costuming, unfortunately for earthlings such as yourself, I do become completely coldblooded. Nonetheless it does enable me to execute, most efficiently, my more nefarious plans, as you will soon come to witness.

"Now you just sit over there, under that tree, and wait; wail and scream if you like—but don't move. Oh, and may I suggest that you don't sit too close to its base; you don't want to leave here without a guide."

"What do you mean, leave without a guide? I don't understand."

"That's where Chowbingo, unexpectedly, began his journey."

"Are we here for a reason? It seems like you're actually waiting for something."

"The boat."

"Boat? What are you talking about, Xeres? This is the middle of the forest."

"Now Val, it's either Mr. Xeres, or Owari that you will call me. I insist upon protocol. I absolutely refuse to allow Father to have my self-respect, too."

"Okay Mr. Owari, or whatever you wish to be called, I know we're quite some long ways from the ocean, or even a large lake, for that matter. Papa taught me that the nearest lake is more than seventy miles from here. The closest I ever came to seeing one was when I looked at some pictures that Mrs. Bellamy showed us, during classroom hours, from her summer vacation over in Switzerland."

"Val, enough of your babble. You will soon be able to see lots of water. You will see a boat and a lake filled with fiery water. Now just seat yourself, over where I first showed you, and, like I said before—don't leave that spot. I've decided that I'm going to arrange for Chowbingo to come here and join us."

"Chowbingo?"

"Yes, I want him to witness your departure so he can see that there is absolutely nothing he can do to prevent you from being taken, by me. Then, following your departure, he will surely show me proper respect the next time the two of us meet in Neveah, especially in front of Father."

"This guy Xeres, he's crazy . . . but . . . faith? Faith is the substance of things hoped for; that's what Chowbingo said. It's the evidence of things not seen . . . I don't want to go with Xeres. I want to be with Mama, and Mr. Dominique, and Mr. Yuri, and Mr. Sam. They've all been so good to me. They don't growl like Xeres. They don't call me 'brat', they like me. And, and Chowbingo, Chowbingo, where are you?"

"I'm right where I am, Val."

"What do you mean, you're right where you are? That just doesn't make sense," exclaimed Val, through a face full of panic-stricken tears.

"Well, I'm kind of tied up right now, myself. The trees have me tangled up in their branches, real tight I might add it's all Xeres' doing."

"How come I can't see you?"

"*Because I'm being held in the clearing where Xeres first grabbed you. Now pay attention so you can hear me clearly. You are not used to our spiritual language, so please quiet your inner-self and try to concentrate.*"

"What shall I do?" Val blurted out inwardly, while outwardly, sobbing hysterically.

"*Val, you need to concentrate on your faith. I can't help you now. I'm all tied up, and even if I were free, I couldn't be of much help. Remember, Xeres destroyed my amulet. It's all up to you now, and your faith.*"

"But, Chowbingo!"

"*No 'buts' allowed, Val. Sometimes circumstances and events just don't work out the way you might like. Then your only answer is to turn to your faith. Fact is, you'll find that things will work better if you start with your faith rather than waiting until later to use it.*

"*Val, where I come from, faith is money. Father also gave a measure of it to you; so use it. There are no banks in Neveah. There, unlike here, the more you use your faith the richer in faith you will become.*"

"How does that help me here, Chowbingo?"

"*Val, you have riches from Neveah that you are afraid to use. So I am going to give you a personal loan. I want you to try spending some of my faith down here where you live.*"

"Is that really what you use?"

"*Yep, I use mine and Lucy the cow uses his, I mean hers. Even Xeres knows about it. He just has too much pride to use his. And since, because of pride, he didn't ever use it, he lost it all. Now Xeres is bankrupt. That's why he's always in a predicament that turns out bad. Where we come from, Val, we call it 'Coin of the Realm', It's what Father uses when He gives us good gifts. This is how He will give you good gifts too."*

"Look, Yuri. There seems to be a clearing up ahead. I think I can almost make it out. Through those two trees, just to the right of you."

"I believe you're right, Dominique," responded Yuri, now shining his flashlight toward the clearing.

"Let's head over there. It can possibly afford us a better sense of direction. Perhaps we might also pick up some trace of Val or the dog."

"You may be right, Sam. If they've been there we might even be able to find us a bit of Puppy's fur from one of the lower branches."

"Good thinking," added Dominique, wishing to impress Angelina, if by no other means then perhaps by expressing his agreement.

"Okay everyone, take it easy, stay in line, and continue to follow me," ordered Yuri. "Continue to keep those other two flashlights searching along our pathway. We don't want anyone spraining limbs out here. We've got ourselves enough of a challenge already tonight."

"I'm still here following up in the back, and I've got everyone covered, Yuri. Dominique's holding Angelina's hand, so I think we're alright for now. Just keep an eye out up ahead."

And so they continued, the discordant little band of rescuers, each traveling for a slightly different purpose, but all united, nonetheless, in their common rescue effort. Angelina, wishing for the safe recovery of her son. Dominique, discovering himself enamored with Angelina, saw not only a suitable wife in her but also a possible business partner for his chocolate truffle business.

Sam, the green grocer, knows that should Val's mushroom find actually be one of white truffles, then the economic fortunes of the village will change overnight. Sam firmly believes that he would be invaluable because of his purchasing and marketing skills. Hadn't he, after all, spent the past twenty years buying, marketing, and selling all of his grocery goods to their village?

Yuri, the butcher, who was leading the gang of would-be rescuers, comfortably found himself to be in no apparent need for additional material wealth. He simply considered himself blessed just to be in the company of friends. He felt privileged that he had been asked to contribute his limited talents and skills to assist in the recovery of Angelina's son, Val, and his pet, Chowbingo.

"What's that sound? It's Puppy. I know it's Puppy! He's barking from over there, right where we're headed."

"Can you be a little bit more specific, Angelina? It appears to be a rather large clearing," added Sam, as he began moving his flashlight back and forth toward the clearing's expanse.

All sense of order abandoned, they began following Angelina's lead as she scurried toward the darkened pasture land. Simultaneously and without warning, each one of them bumped into and fell over Yuri, until finally they found themselves spread in one discordant heap of intertwined limbs and heaving torsos.

"Hey, I thought you were all going to follow my lead, not trample me," Yuri exclaimed with a laughter that served to dispel, momentarily, Angelina's pent-up frustration. "Now could you all please let me up so that we can try to do this in an orderly manner?"

"Oops I'm sorry, Yuri, for stepping on your hand but he is my son and it's getting very late."

"No excuse required."

Unbeknownst to this little band of rescuers, Xeres was not about to allow them to undo his earnest endeavors, that of bringing Val to his earthly dwelling for eternal residency. So, while momentarily seeking to regain their composure, they stood, reassembled, and exchanged sheepish apologies. Xeres, in the interim, was already instructing his minions to block their passage and remove all threats of their intervention into his plans.

Reassembled and again marching forward with determined resolve and a renewed sense of purpose, the disheveled group meandered forward, toward the clearing, with its resonating sounds.

"I can hear the noise. They're right over there, in that direction. C'mon, let's hurry!"

"Whoa there, hold up a minute," cautioned Yuri, as he glanced back at Angie, over his shoulder. "Let's not end up in another pile." He then paused a moment, to volunteer a forced chuckle, with the hope once again, of alleviating any tension that Angelina might be about to experience.

"That sound, I can hear it again over there at the far end of the clearing, by those tall trees." Again she broke away from their tightly knit little cluster. Without hesitation she neatly circumvented Yuri and, once free of the others, she began an open field run, towards the grove at the opposite end of the clearing.

The forest waited. Xeres' team was experienced, if nothing else. Their skills had already effectively been displayed to Chowbingo and Val. However, for this little troop of rescuers, it was to be different. They wouldn't understand. Childhood memories and spiritual discernment had long before been taken from them. Life's challenges had matured each one. It had stripped, from them, the gift of wonderment, while simultaneously squeezing each into the cogs of life's machinations. Here, they were being crushed, pressed, and printed into Xeres' master plan. They, like most earthly adults, had already been introduced to greed, envy, and avarice. Impacted by the progression of time, they would become the finished product of Xeres' processing. Each would be permitted to live out his time, within Earth's domain, before being relegated to his kingdom. There, the final vestiges of faith and innocence would be replaced with a terminal state of doubt and fear.

Angelina and her little group were being processed to respond, in restricted wonderment, to all that each new day would present. Daily they were programmed to march in lockstep as they were continually being prodded. Xeres continued to observe their responses to whatever new stimuli was placed in their path.

Greed, envy, hatred, jealousy; the offerings no longer mattered. Every vice would have its impact and, collectively over time, they were all certain to accomplish their singularly assigned purpose: deliver the earthlings to Xeres!

Place the same mouse in the same maze, for enough days, and its every action becomes predictable. Xeres was an accomplished master. Earthlings were his mice and Earth was his maze.

Xeres knew them to be predictable. All he needed was to litter their pathways with bait. Sometimes it would be attractive or enticing. Oftentimes it would be scary and provide impetus for doubt. No matter, so long as he continued to keep them unbalanced, uncertain, and off-center. Anything to keep them away from Father's instructions and they would belong to him.

"Leave the fools to their routines. Let them have their moments, their limited space, and their time. It will all soon end, and they will then be mine for eternity. Me, the mighty, magnificent, collector! Now Val, he's another matter. The boy has hopes, he has dreams, and he has faith. I must keep him away from his mother, at least until he's mine.

"There's no adult that's ever going to have conversations with a dog, much less attempt to learn the spiritual language of Neveah. But Val; he's a youth, he's smart, and he's different. He talks to Chowbingo as a dog, to Khasmar as a cow, and even to me, in any way he chooses.

"This boy, I definitely have to stop. Should he go straight to Father, now that would cause trouble for me. Trouble, that's my domain; it's something that I am surely more purposed to provide than to receive. Trouble, I give it. No, I don't receive it. Can't allow it. Nope, I absolutely can't allow that. After all I do have me responsibilities."

Immediately, as if on command, the trees again responded to the gentle wafting breeze which, as if on cue, began to increase in velocity while streaming through the lower branches. Leaves and limbs, as they had in their previous performances, began to intertwine. Yes, this net would surely be impenetrable. Not only would Angelina and her fellow rescuers be slowed, like Val and Xeres who had gone before, but ultimately they would be stopped. Absolutely prevented from venturing beyond Xeres' barricade.

"Mr. Valentino, your mother is on her way to rescue you with her merry band of misfits. Unfortunately for you, my little brat, she is destined to fail. I have, quite assuredly, seen to that."

"What are you planning to do with my mother you miserable human being, or whatever it is that you wish to call yourself?"

"Now, now, Mr. Valentino, if there are insults to be thrown about, it is I who will throw them. I am not about to tolerate any such behavior from a brat like yourself."

"I don't understand; insults, what insults? I haven't even gotten started."

"Human being! You called me a 'human being'! That type of name calling is intolerable, you despicable little ingrate."

"So what are you then?"

"I am XERES. I am the all of it and nothing less than all of it."

"Well you certainly don't look like the 'Great-All-of-That' to me. Maybe the 'Great-I-Was' is who you really are. You know, I'm going to do what Chowbingo does. I'm just going to keep calling you Xeres. By the way, where is he? Where is my Chowbingo? You can't still have him trapped. He's way too smart for that. He's certainly got to be smarter than you."

"You say Chowbingo is smarter than me. Well then, my young Mr. Patadarski, perhaps you might wish to ask yourself why 'smarter-than-me' Chowbingo is not here with us now. Well, I'll answer that question for you. It's because your stupid dog is still all tied up."

"Hey, I thought you said that he was going to be joining us. Oh, that's right, I almost forgot—you're just a liar, nothing but a liar. In fact, you're the Father of Lies aren't you, well aren't you?"

"No Val, I don't lie. I just exercise my own truth. You see, Father has His truth and I have mine. Now you can always recognize Father's truth. It is exactly the opposite of mine. Now that you are here, in my companionship, it may serve you well to follow my truth."

"CHOWBINGO, CHOWBINGO, CHOWBINGO, where are you?"

"Will you just be quiet for a second? Your very own, precious Chowbingo, he hasn't moved. Let's just say, that for now he's all tied up in personal matters, or should I just say that his person is all tied up?

"You leave my puppy alone, you big bully."

"If you would stop your complaining and your accusations for one moment, you probably will hear him barking for you, not that it's going to do either one of you a bit of good."

"He's going to come and get me. He's going to come right here. I just know he is!"

"I really don't think that's going to be the case, Mr. Patadarski. You see, unfortunately for you, he's still wearing that crazy dog suit which his friends from Neveah stuck him in before they sent him down here to mess with my affairs. Sure, you can communicate with him now that you've learned our language, but he still isn't getting out of that forest grove where my trees are holding him. That is not unless Father releases him from that suit, and I don't see that happening any time soon."

"Huh?"

"Ah, here comes your little band of would-be rescuers now."

"What band of rescuers?"

"Oh, didn't I tell you? Must have slipped my mind again, I'm sorry—it must be my age. Hmm, let's see, how many millennia must I be by now? Guess one loses count after a few thousand centuries. Oh well, no matter. I thank myself daily for my work. It's what keeps me young of spirit."

"Mr. Xeres, oh—Sir! Get a mirror and look at yourself. You're not young. You're old and you look very, very tired. Now, what was it that you forgot to tell me? What was it, exactly, that slipped your mind? Do you forget things easily like Mr. Ellison, the older man, who owns the dairy? Now Mama says he's very old. Are you that old? Are you really as old as Mr. Ellison? You look like you may even be older. In fact, you . . ."

"Enough of your nonsense. Ah, now I remember. I forgot to mention your mother and her friends."

"What about my mother?"

"They've been running around here half the night looking for you. Oh, and now they're almost here."

"Mom, Mama, M-O-T-H-E-R!"

"Keep yelling, just keep on yelling, Val. It really isn't going to do you any good. Momentarily, you are going to be mine for eternity. Soon there's not going to be anyone to rescue you. They're going to be all 'wrapped up' so to speak. Just like your friend, Chowbingo."

"I hear him. I hear my son. Val, it's your mother. I'm coming."

THUMP.

"Angie, are you all right?"

It was Dominique who was the first to arrive. True, his concerns were genuine, but he did not fail to take personal advantage of the moment. His exaggerated concern for Angelina's well-being was overtly demonstrated to say the least. This moment, at least in Dominic's eyes, was the beginning of a made-to-order courtship.

"Angelina . . ."

"Don't worry, Yuri, I'm all right. Just ran into something here in the dark, and here I am—on my seat once again. Serves me right for running off, I guess."

Her unusual exclamation brought a bit of laughter to the group while Sam was catching up.

"Looks to me like you might have hit some tree limbs, Angelina. Now I'm not meaning to scold you, but again I'm finding that I must make you aware that it's necessary for us to all proceed through this darkness in an orderly fashion."

"But Val! I know that I heard Val calling!"

"Well now, I really don't doubt you, Angie. I believe that a mother's ear, listening for her child's cry, can pierce even the largest of crowds, but in all fairness I have to tell you that the rest of us haven't heard his cry, have we?"

"I can't seem to find any way through this forest. While you've all been talking, I've been trying to find some passage through this mess."

"What do you mean you can't get through, Sam?"

"While you've all been working out how you're going to play follow the leader, I've been trying to find some way through this confounded undergrowth."

"Sam, we've played in these forests as kids. There's always a way through. Might have to get on our hands and knees to find it, but as we know from our childhood, there's always a way."

"You know; he may be right?" It was Dominique calling from about twenty yards to the right.

"What do you mean, he may be right?" exclaimed Angelina, arising to her feet while dusting herself off as best she could. "I've never heard of such a thing. Remember, I grew up here too, and I wasn't always playing with dolls."

"Could have been with cute boys though," chimed in Sam, with a smile on his face.

"Hey Sam . . ." Dominique grasped the moment to sharply address Sam.

"Just kidding, Dominique. Sorry, Angelina."

"It's all right, Dominique. Sam's right, I was a bit of a flirt during my school days."

"Yep, and you got the cute boy, as I remember, Salvio Patadarski."

"Thank you, Yuri. Yes, and Salvio gave me my beautiful son, Val. Now I must find him," cried an emotional Angelina, her eyes continuing to well up with the tears no one had seen before. Had Sam not inadvertently turned his flashlight toward her face, they would have surely continued unnoticed.

Yuri, without comment, continued walking back toward the group after completing his futile search for an open passageway.

"Oh, oh! Angie, you're crying." It was Dominique who first spoke up.

"Yes, yes, I have to find my son," responded Angelina with unabashed honesty. The tears continued to flow down her cheeks, joined now with uncontained hysterical sobbing. "Please help me!"

"Sam, Dominique, I can't seem to see any way through this!"

"Yuri, you've played and hunted in these woods all of your life. I don't understand. What do you mean, you can't get through?"

"Dominique, I don't remember this grove of trees, yet I know I've been here before. Probably many times actually. We only have household flashlights and I really can't see clearly, but these trees seem to me like they don't belong here in this type of forest."

"Well I don't know a lot about forests, but I do know that I'm looking at something very different. I think you all had better take a look at what I'm seeing with my flashlight. Look at those tree trunks, there, in front of us."

"What are you talking about, Dominique?"

"Look at the placement of these trunks. They are all standing in perfect alignment, like someone had planted an orchard. Trees just don't grow this way naturally. Someone has to be behind this"

"Just like a row of soldiers," volunteered Angelina.

"People plant orchard trees in rows, so that their fruit or nuts can be easily harvested. These trees don't produce anything to harvest; besides, way out here, there isn't even water for irrigation."

"Maybe it's an orchard planted for some other purpose, Dominique. Someone, for sure, planted these trees. They just didn't grow this way."

"Okay Sam, now explain the limbs all twisted together. They're so tight we can't even get through. That didn't come from any grower," added Dominique, as he began to take a more active interest in the nature of the obstacles set before them.

"Puppy, it's Val's puppy! I hear him whimpering. It's coming from over there."

"Where, Angelina, where? Sam, come over here with your light. Mine's starting to go dim."

"I'm coming, Yuri. Hold on, I don't want to trip. Okay now, where is he, Angelina?"

"I can't see very well in what little moonlight we have here. But I know I heard him, crying out from over there, in that direction. Puppy, Puppy, I hear you, where are you?"

"Over here, I hear him now," yelled Dominique so loudly that even he was surprised.

Amidst the yelling and the shouts of joy, they all moved toward the whimpering cries, but only to again find themselves abruptly stopped by the forest's impenetrable barricade. Finally, though, they could see the object of their attention. There, on the other side of the tightly knit barricade of live branches and limbs was Chowbingo; he was so tightly wrapped within the intertwining limbs that he dared do nothing more than whimper for fear of suffocation. Not only were his legs tightly entangled within the trees' limbs and branches, but even his muzzle was entwined within the vegetation.

"Puppy, Puppy what has happened to you," cried Angelina.

"Anyone got a knife?"

"I'm sorry, Yuri, I don't think anyone thought to bring one," replied Sam.

"The dog looks okay, for the moment. Where's the boy?"

"Well, Sam, if we can free Puppy, maybe he can lead us to where Val is."

"Okay, let's give it a try; everywhere else here certainly looks like it's starting to come to a dead end."

And so they jumped in, using all of the combined purpose and eagerness that they could muster. Their first attempts were directed toward separating the smaller of the limbs. Once this was successfully accomplished, they would move ahead and bend back those a bit larger. Then they could squirm through and access Chowbingo, or so they hoped. Presently, however, their undertaking was starting to look more like a far-fetched hope than an achievable reality. Unfortunately, Chowbingo still remained entangled in limbs, about thirty feet from where the group had first begun its rescue attempt.

———

"Foolish, foolish humans. When will they ever understand that I am the all-powerful one? Wasn't it I who beat Father in the garden? It's all about me. It always has been. I am the one who fills my properties with the ones that Father lets die because of 'free will'."

"All you are, Mr. Xeres, is a big bag of wind. Chowbingo is going to come and get me. I know he is. My faith tells me that it's going to become so."

"I'm not interested in you right now. So be quiet and don't ever speak the word 'faith' around me again. Father put me into bankruptcy up there. Made a laughing stock out of me, He did. Not going to be able to do it here. Not going to let Him do it here. Nope!

"It's your mother who has my interest now, so be quiet."

"What about her? Why do you say that?"

"Because she and her miserable little group of friends are not far from here right now."

"Mama, Mother, Mama!"

"Quiet, I told you to be quiet. Didn't your mother ever teach you to respect your elders?"

"You're not my elder. You're just a dirty old man."

"Mr. Valentino, allow me to impart some wisdom into your young, simple, mind. I am, as you say—I am Xeres. More importantly, I was a presence before this universe, which you presently inhabit, was first created; and then, I was among the first to inhabit it. So, yes, I rightfully do demand your respect."

"Xeres, I really don't see anything about you that is 'rightful'. Now please let me go. Mama, Mama, hey Mom where are you?"

"I told you, that when you address me, you are to use, Mister . . ."

———————

"I hear him, I hear him. I know that's Val calling me!"

"Where is he calling from? I'm sorry, but I still can't hear anything."

"Of course you can't hear, Dominique. Feel the wind. It just seems to have come out of nowhere. It's almost like someone is trying to prevent us from listening."

"I agree, Yuri. This is all very strange. Very unusual."

"Hey, while you've all been chatting, I've still been trying to strip these small limbs away so we can break through to the pup."

"Sam, how far did you get?" Yuri was yelling over the wind, which was steadily increasing.

"Come over here and see for yourself. Unfortunately, I haven't made very much progress, and I'm almost too tired to go on."

"What are you talking about, Sam? It doesn't look like you've even started. We have to get serious and get that dog out of there. Hopefully, he can help us find Val."

"Yuri, I'm not fooling around. It seems that every time I remove a limb another one seems to pop up to immediately replace it. Strangest thing I've ever encountered. If I didn't know better, I'd say that these trees have minds of their own. In fact, I would say that they're purposely placed here to stop us from moving forward."

"Sam, now we all know that's just pure and utter nonsense."

"Yeah, well then explain the soil right here around us. Look carefully at where my flashlight is pointing. See it? It's all been stirred up. Just like it has been recently plowed."

"I see what you're talking about, but let's be realistic. There's not a disc, I know of, that is capable of plowing between these trees and that close to their trunks. It would have to have been done by hand, using manual tools."

"That's crazy. Who's going to come way out here and hand turn all of this soil?"

"I don't know, Sam. I know it sounds crazy, but it certainly does appear that these trees moved themselves into this position."

"Well, I must admit, I definitely don't understand any of it," piped in Dominique. "I make candy and probably haven't spent as much time in the forest as you men. However, even I know that trees don't move on their own. In fact, I would believe that they can be pretty stubborn, should either of you elect to try and move one. They're 'rooted and grounded' I believe is the way the saying goes."

"Gentlemen, you may all be right in the things that you say, but this discussion is doing nothing toward freeing puppy and finding Val. I just pray that he isn't hurt by now."

"There's just something very, very, strange about all of this; something's not right," murmured Yuri, under his breath. Frustrated, he moved over toward where Sam was working to see if he could help him toward engineering some manner of a breakthrough opening.

Chapter 16

The Departure

Come on, you little brat, now it's time for us to go."

"Go, go where?"

"Down my rabbit hole of course. Over there, beside the tree."

"That's where our truffles are stored. They're over there, the ones that Chowbingo found."

"My boy, those aren't truffles. They are what are known as false truffles, deer truffles to your villagers, or scientifically, for your bright little mind— 'elaphomyces'."

"Elappy what? I don't understand; how can you be sure?"

"Mr. Valentino, I'm the one who planted them there."

"But why?"

"Bait, my boy, bait."

"Bait for what? There aren't any fish out here. Now I'm sure you're crazy."

"No, Mr. Valentino, I'm certainly not crazy. I'm just shrewd. Take a moment and learn. Your mother and her friends believe that all of their problems will be solved when they collect these worthless fungi, which they surely will mistake for truffles; white truffles at that. Their hopes will be elevated, because of their greed, before they discover that what lays here, before you, is worthless; just like everything else that I counterfeit. And then, my innocent conquest, comes my coupe-de-gras. Your mother comes to realize that you are missing—FOREVER.

"Sam Emerson will, of course, be crushed when he understands there will be no real truffles. Mr. Bellingeri will watch his candy dreams fold before him when he finds your mother, forever inconsolable, upon learning that you are missing. The only one who will remain untouched will be Mr. Kolvalenko."

"Why will Yuri remain untouched?"

"Because the only thing that he ever sought was friendship. Now, that is one of Father's gifts and, try as I might, I don't have any power over His gifts. Very, very frustrating, but I continue to press on.

"You see, my naïve youth, greed continues to be one of my favored weapons through which I am able to destroy humans and prepare them for an eternal life with me, or as more food for my precious worm.

The time it takes for me to keep her fed is a bit of a challenge, even for me. Her appetite, Mr. Valentino, remains simply insatiable. All that I've ever encountered, which comes measurably close to her appetite, have been fire, greed, and the craving for power—each one ceaseless."

"Why do we have to leave now? I don't want to go anywhere with you. I don't care what you say. I still believe that you're crazy!"

"I'll ignore your slanderous remarks for now, Mr. Valentino. We don't need to get off on the wrong foot, as your people say. Especially, not since you and I will be spending our eternity together—you know, for ever and ever; that is, unless you displease me. Whereupon, instead of a valued associate, you will simply become worm food, over, the end - kaput."

"Yes, but why here? Why right now?" wailed Val, as the reality of the situation began to embed itself into his inner self.

"Because your mother and her friends are too close.

"My trees are doing an excellent job of holding them in place but, unfortunately, I've been foiled by the creative abilities of you humans before. I'm not going to allow anyone to repeat that again.

"Young man, you're my prize and I'm not going to lose you now, so bend down and crawl into that hole. I know it looks small, but don't worry, I assure you, you'll fit."

"No, you're an insane monster; I'm not going to go!"

"That's it. You've tried my patience; its worm food that you'll now soon become."

Without any further words being exchanged, Xeres, swiftly and firmly, grabbed Val by the back of his neck. The steely, supernatural, grip would not permit Val to see to the right or to the left. All he was able to see was the rabbit hole, which was exactly where he was about to find himself.

———————

The sound was deafening and the light shone brighter than all the stars of the sky. It flashed with the brightness of the sun but the color was not yellow. It was blue-white, the purest light that any of them had ever seen. The sound was unlike that of thunder, but it rumbled nonetheless. It was a sound, similar to an ocean's roar, except that its intensity seemed to be maintained at a continuing, unchanging level. Never had any of them heard such a sound, a sound more filled with power than noise. Moments passed, slowly it seemed, and then abruptly it was over, just as quick as it had begun!

The blue-white star in the sky had disappeared. The once orderly well-groomed stand of trees, they found in ashes before them. Chowbingo? Well, he had been deposited next to Angelina, unsinged and unharmed. Beside Dominique sat Yuri and Sam. The once infamous tree remained, unburned. It had been split in half. The "rabbit hole" was closed and Xeres, for the moment at least, was unavailable.

There they sat, the little band of rescuers, speechless as they looked across the charcoal chasm. Under the fresh moonlit sky sat Val, plopped haphazardly amongst two hundred kilograms of fresh white truffles; not false truffles, but fresh, newly discovered, white truffles. These were of such a premiere quality that they could only be classified as 'yet unknown' to the gourmets of the world.

Dominique was the first to speak. "Bellingeri & Patadarski, we're going to be rich!"

Angelina quietly looked toward Dominique, like a teacher toward a fresh-faced youth who just hadn't yet "got" it. Speaking not a word, she slowly arose from her position, walked through the ashes to Val, sat down beside him, and slowly wrapped her arm about her son with the gentle but firm loving embrace that only a mother can administer.

"Let's go home, Val."

Chowbingo struggled to his feet, shook his fur as he cleared the ash from his coat, and immediately went to each person still seated, intent on licking each hand individually.

Val remained quietly in the warmth of his mother's embrace as he turned his attention, for the moment, to Chowbingo.

"Hey Puppy, are you all right?" he softly inquired, of his companion, in their special language.

Silence. His simple question was met with nothing but silence. He continued to repeat himself until an assurance set in that there was to be no response. His furtive glances, toward Chowbingo, offered no better reassurance. Chowbingo was still engaged in doing those things that would most amuse a dog.

"I guess Chowbingo must be pretty rattled by all of the noise and the bright lights. I'll just form a leash from my belt and walk him home. He can rest by the fireplace and then he'll be good as new tomorrow."

The rescuers, Val, and Chowbingo, leaving the truffles behind, began their trek through the wooded pasture and on toward the familiar trail leading back to Angelina's cabin.

"What was it, Yuri, what happened?"

"I don't know, Sam, I just don't know."

"We're going to be rich." Dominique continued to mumble it beneath his breath, still oblivious to his surroundings. It would probably be some time before the shock and awe of the evening's events would dissipate from his memory.

Sam continued to frightfully glance upward. Only able to recall the unique white star that had been with them, and now inexplicably was absent, his senses, like Dominique's, were not yet prepared to accept the totality of all that had just occurred.

Yuri kicked a few pebbles with his feet, as he quietly led the group back toward the cabin. He was very aware of all that had happened and the magnitude of the inexplicable power that was attached to it. He knew that this was "otherworldly" to say the least. He was a man with a simple lifestyle, yet he was very wise from his observations. Something had happened that was very, very different. He looked over toward Val, hoping to catch his eye. Perhaps Val knew something.

Val seemingly chose to direct his attention elsewhere. His interests were inexorably being pulled, from embracing the looks of gratitude and relief that his mother was expressing, to that of his puppy.

The glow emanating from Chowbingo's fur looked like static electricity, which had stubbornly refused to dissipate. Lasting less than a millisecond, and captured only within Val's sight, it nonetheless appeared to linger, significantly longer. No sooner had his mind accepted its veracity than it dissipated from Chowbingo's body and coalesced into a pure, blue light. Resting without foundation or support above Chowbingo, it later seemed to Val that it had remained there, while awaiting his acknowledgement of its presence.

Then the light was gone; straight up it had moved, the streak of vibrant blue, through the moonlight night, directly into the dark abyss above. There was no tail, as might be expected of a comet, nor did it turn to circumscribe the Earth. It moved straight away, with certainty, and with purpose.

Confused and a bit frightened, Val pulled away from his mother's hold and moved over to kneel beside his precious puppy, whose only interest appeared to be one of unearthing another truffle, from beneath the nearest tree, where it was conforming to its life plan of providing a source of symbiotic nourishment to its host.

"So, you still like digging for truffles?"

No answer. The furry dog just continued with his digging, completely oblivious to the gentle whispering of Val's voice, beside his ear.

Puzzled, Val hesitated for a moment, and then glanced up toward the heavens; just in time to see the same blue light, blinking a last acknowledging burst, before disappearing into the final great void, beyond Earth's vision.

"Val, looks like you got yourself a good truffle dog there."

Yuri, the butcher, had just snapped Val out of his trance of wonderment. Val, still a bit unnerved, looked directly at Yuri, who returned the startled youth's look of amazement with his wise, crinkled old smile.

The wide-eyed youth and the wise old man. They both knew!

THE END

ABOUT THE AUTHOR

Although Philip is not a well-known writer in literary circles, nonetheless, his ability to weave a story will
captivate the most seasoned reader. An author whose life
has taken him from privilege, to despair, to redemption,
Philip is able to translate his journey from the absolute

failure of self-reliance, through the labyrinths of moral confusion, to the redemption of "letting it all go" where he found the happiness and contentment which he enjoys today.

Although a successful construction manager, and construction defect litigation expert witness, his personal life was fraught with the ravages of alcohol, feelings of imminent failure, and unrelenting self-doubt. There was no amount of success that seemed to remedy it nor any amount of failure that could release it.

It was only after he began to weave the imagined tales of Chowbingo for his wife, Diane, to replace the childhood which she never enjoyed, that he began finding answers to fill his own void.

Philip and Diane share their time between New Orleans and Southern California where they maintain two residences. California is native to Philip and the place where he enjoyed his highs and suffered his lows. New Orleans, a city of history and imagination, remains for Philip the inspirational place that led him to write Chowbingo, the adventure of a very special dog who will reveal, for the reader, some of life's very special gifts. Here, Philip takes his characters from failure and confusion to peace and satisfaction; magical perhaps for Chowbingo but realistic for us, no matter if rich or poor, young or elderly.

.

.

For more information about this book, to register your review, or to contact the author, please direct your communication to;

www.philipamos.com